Stand and Deliver

Glancing up into Valerian's eyes, Lydia saw, with fascination, a look of abject hunger and lust which she felt mirrored deep inside herself. A tingling heat thrilled across the surface of her skin, and she felt her breath catch in her throat as he gazed at her with unsmiling intensity.

'You cannot escape me, Lydia,' he purred. 'You can run. Indeed, you excite me with your running, and I shall always give chase. But I will catch you. Every time.'

Stand and Deliver

HELENA RAVENSCROFT

BLACK
lace

Black Lace novels are sexual fantasies.
In real life, make sure you practise safe sex.

First published in 1999 by
Black Lace
Thames Wharf Studios,
Rainville Road, London W6 9HT

Typeset by SetSystems Ltd, Saffron Walden, Essex
Printed and bound by Mackays of Chatham PLC

ISBN 0 352 33340 5

Chapter One

*L*ydia paused as she approached the front steps of the house, her senses suddenly alert as the gravel of the walkway crunched behind her. She turned around and fixed her gaze on the highly polished black riding-boots; she knew who wore them without having to raise her eyes to his face.

She watched his striding approach, carefully disguising her hostility with a neutral smile; Valerian Hawkesworth was cruel and only someone distinctly lacking a sense of self-preservation would deliberately provoke him. His arrogant nature showed in the imperious tilt of his head and the way he stared down his aristocratic nose with cold, dark, almost black eyes which seemed to slash straight through her long petticoats and trace the curves of her body beneath.

He had his late father's height and lean dark looks. Although he was the younger of Lord William's two sons, he exuded a natural air of command and had quickly assumed the role of lord of the manor, riding rough-shod over his dying father's last wishes and imprinting his malign influence as soon as the burial vault was sealed.

He stopped in front of her, so close that her nostrils flared as she caught the citrus tang of the pomade that slicked his ebony hair back from his wide brow and tamed it in the satin ribbon at his nape. She kept silent and he raised one dark eyebrow.

'Cousin.'

His drawl was lazily measured, low and thick as treacle. If he weren't so unpleasant he would be very attractive, she thought, as she tried to anticipate his next move. Living with Valerian was like being involved in a perpetual game of chess, except that her pieces weren't marked and the board kept tilting out of reach.

Glancing swiftly over his shoulder as if to check that they were not being watched, he stepped forward and suddenly grasped one of her breasts with one hand, his other snaking around her waist to pull her to him.

'What an unexpected pleasure.' His finely chiselled lips curled in a malevolent smile and, through the tight lacing of her bodice, he massaged her nipple with a rough thumb and forefinger. Lydia slapped his hand away and spat her words into his face.

'Pray don't touch me, Valerian. You may have set yourself up as lord of the manor, but you are not master of all you survey!'

'Oh, but cousin, I am. Much as I hate to contradict you, I must remind you of the situation.' His fingers tightened on her and she felt a sharp stab of pain as he squeezed her breast. 'My father shuffled off his mortal coil without leaving a will, and therefore you are unprovided for. You remain in this household on my sufferance. Perhaps you should be a little more gracious if you expect me to provide a roof over your head and a bed for you to sleep in.' His malignant tone lingered on the word 'bed' and Lydia felt her cheeks flame.

'But you are not the sole heir.' She controlled her breathing with as much calm as she could muster, willing herself to ignore the insistent thumb pressing at her nipple. 'Drummond will be found soon and as the elder son he will inherit the estate.'

'Forget Drummond! My esteemed elder brother is dead. Naval recruits are notorious for becoming cannon

2

fodder, and the recent battles with the Spanish have been vicious. Oh no, my sweet cousin, he won't save you this time.'

He sprang forward suddenly, grasping her waist and jerking her into the unyielding circle of his arms. His hard mouth crushed down on hers as she opened it to scream, his hot tongue probing while one hand swiftly lifted a handful of her petticoats to grasp at the bare flesh beneath. He stabbed shockingly between her thighs and Lydia struggled, horrified at her own responsiveness. She stiffened against him and tried to wrench herself free, but he held her tighter, imprisoning her arms and insinuating the tip of one forefinger into her.

'So, my little cousin. You are virgo intacta.' He laughed softly, his black eyes filled with spite. 'I often wondered whether Drummond had plundered the treasure during your walks together in the forest. I am thrilled to discover that he left that pleasure to me. And it will be a very great pleasure, Lydia, to deflower you and mould you to my desires.'

Hot dry lips grazed her face and he gripped her sex, pinching and twisting the swelling flesh. Lydia arched against the rigidity of his muscular body and closed her eyelids, feigning surrender. As if encouraged, he raked his hands around her, grasping her smooth buttocks and wrenching her closer, trying to mould her body to his as he curved her backward like a flexed bow. The potency of his hard cock strained against her thigh with painful insistence. Lydia struggled one arm free. Bracing herself against him, she swung her hand back and slapped his face with the full force of her anger.

'Bitch!' he hissed.

She almost fell as he dropped her to clutch his cheek, but seeing an escape route open up before her, she staggered on to the lawn, turned quickly, and ran into the main house, her footsteps echoing eerily on the stone-tiled floor of the great hall.

She heard him shout after her: 'I'll allow you to

escape, this time! It excites me to see you run. There's no hurry, I'll have you yet.'

His derisive laughter echoed on the latticed windows. Lydia tried to ignore it as she ran up the sweeping staircase two steps at a time, bunching her skirts in one hand. Pausing as she went along the dark gallery, she glanced briefly over the balustrade to see if he had followed.

He had not.

Up on the next floor, she hurried to her room and swung the heavy door closed behind her, resting against the polished oak to steady her legs. Hatred for Valerian – and something darker, something nameless – wrenched at her gut, and she glowered around the room, stepping forward to search for something to break. A tiny statuette wobbled on a spindly table as she brushed past and she grabbed it, raised her arm to throw, and then paused, remembering that it was one of the few mementoes of her own family. She set it carefully back down and sniffed hard.

The four-poster bed with its vast snowy coverlet beckoned and she threw herself headlong on to the quilt. Face down in the bolster, she burrowed into the depths of the mattress and exhaled hard into the pillows, enjoying the hot return of her own breath.

She hated Valerian, had loathed and detested him since the day of her arrival at Hawkesworth Manor as an orphaned child. The fire which had engulfed her home and parents had spared her, allowing fate to sweep her from one impatient neighbour to the next. Finally someone had seen fit to contact her late father's brother, and had deposited little Lydia Hawkesworth and her solitary trunk of belongings on a stagecoach bound for the West Country.

Valerian's wicked, mocking face floated before her closed eyelids. Loathing tempered with fascination welled up in her; he was as familiar as a brother, and she had watched him grow from a vicious little boy into an unpredictable man, yet every time she was in his

4

presence she was spellbound. She twisted her head and clamped her teeth on the linen of the bolster, feeling her body tense at the memory of his brutal touch.

Slowly, in an action which mirrored his, she slid her hands under the layers of her petticoats. Her fingers slid over her sex, still moist from Valerian's ministrations. She rolled over on the bed, kicking at the pillows and spreading her legs, tentatively rubbing a finger over herself. Languid waves rippled through her relaxed body and she tipped her head back over the edge of the bed.

A sudden movement across the room caught her attention and her heart leapt for a brief moment, until she realised that it was her own reflection.

She stared at the image in the gilded cheval-glass. The scene was sensual: an odalisque reclined upon pale scattered pillows, one leg hooked about the vertical column of the bedpost, her head tilted back so that long ebony curls spilled over the side of the mattress almost to the floor.

Aroused by the sight of herself, she repeated her hand movements until she felt herself slick and wet; then, mimicking Valerian, she plunged a finger into the tightness that ached so delectably. She imagined that it was Valerian who touched her – a gentle and tender Valerian – and she found herself arching her back and gasping his name.

Looking into the mirror made Lydia quiver and her skin prickle. She concentrated on her reflection as slow rhythmic waves began to ripple through her and a delicious feeling of coolness brushed across her skin, while inside she was burning and drowning in a pool of searing golden sensation. She tightened on to her own finger, her mind conjuring images of Valerian with his stern jaw and hypnotic, jet-black eyes. She tried to grasp the sensation, but it slipped away, elusive and desperately sweet.

Ultimately unsatisfied, she fell into a drifting, disturbed sleep, peopled with men who ground their hips on hers and whose faces were versions of Valerian's. Then came Drummond. He walked into her dream like a dark shadow, and his half-remembered mouth bore down on hers. He became passionate, ardent, pulling her legs quickly up and around his muscular back, burning kisses on to her eyelids, her cheeks, and her straining breasts. She could feel his hands stroke her thighs, and he ran a tingling finger from hip to ankle and back up again.

A light breeze from the open window disturbed her sleep, and Lydia shifted as the coolness fanned across her hot skin. She sank deeper into the vivid, achingly sweet dream. Beneath her questing lips the salty tang of the sea mingled with the masculine muskiness on Drummond's firm skin. He pushed her back on to the quilted counterpane and parted her legs with strong fingers, dipping his head and flicking his tongue over her.

Lydia opened her eyes to gaze unblinking at the canopy of the four-poster. She was awake, the dream rapidly receding from memory. But the deliciously warm, probing tongue remained. Lifting her head, Lydia gazed down over her own stomach to see a blonde head buried between her thighs. As if sensing her wakefulness, the owner of the sleekly combed saffron hair looked up and smiled.

'Oh, Miss Lydia. You looked so inviting lying there in your undress. I simply couldn't stop myself.' Angel, the diminutive upstairs maid, smiled and parted her pink lips slightly; Lydia could see the fascinating pearliness of her teeth. 'I can sense you don't object.'

She slowly dipped her head, locking Lydia's eyes with her own, and lapped tantalisingly with the tip of her long tongue. Surrendering, too languorous to protest, Lydia closed her eyes and let her breathing gradually slow to shallow gasps, tentatively winding her fingers into the abundant golden hair and loosening its restraints.

As if feeling Lydia's enjoyment, Angel pressed with

her tongue, making tiny movements until Lydia felt that she would expire from pure, delicious sensation. Then she felt Angel probe with her hands and suddenly, deeply, insert her warm tongue and one finger.

Lydia sighed and arched her back, tilting her hips and bracing one foot against the bedpost. The pulsing rhythm of Angel's hand and mouth radiated through her body and she cried out as the elusive sensation she had so desperately chased earlier finally gripped her and she was bathed in pleasure, bittersweet and as hot as a blacksmith's forge, with swirls of ecstasy echoing inside her head, and searing, bubbling, racing, all the way down to her toes.

She lay still, rawness constricting her throat, while her whole body felt exuberant and tinglingly alive. The other girl raised her slender form and rested her weight lightly on Lydia's sated body, smiling down and tracing a finger across the velvet cushion of her partly open mouth.

Drummond Hawkesworth, muscular legs firmly braced, stood on the rough wooden deck of the ship and revelled in the brisk salt wind as it ruffled his already tousled brown hair. Shielding his eyes with one bronzed hand, he directed his gaze towards the thin strip of land which curved, barely visible, on the distant horizon.

The shores of England at last.

His heart swelled at the thought of home, a tantalising prize at the end of an uncomfortable sea voyage. The unvarying diet of biscuits and salt beef had begun to pall by the second week, and Drummond was desperately in need of a hearty meal. He had travelled far since receiving the belated, much forwarded letter from Lavendale's Solicitors. The marked and torn yellow parchment with its barely intact wax seal had taken months to reach him, and when he had finally read its melancholy contents, his father had long since been sealed in the family crypt.

His ever-restless mind wondered how Lydia was

faring at Hawkesworth. In his absence, Valerian would undoubtedly have seized control of the manor and all who lived under its gabled roof. Lydia was a young woman of twenty-one now; she would have changed in the five years of his self-imposed exile, and he smiled at the incongruous thought of the chubby girl with untameable hair and wild ways growing up to be a woman of poise and dignity.

Drummond stared down into the stormy sea, casting his mind back to when he had seen her last. The morning of his departure, he had crept along the dawn dark corridors into the womb of the house, and had gently pushed at the barrier of Lydia's room door. She had been sleeping, as he had expected, but he could not leave without bidding his own farewell.

Drummond had dropped a feather-light kiss on her lips and stroked a vibrant curl as it sprang from her brow to tangle temptingly across the white pillow. The hot June night had been too sultry for bed linen, and Lydia had kicked away the coverings in her sleep, leaving a pale expanse of delectable calf to glow in the soft bloom of the dawn.

Drummond had gazed, entranced, at his childhood friend, and saw no longer a tomboy hoyden intent on climbing trees and making sling-shots, but a ripening, fragrant fruit, the swell of her breasts tempting and succulent beneath her virginal Dutch linen nightgown.

His hand had stolen across the bed, almost of its own volition, and he had felt as if he were watching someone else, voyeuristically enthralled as the hand lifted the hem of her chemise. He had swallowed, his mind reeling with possibilities hitherto undreamed of.

She had stirred slightly and rolled on to her front, pressing her hips down on to his hand so that it was trapped beneath her. He had savoured her warmth for a moment, feeling the heat of her sleeping body and the pressure of her thighs on the back of his hand. Then, desperate not to wake her, he had eased his hand free and tiptoed backward across the room.

Now, almost five years later, he was finally on his way home, and he wondered how that promising fruit had ripened. Aware that the memories had stimulated a hardening in his tight breeches, Drummond pulled the wide skirts of his travelling coat more closely around him and leant forward on to the blistered rail of the ship.

In the candle-lit darkness she arched her body above him, tipping her head languorously back to reveal her snowy throat, and pushing the full silken orbs of her glorious breasts forward. Her hair tumbled, unbound, behind her, and he could feel its satin weight stroke across his thighs and balls, causing him to contract and push his cock deeper into her.

He gripped a handful of the silken skeins and gently eased her head further back, admiring the tilt of her chin and the velvet pout of her lips which had so recently been clamped caressingly around his rigid member. A tiny groan escaped from her and he smiled, moving beneath her body with deliberate intent.

Stroking his strong hands around her hips and gently up to her tiny waist, he eased her willing body up and down the long length of his cock. Her full breasts invited him to cup them and he lightly massaged their heaviness, feeling her deep arousal as her nipples sprang to life beneath his thumbs and forefingers. Her pale hands began to mirror his, and the bronze discs of his own nipples puckered into erectness as she squeezed them. She was gorgeous, and his eyes gloried at the sight of her soft, milky-white skin contrasting with his own burnished copper musculature.

He lifted her, gently gripping the sides of her hips to raise her to her knees. Kissing the curve of her belly, he began to trail his tongue to the hollow at the top of her thigh. He could feel her skin tingle beneath his touch, could almost sense where she wanted him to kiss, and his lips burnt with the knowledge of her pleasure.

She moved forward, lifting a knee over his broad

shoulder to position herself directly above his face. Tonguing gently, he explored her sex with his lips, breathing her scent. He spread his hands wide on her behind and gently pushed her forward until she repositioned her other knee beside his face, gorgeously imprisoning his dark head between her thighs as he lapped at her, as with the thirst of a man who had spent years in the desert.

He kneaded the twin ovals of her buttocks with his hands and suddenly pushed his tongue deep into her, making her cry out and arch above him as the dark stubble surrounding his mouth grazed her.

'You're so wet: you taste like honey,' he murmured, his thumbs stroking and smoothing. She seemed unable to speak, trembling above him and pushing down on him for more.

Sliding further under her, he nibbled gently at the curve of her buttocks, taking gulps of her smooth flesh, caressing with his searching, searing tongue. Easing out and round behind her, he twisted agilely and came up to press his muscular chest into her smooth back. Biting softly at her neck, he lifted heavy handfuls of her hair so he could suck and nibble her shoulders and nape.

She leant her weight back against him and he held her imprisoned for a moment, the length of her straining body stretched against his; then he snaked one forearm around her waist while the other leant weight on her shoulders, arcing her forward until she buried her face into the welcoming softness of the pillow.

'Please! Please!' Her hands kneaded across the bolster to grip the brass rails of the bedstead.

Stimulated almost beyond control by the sight of her tiny waist above the beautiful flare of her hips, he held her close with his hands. His fingers slid to her tight anus and he circled it with the tip of his thumb, his short square nail rubbing and making it pucker tightly. He felt her tremble, and he moistened his middle finger with his own saliva, holding her buttocks wide and gentling her.

10

'Oh God, no,' she murmured. 'It'll hurt me, won't it?'

'Let me try,' he whispered, almost unable to stop as his finger slipped and twisted at the barrier to what he knew would be a smooth, tight haven.

She nodded, her reply muffled by the pillow under her face, and he moved before she could change her mind, pressing inside, passing the constricted sphincter into the warmth beyond. He heard her gasp and he smiled as she pushed herself back towards him, opening her bottom and almost sucking his finger in.

He reached underneath and caught his own tight balls in one hand, holding and squeezing for a moment, then running his fist along the length of his straining cock. When he judged she was ready, he pressed into her sex, his eyes fixed on the tumbled hair which spread wide on the sheets, obscuring her face.

She could be anybody.

The thought of taking an anonymous woman almost pushed him over the brink as he felt her velvety warmth envelop him. He was able to slide his finger deeply into her anus now, she was so ready and aroused, and he could feel the steely glide of his own cock through the paper-thin membrane that separated her inside.

His free hand raked around her, and gripped one of her breasts so tightly that she groaned. He rode her, staring down at the glisten of her juices, his mind clouded with the sweetness of each inward stroke. He had a sudden desire to see her come, to watch her face contort as she submitted to him.

'Turn over. You feel so good, but I want to see your face – I want to watch you come – I want to see you cry out.'

He released her and then quickly twisted her on to her back. She encircled him with her thighs as he pulled her on to him. The silken wetness of her sex shimmered as he rocked his hips, slowly pulling himself back and forth within her.

Gradually building his speed and rhythm, he gained momentum, feeling an exquisite sensation as the satin

skin of his foreskin was stretched by her firm grip. He
could feel himself spiralling inside her, twisting and
ramming with increasing speed, a fine sweat beginning
to sheen across his shoulders and chest. He pressed her
with one thumb, seeking and finding the exact spot he
knew would tip her over the edge, and he ground his
knuckle against her.

She cried out as her deep orgasm engulfed her, sending pulsing waves through her and on to his slickly
encased shaft. He smiled, enjoying the sight of her as
she tensed on the bed beneath him, her hands clawing
sideways to grasp handfuls of the creased sheets and
pull them up to her chest.

At last Drummond began to pant, gasping and thrusting deep into her as he felt a curious sensation of
constraint and release. His climax burst over him like a
broiling tide of pleasure and he cried out: 'Lydia!'

He was aware of a rush of displaced air the instant
before her balled fist struck him hard across the side of
his face.

'Who the hell's Lydia?' spat the innkeeper's daughter,
her face flushed and angry. Raising his hands to protect
himself against the slaps which rained upon his face
and chest, Drummond felt his mind spin with confusion
and disbelief at his own outburst. He caught at her, but
she fought him wildly, and he needed all his strength to
grasp her hands and still them. Gripping her wrists, he
pushed the girl down into the softness of the mattress
and silenced her with a hard kiss.

'Hush, Bess. You know that a man must have more
than one lover in a lifetime. How else would I have
learnt to satisfy you so well?'

He nibbled her lower lip caressingly and she frowned
up at him, searching his brown eyes. He thought for a
moment that he would have to say more to convince
her, but abruptly, like a summer storm, her temper was
gone and her cheeks dimpled.

'Oh, sire.' She caught and held his head between her
hands. 'I don't rightly care how many you've had. 'Tis

a rare treat for me to tumble with a gentleman like you. My usual bedfellows are bald of pate and thick of waist.'

She pulled him down and kissed him deeply, her mouth opening beneath his and her tongue moving to test the tender nerves in his lips. She began to move suggestively beneath him, wrapping her arms and legs around him, binding him to her and scratching her nails softly down his back.

'Remind me again what you've learnt from your other lovers.'

She giggled as he rose above her again in the crumpled bed, his cock jerking obediently against his navel.

Once on the road, astride the black mare that he had purchased that morning in the harbour town, Drummond reflected on his unguarded cry of his cousin's name the previous night. For weeks she had flickered around the deeper recesses of his mind like a ghost, her spectral image growing stronger as he came closer to home.

The mare bridled suddenly under his breech-clad thighs as muffled cries came unexpectedly through the dappling tree branches. The copse was small and lonely, but the road below him looked well-travelled, and he knew that the route was popular with cross-country travellers. Spurring the mare on, he rounded the curve of the wooded path to see that the road forked ahead of him. Two horsemen, slung low in their saddles, sprinted away at a gallop down one lane, while on the other, shadowed by trees, he could make out a distressed band of travellers and a stationary carriage.

As he drew closer he could see that there were at least four men on the roadway, all on foot. One was bound with rope; another two staggered on the wayside with cloaks tightly wrapped around their heads and faces. The coachman struggled in his attempt to loosen the rough bands which looped around his barrel chest, a blend of rage and fear washing across his ruddy features as he perceived the lone horseman approaching from the darkened archway of the forest.

Drummond dropped nimbly from his saddle and strode to the quailing group, holding his open palms up to show his lack of weapons. His stout boots sank into the mud which swamped the rough track.

'Are you stuck in this damned mire, sirs?' He glanced curiously at their various bindings, trying to decide which to help first.

'A mire it is, but not of mud!' spluttered a white-coiffured man of apoplectic complexion. 'A mire of rogues and thieves! Footpads and vagabonds! No road is safe for travellers!'

The coachman, having rid himself of his hempen cords, jumped down from the stagecoach and began to untie his beleaguered passengers. Drummond helped him, pulling the cloth from the head of the man nearest to him.

'Do you mean that you've been robbed?' He was surprised that the thieves had struck in broad daylight.

'Aye, it was the tobymen. Two of them, the blighters,' replied another whose black garb and high white collar marked him out as a parson. 'They've plagued this highway for months. They should be caught and strung from the gibbet, like that good-for-nothing Dick Turpin.'

Drummond helped the party back into the coach as he listened to their tale, wondering whether he should have given chase to the two men he had seen fleeing on the other road. Thoughtfully, he watched the mud-spattered coach as it wound its way towards the dark tunnel of trees, then patted his ebony mount.

Swinging his long leg over her back and settling into the saddle, he decided that when he reached the next town he would invest in a pistol or two. He hitched his warm circular travelling cloak closer around his power-ful shoulders and urged the mare forward, anxious to finish the long journey home.

* * *

Four days in the saddle had rendered Drummond weary and travel-stained. But the sight of the familiar town which nestled in the sunlit valley below cheered him, and he pulled the horse up so that he could gaze at the land. It rolled away like a verdant carpet, stretching and arcing in the sunlight. A far-flung prize hid just out of view over the brow of a distant hill: Hawkesworth Manor. His home was clear in his mind's eye as he dropped from the saddle and led the horse down into the valley.

When he reached the town, Drummond mounted again, shortening the reins and trotting the obedient horse through the edges of the busy market, carefully avoiding the pedlars with their laden barrows. The dry summer had made the roads dusty, and he watched the clouds of brown chalk puff underfoot and grime the hooves and legs of his mount.

A ragged group of filthy beggars held out grimy palms as he approached. The familiar gap-toothed smile of one caught his attention, and he reined in before them, searching in his pouch for coins. As he dropped a few shillings into the scarred and blackened hand, the beggar dropped a curtsy.

'Thank you, sir.' Her voice stirred his memory, and Drummond leant forward, frowning into her lined, defeated face.

'You are a Hawkesworth servant, woman. Why are you begging in the streets?'

She stepped away from him slightly, squinting up and twisting her hands in her grimy shawl.

'I'm no longer at the manor. The new master prefers his own staff.'

Valerian. So this was his brother's doing: purging the household of their father's faithful retainers and replacing them, no doubt, with hand-picked mercenaries.

'But why are you begging? Surely your references are good enough to secure you another post? And your severance pay, what have you done with it?'

The woman barked a laugh, bitter and mirthless.

'References? Severance pay? I don't know where you hail from, sir, but the old master is dead. There's a new liege at the big house now. He don't waste time with nonsense like that.' With a wracking hawk, she spat on to the ground at his feet. Before Drummond could sufficiently recover his wits to speak, she had gone, dragging her pale, wraith-like children behind her.

'Wait!' he cried, but she ignored his call, turning abruptly at the corner and disappearing down a dark, stinking alleyway.

He had intended to go straight to the house and announce his return, but he found himself loath to do that now. Heaven alone knew how his unpredictable brother would react at the loss of his assumed power. Drummond needed more information before he could declare himself.

Rubbing the coarseness of his unshaven chin with one hand, he thought of Jim Handfast, a retired gamekeeper and his father's oldest retainer. Jim was the only one he could trust to keep the secret of his return, and he would probably know enough to update Drummond on events at the manor. Turning the horse, he took the road out of town and began the short journey to the dilapidated cottage on the outer reaches of the Hawkesworth Estate.

'Lad, it's good to see you. Those at the big house have given you up for dead, but I knew you'd return someday.'

The old man clasped Drummond's firm hand in his gnarled grasp and shook it, his lined face full of pleasure.

'Master Valerian has been asserting himself and now most of the servants fend for themselves. He's replaced a lot of them with his own henchmen and cheap untrained labour. The poachers take a lot of the deer, now.'

He thrust a mug of sour ale on to the rough surface of the wooden table and looked at Drummond, concern in his pale, rheumy eyes. They sat silently for a few minutes, then the old man coughed before he spoke again.

'I know why you left, lad. Valerian hasn't changed one whit. A man of injustice and cruelty whose actions helped send your poor father to his early grave, God rest his soul. A sniff of your return and that young whippersnapper will be on your tail again, and this time he won't fail, unless you've gotten faster than him with the sword.'

He nodded at the pale scar which marked Drummond's left cheek, a constant reminder of the events which had led to his dawn departure. Rather than carry tales to their sick father, Drummond had left home and taken the King's shilling. Life on the sea had been exciting, and he had revelled in the roving life style which suited him far better than his old life of pampered ease. He had seen most of the world, won a few battles, and conquered his own demons. There was no way that he could let his brother take the one thing he wanted more than anything else: his birthright.

Drummond banged a clenched fist on the table-top.

'I'll challenge him!' he declared. 'I've learnt to wield a sword better than any man I know.'

'Aye, but desperation will sharpen his point. He has more to lose now,' Jim reminded him. 'No, Master Drummond, you must bide your time. It's the eldest surviving son who inherits when a man dies intestate. And, as far as everyone knows, you're dead. The will is missing and it's you who has to find it. Master Valerian is hardly going to help you: methinks he'd rather be branded a murderer than hand the inheritance to you. Where do you think your father would have put it? Can you remember the whereabouts of his strong-box?'

They talked late into the night, and when Jim finally pulled a straw palliasse from under the truckle-bed, Drummond found he was past tiredness. Through the small hours he tossed fitfully on the prickly mattress, his mind twisting and turning, picking at his dilemma as if it were an itching scab. He was determined to regain his inheritance and desperate to help the servants who had been deprived of homes and livelihoods.

As an early pink dawn stole over the thoughtful planes of his face, an idea germinated and slowly flourished. Remembering the travellers that he had helped on the road, the victims of two fearless highwaymen, he rolled over and folded his arms under his head. He would find the will, but in the meantime he had conceived a plan – daring and dangerous, but entirely necessary – to redress the balance and put Hawkesworth money back into the pockets of those wronged workers.

He would haunt the roads, and each time he encountered his brother's carriage, he would hold him up and take the equivalent of one servant's wages in gold or jewels: no more, no less. It was a fair, albeit temporary, way to settle it.

As he drifted to sleep, a smile curved across his mouth: the image of himself in a black mask and a hat pulled low over his brow had a certain romantic appeal, and he was impatient for the first confrontation.

Chapter Two

'*S*tand and deliver!'

The command rang clearly through the crisp air, and the coachman pulled the horses up, his eyes rolling with shock and fear. The highwayman, darkly masked and cloaked, dismounted and gestured with his pistol at the man's chest.

'Your weapons, man. Give me the arms you bear.'

After stripping the coachman of his only protection, he swiftly bound him to his seat and tied the cloth of his long coat over his head, rendering him helpless. The man continued to struggle and cry out, yelling loudly for help. The highwayman hesitated, his body taut with indecision. Then he swung his pistol round and brought the heavy handle down across the coachman's neck.

There was silence.

As he approached the carriage, Drummond glanced at his own family coat of arms so familiarly displayed upon the highly polished timber of the door. He took a deep breath, bracing himself. What had seemed so easy in his thoughts, in the dead of night, was much harder in the cold light of day.

He ducked his head and looked through the open window to see a velvet-cloaked woman shrink into the shadowy recesses. There were no other occupants and

Drummond was disappointed at his brother's absence. A mere woman: one of Valerian's mistresses, no doubt. Maybe her jewellery would be worthwhile.

He glanced into the carriage and sighed. This was not quite as simple as he had anticipated.

'Come, madam. I will not harm you. Give me your money and your jewels and I'll be away.'

He extended a leather-gloved hand and was relieved when a kid pouch of jingling coins was placed on his outstretched palm. There was a long pause.

'And your jewels, madam,' he urged.

'I can't. They are precious to me. A gift. Please don't ask me for them.'

Her voice, although taut with fear, was soft and low, the words caressing him like swansdown as they curved towards him from the shadows. His head swam and he shook it to loosen the hypnosis.

'Your jewels or your life.' The words sounded harsh even to his own ears.

There was a long silence, then a small hand reluctantly placed two pearl eardrops and a slender circlet of gold into his grasp. Recognition lanced through his body in a shocking wave: the bangle was his own birthday gift to Lydia when she had turned twelve, and he had never seen her without it. Grasping the still-extended wrist with a vice-like grip, he jerked her forward into the light.

Wide eyes met his, thick lashes shading the fear in the emerald depths. Her beauty took him by surprise, and he gazed, spellbound, drinking in the opalescent skin of her face and neck, and the carefully tamed black ringlets which clustered around her cheeks under the dainty tricorne hat.

Shock made him speechless, and he could only hold fast to her arm, his breathing rapid and his thoughts confused, as he waited for her to recognise him.

Lydia, who had heard whispered tales of fearless highwaymen, stared back. She held her breath as he drew her fingertips to his chiselled lips and kissed each finger lightly, caressingly, before relinquishing her hand. His eyes glinted through the slits in his black mask and he nodded, a smile quirking the corner of his generous mouth.

'A fairer jewel than any other is seated in the carriage before me. With your permission, madam, I will step inside.'

'No. You can't. I'm alone. I – I have no chaperone.' Lydia tried to quell her nervousness by twisting her hands into the soothing velvet of her cloak. His eyes narrowed. Ignoring her words, he pulled the door open and stepped up into the carriage.

'Without your permission, then.'

Lydia's heart hammered as she shrank into the farthest corner, putting as much space as she could between them. When he sat on the seat beside her, his long muscular legs stretched the tight seams of his knee-breeches and she felt her throat tighten and constrict at the evidence of his physical strength. There was a tang of danger in the close air of the carriage as he stripped off one leather glove and placed a strong hand under her chin, tilting her head back to gaze searchingly into her face.

He raised one eyebrow.

'No chaperone? What a tragedy. Your mother should know better.'

'I – I have no mother.' She froze as she felt his hand caress her face, his thumb travelling lightly across her lips and down under her chin, lighting a fire under the passage of his touch. She reached up to push his hand away, but he grasped her wrist in his iron grip and forced her hand down to his thigh; she jerked it away as if he had burnt her.

She squeezed her eyes shut as he left her chin to travel down to the fastening of her cloak, and she felt the fabric part as he undid the clasp. The heavy velvet slithered from her shoulders and she suppressed a shudder. She clutched at the mantle, trying to pull it back up but he casually knocked her hand aside and pressed her into the corner until her back arched painfully against the hard timber behind her.

With sudden vigour he crushed her to him, pulling her bodily into his arms to kiss her hungrily. Lydia twisted her head to escape him, but he held her fast and she felt the first stirrings of fear laced with an uncontrollable arousal at his kiss. As she fought against the iron hardness of his chest, he jerked the hat from her head, and with one hand fumbled at the pins and ribbons which held her hair until it tumbled, unfettered, down her back.

He became fierce, ardent, shocking her as his tongue probed between her teeth, and she struggled harder, sensing a rapacious hunger which was barely under control as he forced her further back into the corner of the coach. She tried to cry out, but his lips sealed hers with the effectiveness of a gag, and she could only twist her hands against his unyielding body and bite him, sinking her teeth into the fleshy pad of his lip.

'You little vixen.' He drew back, wiping his mouth with the back of his gloved hand. There was a streak of crimson blood on the black leather and a corresponding bead on his lower lip. He stared at her, his eyes, cinnamon lit with gold, devouring hers with frightening intensity. Lydia was the first to drop her gaze.

She was unprepared for what followed.

One strong hand slid to the back of her neck, his mouth descending on hers as his knee forced between her legs and his hard leather boot knocked her feet apart. He grabbed her wrists and forced them behind her back, pulling one of the remaining ribbons from her hair and winding it tightly around to secure her hands. She struggled, but he was much stronger than she was; he jerked her shoulders back, making her sit upright, and she was aware of her breasts straining against the lacing of her bodice. She could almost see herself through his eyes, helpless but glowing, her eyes bright and her skin feverish, her breast rising and falling with rapid panting breaths. She knew that he wanted what he saw, and that she would have to fight hard to prevent him taking it.

As she glanced at the swollen bite-marks on his lower lip, a tiny voice in her head seemed to ask her if she really wanted to stop him. He was so handsome, uncompromising, and virile. Surely there were worse fates to befall a girl?

'Please,' she said, trying to speak calmly. 'If it's money you want, then I have plenty at home. I'll fetch it for you. I could bring it back here. Please let me go.'

'The only thing you'd bring back is a magistrate, and a length of rope to hoist me to the gibbet. I don't want your money. I want you.'

His hands went to the neckline of her gown and he plucked the lacing open with the speed and expertise of someone well versed in the intricacies of women's clothing. The chemise below was fine muslin, and, placing a finger at the top of the delicate fabric, he tore it from breastbone to navel in one fluid movement. Lydia gasped and flinched, her shock mingled with admiration for the determination which hardened his handsome face. He gripped the two edges of her bodice and jerked them back and round, trapping her arms more firmly and effectively than any ribbon.

She was his captive.

'Sweet Jesus, you're beautiful.'

Before she could take a breath he had leant forward and opened his greedy mouth to her breast, using his hands to shape the rounded form, his lips questing over the sensitive flesh and fastening on one nipple, which tightened beneath his teeth. He circled it with his tongue, then drew it into his mouth, licking and sucking until it gleamed and lengthened, and Lydia felt hot needles dart from her breast to her thighs.

She arched her back slightly, pushing herself out to his mouth and drowning in exquisite sensation; her body ached as it had when Angel had touched her, but everything was somehow hotter, her skin more alert, her mind more clouded. She breathed shallowly and softly, afraid to disturb his caress, but her nose was still full of the smell of him: the masculine scent that emanated from his hair and clothes as he moved across her lap, a half-familiar soapy muskiness, tinged with woodsmoke, that she had smelt before but could not place.

'Look at me! Kiss me!' It was a command, not a request.

She shook her head, her eyes tightly shut. He gripped her jaw, squeezing her cheeks until they hurt and turning her face up to his.

'I said, kiss me. Kiss me now.'

She opened her eyes and risked looking at him. His tousled hair had tiny sunlit streaks, and it was tamed and flattened at the sides by the coal-black mask he wore. The breadth of his shoulders almost blocked the light from the window, and the carriage seemed small and very dark. She could feel the heat of his breath on her face where his mouth was close, so very close to hers.

It would be so easy, she thought. And there was a part of her that desperately wanted to feel his mouth with her own.

She took a deep breath and leant forward, tentatively touching. He did not kiss her back at first, staying very still as her lips flickered across his with a butterfly touch. When he did respond, the kiss was long and deep, his mouth hard yet soft against hers, and she was left gasping and disappointed when he pulled away from her. He stood up, so tall that his head brushed the roof of the carriage.

Watching her, as if assessing her reaction, he pulled at the buttons which joined his shirt-front and impatiently jerked the shirt-tails out from the waistband of his breeches. Lydia stared at his bare skin, at the satiny, sun-kissed bronze of his chest and the line of crisp, golden hairs which snaked between the muscular curves of his pectorals down to the bulge that pressed insistently against the fastening of his breeches. She felt

a sharp, jolting kick in her stomach as an almost unidentifiable feeling – excitement mingled with fear – flooded
through her body. He popped the first button of his
breeches and her eyes shot to his face: she saw that
there was never going to be a chance of escape.

He took her bound and half-naked body in his arms
and lay her back until she felt the cool firmness of the
leather seat beneath her skin. One hand ran lightly from
her neck, down over her breast, to the flatness of her
stomach; then he pulled her skirts up, his fingers
probing between her thighs and sliding over her with
practised ease. Lydia tried to press her knees together.

'Please – oh, please!' She was unsure whether she was
pleading with him to stop, or carry on. His mouth
became stern as he firmly prised her legs apart again
and curved a possessive hand over her. She shut her
eyes, her body trembling as his weight pressed down
on her and burning kisses rained across her face, her
neck, her breasts.

'You're beautiful, so beautiful. I won't hurt you. Let
me stroke you, you're gorgeous. You smell so fresh.'
His lips were soft and questing as they moved to her
eyelids, kissing and pressing the delicate skin as he slid
his hands over her trembling body.

He was insistent but gentle, and she felt herself
respond. A primitive throb swelled somewhere deep
inside herself, and she tried to push it away, to deny it,
but it grew stronger and thicker. The unwilling stirrings
of desire swelled and grew as he stroked her tingling
flesh, lingering on the smoothness of her thighs and
then moving inward to her sex, touching the tight
opening, gentling her.

She lay still, shaking and afraid but warmed by his
embrace, concentrating on the sensation of the tips of
his fingers: she felt that she was swollen and open, and
so soft under his touch.

He held his weight above her body with one sinewy
arm while unbuttoning and releasing his cock, rigid and
taut as it sprang eagerly from the constraints of his

clothing. Lydia glanced down, and then quickly away, unable to believe that a man could be so different from herself. She held her breath as he curved his hand over her sex, parting her. When she felt the throbbing heat of him, her self-possession deserted her and she felt her bound hands trembling under the small of her back, her fingers tingling and fluttering inside their bindings.

As he entered her she struggled: too late. They were both beyond the point of no return, and Lydia let her head fall back on the cushion of her discarded cloak, her eyes fixed on his.

He stopped abruptly at the unexpected barrier, his pupils constricted to pin-points.

'Have you – ? Are you – ? Oh, Christ!' He paused, panting, as if teetering on the brink of an enormous precipice. Then, as she instinctively lifted her ankles and wrapped herself around him, he closed his eyes and pressed firmly through.

Deep into her.

Lydia was lanced by sharp pain, and tiny hot tears smarted at the corners of her eyes. The highwayman whispered in her ear, words of endearment that she could barely hear or understand. She thought he said her name, but sensation clouded her senses and she stopped listening, aware only of the feel of silken lips soothing her face and neck, satin hands sliding over her hips as he moved.

He was almost impossibly gentle, shifting slowly above her and cradling her in his arms. She felt the harsh rawness gradually superseded by a sweet pleasure as he drew his length back and then drove luxuriously into her again, his strokes developing into a voluptuous rhythm as she gradually relaxed beneath him and began to rock her hips against him, her mind centred on the exquisite torture of his touch.

She arched her back against the red leather seat, her heart beating faster, with feverish waves radiating outward over her whole body and raising the myriad downy hairs on her skin. She could feel a tingling which started in her toes and fingered up her spine to pulse across her scalp, and soon she was foundering, sinking, drowning. Senseless, totally hypnotised by dark sensation, she gripped his waist with her knees, almost unaware of the sudden low groan that the highwayman gave as he climaxed, shuddering into her with muscular thrusts of his taut pelvis.

She felt his cock resonate and jerk, and gave herself up to the sweetness of her own sensation, fluttering and rippling beneath the weight of his body. A curious relief seemed to free her, and she wished that her hands were not bound so that she could reach around him and anchor herself firmly to him before she floated away.

They lay spent, and she inhaled the seashell scent of their embrace. Drummond raised himself above Lydia, resting on one elbow, his smooth biceps bulging against the taut cotton of his shirt.

He bent his head to hers and kissed her swollen lips tenderly, almost lovingly, his eyes bright with some emotion that Lydia could not decipher. She would not, could not, kiss him back; her mind was too full. She lay still beneath him.

'I must be away. I have stayed too long.' His voice was low, intimate, and sweet to her ears. She shifted beneath him, conscious of a cramping in her bound hands.

He lifted her, pulling her torn chemise and the unlaced bodice forward. When her hands were free, Lydia tidied and re-pinned her hair in silence, conscious of his inscrutable gaze tracking her every move.

When they had dressed, she glanced at him, a small frown creasing her brow.

'There is something I must do,' she said, standing up and turning to face him.

There was a pause, then Lydia raised her hand and brought it down with the full weight of her body, landing a slap on his cheek which cracked as it hit him. He recoiled with shock, but in the depth of his eyes was a silent understanding; he did not touch the livid finger

27

marks which flushed on his jaw, but simply reached out and fingered a tiny lock of hair which coiled across her temple. He opened his mouth, drawing breath as if to speak, but suddenly turned away and jumped down from the carriage.

He turned to look at her through the open door, then reached forward and grasped the hand that had struck him, pressing his lips into the palm.

'Good day to you, madam. A safe passage.'

Abruptly, he was gone, running light-footed to his ebony steed. He was up and away at a gallop before she could cry out. Leaning her head and shoulders out of the carriage window, she watched him as he crested the hill, his silhouette dark in the morning sun. Then he disappeared from sight.

Liberty, thought Lydia, that's what it is. She smoothed the fashionable dark green stocking up over her knee and paused to check her reflection in the mirror. Her leg was as sleek and shapely as it had been yesterday morning, but somehow everything about her body looked different. Everything was different, everything had changed. Now she knew. Now she was no longer – what was it that Valerian had called her? – virgo intacta.

She dropped the petticoats over her stockinged legs and ran her palms across her skirt, her eyes still fixed to the glowing reflection in the mirror. If she leant forward she could see that even the colour of her eyes was different: lighter, brighter, a glinting emerald with tiny pin-point pupils, constricted by the morning sun which lit the surface of everything around her.

She wondered what he was doing, where he was.

The ruthlessness of the masked highwayman had given her first full sexual encounter an added zest, and his anonymity made her memories all the more heady.

Who was he?

She rubbed one finger over the fullness of her lower lip, imagining the swollen wound, the bite mark, which would mark his mouth for several days.

Would she ever see him again?

Her body, melting and honey-soft at the core, hoped that she would, and soon. Now that she had found sex – had not even had to seek it – she was filled with an unquenchable desire to experience more of its pleasures.

She gave one more pouting glance to her reflection, then went down to breakfast, wondering whether any-one would notice how different she looked and ask themselves why.

Leaving the overnight guests to fortify themselves with breakfast before the hunt commenced, Lydia stepped out on to the stone steps. Ghostly tendrils of morning mist fingered lightly around the sturdy oaks in the panoramic gardens. The cold dampness of early autumn caused several of her stray curls to coil around her face, and she tucked them impatiently into the hat which tipped low over one eyebrow.

Flexing her supple crop between leather-clad hands, she strode purposefully around the gable end of the house, the full green skirts of her riding habit swirling around her legs. She could hear the hounds in the yard, baying as they milled around the shining legs of the mounts.

As she rounded the corner she saw Valerian, resplendent in close-fitting breeches, his pale satanic beauty enhanced by the scarlet coat which stretched across the breadth of his shoulders. His right arm suddenly flung up and back, as he brought his whip down on the cringing shoulders of a young stable-hand.

'Damn you,' he snarled, raising his arm to strike again. 'When I say polish it, I mean polish. Look at it, boy, look at it! I will not be seen in public with such a filth-encrusted bridle.' He drew himself up to his full height. 'Clean it again or I'll thrash you to within an inch of your life.'

'But, sire, I –'

'Don't be impertinent: I am your master!' Valerian shrieked, fury and petulance stiffening his body as he

29

raised his whip to lash again. The young groom cried out as the stinging tip caught his outstretched hand, and Lydia ran forward to pull Valerian's arm down with both of her own, dropping her crop to the ground.

'Valerian! No! Don't beat him. Please!' She pulled at him, willing him to face her. The groom scrambled to his feet, hesitated, and then fled as Valerian swung his enraged body round, his narrow lips forming a gash across his face, the deep pools of his black eyes glazed and bloodshot.

'Valerian,' urged Lydia. 'Please, cousin, look at me.'

She had seen his rages, knew that he would become unrecognisable, unaware of his surroundings, focussing totally on the violence that raged within him.

Suddenly his stormy eyes snapped on hers, and he curled his lips venomously as one strong hand flipped quickly up and grasped the frills of her shirt-front. He jerked her roughly towards him, and as she felt his foetid breath fan her face she flinched, fear worming in her belly. He shook her by the neck like a drowned kitten, then abruptly threw her away from him so that she landed heavily on the stone floor of the yard, skirts flung up around her knees.

Valerian raised his leather whip before awareness dawned in her, and he brought it down, missing her by a hair's breadth. Panting with disbelief at his violence, Lydia screamed and cast wildly around, hoping someone would help her.

There was no one. The guests were still breakfasting, and even the hounds were cowering, away at the end of the yard, as far from their master as they could get.

Lydia was suddenly aware of a highly polished boot kicking her legs apart. Firm hands grasped the edges of her skirts, paused, then tore their length from hem to waist, revealing the green stockings which encased her legs, all the way up to where an inch of pale, smooth flesh was vulnerably visible.

Seeing the intent deep in Valerian's coal-black eyes and the rigid rod of his cock bulging in his breeches, she scrabbled furiously away. Grazing her hands on the ground as she moved crab-like from under him, Lydia turned, half crawling, and pushed herself to her feet. Panic began to swell in her breast as she heard his muttered expletive and felt the talons of his fingers swipe at her hair.

Then suddenly the gate was before her and she was over it, her torn skirts flinging wide as she swung her legs. She glanced back to see Valerian's smooth boot bottoms skeetering over the cobbles as he tried to regain purchase.

'Stop!' he shouted, the frustration audible in his throat. 'Come back here or I'll set the hounds on you!'

Without pausing, Lydia jumped from the top of the five-barred wooden gate, twisting her ankle slightly on her heavy landing. Trying to regain a footing on the dewy grass, she slipped a little and, holding her ruined skirts up, raced headlong, dodging through the sparse trees of the estate grounds. At last, out of breath, she reached the edge of Hawkesworth Forest, where dark sanctuary waited.

Lydia paused in her flight, rubbing her fingers along her ribs where a burning stitch tore at her side. She felt as though she had been running for hours, although it must have been only twenty minutes. She had skirted the edge of the shadowy woods at first, afraid of the silent interior, but when she heard the hounds give tongue as they were loosed from the yard, she had pushed her superstitious fear to the back of her mind and plunged into the dark green heart of the forest.

As she ran through the undergrowth, brambles and thorns scratched at the flesh of her calves until tiny droplets of crimson blood beaded the surface of her skin; the autumn-bare branches snatched at her hair, tangling into its already tousled fronds as she impatiently pulled herself free. The ground before her sloped down, its loamy surface covered with a carpet of crisp leaves: russet, gold, and brown.

Lydia slipped and slid, sideways and downward, the forest growing darker around her as she progressed down into what appeared to be a ravine with a tiny gurgling brook in the bottom. The morning sunlight hardly penetrated the gloom: just a few dusty fingers filtered through the lofty branches as the trees curved protectively overhead.

She reached the brook and stood, breathing heavily, leaning on a tree-trunk to steady herself.

There was silence. The deep, ominous quiet in the cathedral-like clearing was broken only by the sound of the brook, and the creak and scrape of brittle branches. A dead leaf floated down and lightly brushed her arm, making her jump and glance round. Behind her the slope was steep and the tracks of her descent clearly visible; Valerian would have little difficulty following and finding her, and she was certainly no match for his dogs.

As if on cue, the distant hounds gave tongue again, picking up her scent on the edges of the forest. Fear made her heart beat thunderously and the blood swished in her ears. She picked up her torn skirts and stepped determinedly into the stream. The icy water made her gasp and smarted the tiny scratches on her legs, but she pushed on, knowing that if she could follow the water for long enough then the dogs might lose her trail.

She splashed over stones and fallen branches, staying in the centre of the brook and travelling against the current. She wondered where the spring originated, hoping that it would bring her round and behind the hounds. She could then double back to the manor, to warmth and safety.

The thought of home was so inviting that, losing her concentration, she stumbled, tripping over a boulder and falling to her knees in the freezing water. Her hands went forward to break her fall and her palms scraped across the rough edges of the huge rock. She could hear the dogs gaining ground behind her, crashing through the ferny undergrowth and sliding – some yelping as their paws caught on sharp stones – down the ravine towards her. She scrambled upright and forged ahead, heedless of the pain in her twisted ankle and the heavy sodden fabric of her skirts.

Veering to the left, she splashed out of the water and up on to the bracken-covered slope where she ran more freely, casting a terrified glance over her shoulder. The leader of the pack was gaining ground, frothing saliva drooling from its yellowed fangs as it sensed the despair of its quarry.

Lydia screamed, long and piercing.

'Halt!' commanded a rough foreign voice. Turning, she collided with a solid expanse of muscular chest, and two powerful arms held her, almost lifting her off her feet.

'Help me! Oh, please, help me!' she gasped, briefly grateful, thinking she was safe until she looked up into the hard, uncompromising face of Conrad, Valerian's Nordic manservant.

He surveyed her calmly, then without a word he swept her up and threw her over one of his broad shoulders, kicking at the lead hound as it launched itself at her. Drooping over his shoulder, her long hair streaming almost to the ground behind him, Lydia shouted and beat her fists against the rigidity of his back as he turned and splashed across the brook, his powerful legs making short work of the journey back up the ravine.

Valerian waited, astride his huge chestnut stallion, a second manservant patiently standing at his side.

'Run to earth then, dear cousin?' he asked, a mocking lilt to his calm voice. 'Thank you, Conrad. A job well done. I shall reward you appropriately.' He reached into his scarlet jacket, drew out a pouch of sovereigns and tossed it. The tall Norwegian, hardly breaking his loping stride, caught it easily with one huge hand.

'Put her up behind me,' commanded Valerian. The servant deposited the struggling Lydia on to the stallion, where she instinctively held on to Valerian, gripping the waist of his crimson coat.

'Bring the pack home.' He nodded at the henchmen, then spurred his horse, turning and heading through the forest. Lydia clung to him, her despair turning to relief as she saw that they were heading home.

Chapter Three

*T*he trees thinned and they trotted across the open parkland of the estate. The chimneys of the house were just visible, a welcoming drift of smoke curling out of the tops. As they approached, Lydia saw Anderson, the butler, waiting at the gate by the stable-yard.

'My Lord,' he said, clearing his throat tactfully. 'The guests are wondering about the hunt.'

'Send them home,' replied Valerian curtly. 'Inform them that my cousin has a minor indisposition and that she requires rest and quiet. Here, Sam!' He beckoned the groom whom earlier he had so cruelly chastised. 'Take my horse.'

The youth touched his calloused hand to his forelock and hastened to do his master's bidding. Dismounting, Valerian pulled Lydia into his arms and bore her indoors, through the great hall and up the sweeping staircase. Lydia struggled slightly as they passed her room door without stopping. She searched the hard planes of his face but did not speak, a tiny flame of excitement flickering within her as he kicked open the studded door of his own room. Lydia had not been inside since childhood, and glanced around with interest, half expecting it to be littered still with the trappings of boyhood.

Heavy scarlet drapes were pulled across the wide windows and the room was in partial darkness, lit only by the embers of a dying fire in the grate. The ebony floor was devoid of any coverings save one large tiger-skin stretched before the grand, black marble fireplace. An upright wooden chair, throne-like, stood at the side of the rug, with brass studs securing the raven leather of the seat and armrests, and lengths of soft cord looped around the front legs and each armrest. Beside the throne a bound casket rested on a footstool.

Across the room Valerian's huge bed dominated the space; it was at least seven feet across and raised, altar-like, on a dais, black and red silken drapes concealing the softness of the mattress. Ebony wood legs held it aloft, and yards of drifting crimson voile formed a canopy, suspended from a perfectly circular cast-iron loop set into the beamed ceiling. The starkness of the room and the scarlet and jet hues of the fabrics stimulated Lydia's sensuality. She found it hard to imagine Valerian sleeping here: it was a room designed not for restful repose but for some other, far more disturbing, activity.

Glancing up into Valerian's eyes she saw, with fascination, a look of abject hunger and lust which she felt mirrored deep inside herself. A tingling heat thrilled across the surface of her skin, and she felt her breath catch in her throat as he gazed at her with unsmiling intensity.

'You cannot escape me, Lydia,' he purred. 'You can run. Indeed, you excite me with your running, and I shall always give chase. But I will also catch you. Every time.'

He sat her down, almost tenderly, in the throne-like chair, placing her hands on the armrests so that she instinctively gripped the carved globes at the ends. Looping the silken cords around her wrists, he tightened them securely before moving down to do the same to her ankles.

Lydia watched him, unsure whether to struggle or cry

out, wondering what he planned to do. The chair was broad and her legs were parted under her gown, her ankles tied firm and wide; she felt exposed and open despite the coverings of her heavy wet skirts.

Valerian knelt before her, surveying his handiwork with satisfaction, apparently pleased with the enforced uprightness of her position and the rigidity of her spine which thrust her breasts towards him. He reached down and eased her sodden shoes from her feet, tossing them abruptly aside. Lydia tried to remain impassive, her feelings confused at his intimate behaviour, as he unfastened the hooks at the side of her skirt and pulled it down over her hips.

'Lift.' It was a command that would tolerate no disobedience.

Lydia lifted, bracing her hands and raising her buttocks from the seat. He slid the skirt and petticoats off as one piece, briefly unlooping her ankles from their bindings to free the garments before they joined the shoes, forming a wet, torn, untidy pile across the room.

He stared at her, feasting on the nakedness of her lower body, clad only in dark stockings. She could feel the bare skin of her buttocks sticking slightly to the leather seat, a slick juicy patch slowly forming where she rested on the firm surface.

She watched Valerian as he opened her coat and blouse, then unlaced her corsets to free her breasts; he did not touch her, content to caress her with his eyes alone. She sat quite still, naked to his inscrutable gaze, a liquid stream of hot desire coursing through her as she longed for the feel of his hands, for him to touch her, take her, do something.

Still he did not. Instead, he peeled the stockings from her scratched legs with great care before rising to his feet to walk to the far end of the room. She watched him as he lifted the ewer and poured water into a china bowl. Kneeling before her once again, he gently washed her wounds with the cool water, his fingers hardly

37

touching her feverish skin which jumped and goose-bumped under his tender ministrations.

Finished, he pushed the china bowl of rose-hued water to one side and grasped her ankles with his firm hands. Holding one cleansed foot, he surveyed its pale length, softly stroking the underside with the pad of his thumb before suddenly engulfing her toes with the melting velvet of his lips, sucking and drawing.

Lydia stiffened, finding the exquisite sensation almost too much to bear, and she dropped her head back on to the high curve of the chair back. She could feel his lips following the arch of her instep to her ankle where his tongue rasped her pale flesh, and her fingers tightened on the wooden globes beneath her hands.

She abandoned herself to the delectable pleasure his mouth induced, as he supped, moving his mouth gradually and inexorably upward, the salty tang of his saliva stinging her bramble scratches. She winced and he smiled secretly, enjoying the tiny evidence of her pain. Continuing up her leg, he moved his face to the soft pad of her inner thigh where he inhaled deeply, savouring the scent of her excitement.

'You smell like a bitch in heat.'

Shocked by his sudden crudity after apparent tenderness, she snapped her head forward, glaring at him through narrowed lids.

'I thought you kept mangy curs away from your bitches!' she retorted.

With unexpected power he suddenly grasped her hips and jerked her pelvis forward to the edge of the chair, exposing her to his close scrutiny.

'Only the best stud dogs take them,' he muttered.

She could feel his hot breath upon her as he dipped his head, and she wriggled back, remembering belatedly that this was Valerian and she disliked him intensely, considered him the enemy. He had been the mortal foe in their game of cat and mouse in the forest.

He regarded her with a dark, brooding intensity, his sloe eyes half closed and glittering with sudden fury.

Coldly, deliberately, he grasped her again and pulled her firmly to the edge of the chair once more, then freed one hand and encircled her neck with a vice-like grip. Lydia stared at him, fear mingling with desire at his authority. He bent forward and took her mouth with his, crushing her lips against her teeth.

'You're hurting me,' she hissed, twisting her head to one side. He grasped her face and jerked it back until her eyes met his.

'If I want to hurt you, then I will,' he said. 'You don't seem to have realised, yet, that I can do what I like to you. You belong to me.'

Maintaining his collar-like grasp, he bent his head to her thighs, plunging, penetrating, and thrusting his insistent tongue into her burning flesh. Her senses swirled and she arched her back, tipping herself forward and on to his face, desperate to feel more, trying to grind herself on to him. He sucked and licked and teased, until the familiar waves trembled at the edges of her awareness; as if sensing her impending climax, he withdrew.

'Oh, no! Please!'

She surveyed him through half-closed lids, her lashes casting a shadow over her flushed cheeks. He curved his thin, hard mouth in a semblance of a smile, patently revelling in his control over her. One hand slid lightly up her inner thigh, and suddenly he thrust two fingers deep into her. She arched her back against the hardness of the throne and cried out, jerking her pelvis and clenching on to him in a vain attempt to retain his fingers, but they were gone, leaving her empty and incomplete.

All thoughts of her hatred for him gone, Lydia swallowed her pride and whimpered, imploring him wordlessly to release her from her exquisite frustration. He raised himself up before her, leant close and whispered in her ear.

'You'll have to beg, dear cousin. I want to hear you beg.'

She shook her head vehemently.

'Never!' She twisted her wrists in their bonds, but the tight cord burnt weals into her flesh and seemed to grow even tighter. Valerian knelt between her legs, his eyes fixed on her face, studying her reactions with the scrutiny of an alchemist experimenting with the philosopher's stone.

She stared back, tracing the line of his straight nose, the curve of his upper lip, the shadow that stubbled his jaw despite the fact that he must have shaved only a few hours ago. She saw the cleft in his strong chin deepen under her gaze and felt an overwhelming desire to lean forward and put her mouth there, to bury her tongue in the fissure and lick his chin. Holding her breath, she resisted the urge, knowing full well that he would not tolerate such a gesture of tenderness.

Smiling, a malicious pleasure washing over his face, Valerian walked across the room and stood by the raised crimson dais, apparently deep in thought. Suddenly he snapped his fingers and came stalking back across the bare floor, his boots ringing on the varnished surface. He threw open the lid of the casket and reached in. As he withdrew his hand, she saw something small and metallic glinting in his closed fist.

Before she could protest, Lydia saw him fix her erect nipples with tiny beaten silver stars. They clamped tightly around the puckered peaks, thrilling her with delicate, almost unbearably painful pleasure. Gasping, she thrust her hips forward in an involuntarily wanton gesture, and Valerian laughed cruelly, leant over, and engulfed her ready mouth with a hard and possessive kiss, plunging his rigid tongue deep into her throat until she almost gagged, sick with desire and penetration.

He stood back, admiring his handiwork before reaching again into the casket and withdrawing a small corked crystal decanter. He grasped the stopper with his teeth, jerked it free, and spat it into the fire where it smouldered briefly and then burst into licking orange flames. He tipped the bottle, and an amber liquid dripped, almost sinuously, over her breasts, inflaming her nipples before drizzling down to the scoop of her navel; it collected there briefly, a shimmering copper pool, before pouring down to wet her dark curls. The liquid burned her already incandescent flesh and she squirmed, gasping at the pleasure which bordered on pain.

Valerian leant his muscular body forward, leaning dominantly over her and dipping his lascivious mouth to the rivulets of brandy, sucking her imprisoned nipples into steel peaks before following the stream of cognac downward, inserting his tongue roughly into the conduit of her umbilicus, drinking the nectar from her belly. His mouth burnt, accentuating the scald of the amber liquid as he drew the tiny dark curls of her pubic hair between his teeth, tugging them with a ruthless ferocity before unleashing his tongue on her. He licked and sucked, plunging his muscular thumb into her before suddenly withdrawing moments before she came.

Wild with the need for sexual release, Lydia bit her lips, desperate not to submit. She closed her eyes to force back tears of frustration, willing her sensual need to dissipate. She hoped silently that he would not be able to hold himself back, that he would need to spend his passion upon her; but, glancing through the slits of her almost closed eyelids, she observed his control and restraint as he stood before her, his hooded stare vigilant and watchful.

Raising one dark, winging eyebrow, he half smiled, enquiringly, but Lydia shook her head, refusing to capitulate. An impatience washed across his features, and he bent forward to briskly tighten the leashes which bound her wrists and ankles. She pulled fiercely against them.

'This hurts, Valerian!'

With a satisfied nod he tilted her chin and ground her mouth with a bruising kiss, before squeezing her left breast with rough brutality. He raised his arm and struck her forcibly across the face with the flat of his palm and, hardly pausing, ripped open the fine cotton of his white shirt to reveal the pale-skinned masculinity of his hairless chest.

The sight of him exposed excited her already taut nerve endings and she feasted her gaze on his musculature, the smooth pink discs of his aroused nipples, and the line of dark hair that tapered from his navel down into the taut sleekness of his riding breeches. His arousal was evident in the bulge that pushed at the finely woven fabric; she imagined his rampant cock exposed and almost fainted with desire and unsatisfied lust, wanting only for him to possess her, to invade her flesh. She moaned slightly as he slowly unbuttoned himself. His cock was glorious and swollen, the statuesque length rearing from his trousers as he advanced towards her desperate lips.

'Suck me,' he commanded.

Opening her mouth to encase him, Lydia abandoned herself, revelling in the salty taste of him as she strained her neck forward to take as much of him in as she could. She opened her mouth and throat, drawing him in and sucking his strength, imagining that she could leach his power and enslave him to her own desires. His hands steadied her head, and she felt his thumbs caress her ears and then her temples as he gave a sighing exhalation above her.

He was giving in. Submission trembled in his fingertips: she could sense it as clearly as if he had spoken. His hands became gentle, tenderly moving over the satin of her hair and smoothing the shape of her head. She could feel his thumbs making tiny circular motions on her crown, and she deepened her hold on his cock, lapping her way to the root and pressing her nose against his belly.

He jerked back without warning, leaving her mouth suddenly bereft, one hand pushed against her shoulder as if to subdue her into the chair. Recovering himself, Valerian stared down at her.

'No,' he said, laying a long forefinger on her cheek. 'That's my game, not yours. I am the master. Now beg, just say it. Say "I want you". Say "Give it to me, Valerian". Ask me, damn you!'

He suddenly became angry, a scowl marring his features. He reached into the casket again and withdrew a thin silver thread the length of his longest finger. First looping it so that it formed a ring, he then bent, and Lydia flinched as she felt his fingers harden on to her clitoris. He tied it, encircling the hard little bud with the loop and pulling it tight. She felt as if every sensation had been forced into that tiny part of her: lances of hot pleasure darted around her sex and she cried out when he touched the very tip of her with his long fingernail.

'Ready to beg, cousin of mine?'

Seeing her quick shake of refusal, he took her clitoris between the nails of finger and thumb. Scratching, flicking, and squeezing, he stared into her eyes and she felt her own fill with tears of frustration. Hatred and longing swelled her breast and she thought she would burst as she felt him tighten the silver thread. Her mind raced.

'Damn you. Come on, just say it.' He grasped her shoulder and shook her roughly. Through the haze of pain and desire, she heard the last word that he said: 'Please!'

She knew then that her submission was also his.

'Fuck me, Valerian. I beg you.' It was a honey-clad whisper of defeat and victory.

With a cry of savage triumph he fell upon her, biting her full lips with possessive fervour, gripping her thighs and pulling them wide before sinking to his knees to plunge the full length of his hard cock into her. He ruthlessly plundered her, gaining speed and rhythm until she thought she could bear it no longer and she bucked her hips against him, matching his boundless energy.

Once she gasped at him, begging him to stop, and obediently he paused, long enough for her to sob, 'No, don't stop!' Then he slammed into her again, pulling

43

her forward, crushing her against his chest until they both climaxed, quaking on to each other for what seemed like hours before subsiding limply, damp foreheads leaning together in harmonious fatigue.

Presently Valerian withdrew and tilted her chin for a tender, graceful kiss.

'Well, cousin. You are a fine lay, but no longer a virgin, I discover. Pray explain your lack of maidenhead.' His dark eyes probed hers and Lydia was the first to drop her gaze.

'Temptation surrounds me,' she murmured submissively.

'It should have been me!' he cried. 'You belong to me, Lydia!'

Angrily he untied her with rough hands and, picking her up, bore her to the crimson bed, pushing her willing body face down on to the softness of the coverlet.

'I regret, cousin, that I must punish you.'

He grasped her wrists, pulling them up and above her, winding a length of the crimson voile around and between her fists before jerking her up to her knees. He passed the voile through the wrought-iron loop and pulled on it until she was suspended from the low, beamed ceiling, her body limp and exhausted, her knees barely skimming the slippery satin of the bed.

'Now, you little slut. You will take your punishment.'

'What are you going to do to me?'

'Watch me.'

She felt him reach for something just outside her field of vision, then jumped as the lash of a long whip stung her. He whipped her repeatedly, punctuating his flagellation with hard scratching of his nails down the length of her back, and she sighed, overcome with the exquisite pain as the tip of the whip burnt her skin. It was like a lashing tongue that caught her just below the buttocks, in the tender crease which sloped to her thigh, and she felt it pushing her into paroxysms of pleasure.

She felt Valerian take her hair and wind it around his wrist, pulling her head back and down. The whip seemed now like stinging kisses, tiny puckering embraces that printed fiery weals across her body. She was caught by a thrust of desire that pulled at her, and she hung by her wrists, sobbing and writhing until she heard herself beg him to take her again.

This time he entered her from behind, filling her with his engorged length, taking her roughly until she was almost there, then suddenly, unexpectedly, pushing the knotted handle of the whip into her anus. And she came instantly, utterly filled and shocked to the core.

When Lydia awoke, she had no idea of the time, for the room was in silent darkness which stretched infinitely outward. Her whole body ached with unaccustomed use and she gave a secret self-satisfied smile which lent a feline slant to her eyes.

Stretching her arms outward across the rumpled linen, she found the bed empty and sat up, straining her ears against the inky blackness. There was a scratching metallic sound, and then a light flared as Valerian lit the candelabra next to the bed. He moved about the room, lighting candles of all sizes which had been set on every available surface as well as in banks across the floor. He came to stand by the bed, towering over her, the tapers flickering and casting eerie shadows on his face; his mouth curved in a smile which hardly reached his eyes.

'Awake at last? I trust that you are rested.'

'Yes, but I'm thirsty.'

He moved across the room, lighting the last few candles which stood in tall black iron stands at the end of the dais. In the golden glow she watched him as he moved with the muscular grace of a leopard; he uncorked a bottle of ruby liquid and poured four goblets, turning slowly to place one in her outstretched hand. Lydia drank deeply, the alcoholic fire burning her mouth and throat as she swallowed. Valerian urged her to drain the goblet, then he refilled it.

She sipped the second glassful more slowly. A warm glow seeped through her and she relished the lightheadedness she felt. Recklessly, she tossed back the contents of the glass and gestured for more. Valerian smiled, poured, then watched as she drained the goblet.

'You were thirsty,' he murmured. 'You've almost emptied the bottle. I shall have to send for more.' He strode to the door of the room, threw it open, and beckoned to someone outside. Conrad, tall and serious, entered the candle-lit chamber, and Lydia pulled the silken sheets up around her.

'Come, don't be shy.' Valerian grasped the sheets and pulled them away. 'Conrad will be seeing much more of you than that soon enough.'

Lydia looked up at him, confusion clearing as her gaze slid sideways to the two spare goblets on the table. Conrad lifted one of them and it was instantly dwarfed by his huge hand. He raised it to her in a silent toast and drank deeply and appreciatively, his blue eyes remaining fixed on hers.

She stared back challengingly, the wine lending her extra bravado. So Valerian wanted his manservant to witness his prowess; well, she was not averse to that. In fact, she thought, squeezing her bare thighs together and enjoying the pressure, it might prove very interesting.

What transpired was more interesting than she could have imagined in her wildest dreams. She allowed Valerian and Conrad to spread her arms and legs wide, then bind each ankle and wrist to the four corners of the bed so that she lay like a starfish, open and vulnerable on the sliding black sheets. She closed her eyes, breathing shallowly and curving her head back to savour the moment before Valerian came into her.

She felt his weight dipping the mattress as he knelt between her spread legs, and her flesh tingled as his fingers rested briefly on her narrow waist before trailing a line of fire down over her stomach. He gently spread her, and she felt herself grow moist and full as he inserted a finger, then two, twisting them inside and sliding out before repeating the action.

She tilted her hips up, pushing towards the source of pleasure. He pressed deep within her twice more, then slowly withdrew the fingers to replace them with the hard, hot tip of his cock. The creamy fingers slid a trail up over her belly to anoint her hard nipples and then dip over her chin to her mouth. At first she was repulsed, imagining the taste of herself to be unpleasant, but the fresh muskiness made her open her lips. One slick finger was pushed inside her mouth and she caught it with her tongue, fascinated and allured as she tasted herself.

She kept her eyes shut, visualising Valerian as he arched above her, with his manservant watching from the far end of the room, aroused but impotent. Ostentatiously, she tossed her head from side to side, moaning with genuine delight and straining her hands against the leashes to tease the watching Viking further.

Suddenly she was filled with a man who stretched her impossibly wide and she cried out, widening her eyes in shock to see that it was not Valerian between her open thighs but Conrad himself, huge and muscular, his mane of red-gold hair framing his strong features as he stared down at her.

He paused a moment, as if relishing the rigidity of her suddenly contracted sex and the look of horror upon her face, then he moved with long, generous strokes. She held herself firm, refusing to capitulate to the sensuality of his movements, forcing herself to deny the slow build of pleasure that he created.

She felt his big hand stroke her waist and then slide over her hip. He teased and caressed her satin skin, making her feel deliciously small and extremely relaxed. The gentle thrusts of his hips, combined with the soothing strokes of his huge hands, made her sigh and slowly melt, surrendering herself to blissful sensation. He rode smoothly above her, moving gradually faster with practised ease and athletic stamina until she was gasping, drowning in pleasure, then he withdrew abruptly upon Valerian's softly spoken command.

'Please, let him finish.' Her eyes sought Valerian's, but he ignored her and strode once again to the door. This time he drew his second manservant into the room.

Joseph, short, squat, and powerfully built, paused inside the door. At a word from Valerian he shrugged out of his clothes and Lydia watched him advance across the room, fascinated by the way the candles burnished his oiled black skin, lending it the lustre of ebony wood. She was filled with a mixture of fear and arousal by the sight of his burly form as he approached the bed, deftly lifted her hips with one hand, and pushed a scarlet cushion under her. She felt utterly exposed and open, and tried to pull her legs together a little, but the bonds which held her were firm.

As if to ensure that she would not escape, Conrad and Valerian each took one ankle and firmly pinned her into the soft down of the mattress, while Joseph positioned himself and then entered her, long and hard, until she was full, then pushing in a little more. She realised that he was so large that she could not accommodate him. The gratifying sense of fullness intensified almost to the border of pain, and she arched her back, trying to curve on to him to take him further in. He fucked her gently, almost lovingly, and she came sweetly, biting her lips to keep her climax a triumphant secret from Valerian.

Quickly, before she had recovered her senses, she felt the many hands of the three men untie her. She was held upright by Joseph, his bulging biceps easily supporting her weight beneath her arms. Valerian grasped her legs, almost roughly, and jerked them round his waist as he entered her from a standing position, sliding effortlessly in, so wet was she from her own and Joseph's juices.

He plunged the heat of his cock repeatedly into her, and she was captured by the easy glide of him as he achieved a steady rhythm, delicate pearls of sweat beading his brow. She felt herself impaled by his eyes, narrow and dark as they stared, their expression unreadable.

Then he thrust hard into her and stayed still, his shoulders drooping and his cock twitching inside her. She was unsure whether she could come again so quickly, but the sight of him so near to her, his eyes closed with the force of his climax, and the other two men breathing heavily on to her shoulders and belly in the candlelight, made her tremble and find the spot in her mind where ecstacy hid.

Valerian lowered her legs down. She knew that they were too tremulous to support her weight, so she hung, grateful for Joseph's strength as he held her, her mind blank and her body sore, her sex chafed. Conrad poured more wine into one goblet and all four drank deeply from it. Just before she drained hers, Valerian dipped his thumb into the dregs and smeared it across her forehead, almost as if he were baptising her.

'You're mine now. Always,' he whispered.

When the bottle was empty, Conrad lay down on the bed, his proud cock rigid and standing erect from the circlet of red-gold curls which covered his loins and upper thighs. He beckoned Lydia, and Valerian pushed her towards the bed, his hand cool in the small of her back. She walked to the bed, obediently straddling the Nordic giant.

She poised momentarily over him, then slowly lowered herself, feeling her plump and slightly sore lips unfurl over him. She raised herself and lowered again, enjoying the raw sensation of her flesh sliding over and gradually encasing him, almost sucking him in. She felt a hand grip the back of her neck and push her down until she was lying full-length along Conrad's body, her face pressed on to the hardness of his golden-haired chest, her toes resting halfway along his wide calves.

She felt a weight press upon her from behind, and Joseph mounted the bed, parting her buttocks with his firm black hands. She tensed as she felt him probe the entrance to her secret, most private place, holding her

49

breath and anticipating the exquisite pain as he pushed firmly and unhesitatingly between her buttocks.

'Please, no,' she murmured, part of her not wishing for him to hear her, or heed her request.

There was a long pause before he breached her, and she tensed, almost sobbing with fear and lust as she made herself open for him. Then he pushed and she was slowly filled and stretched, Joseph easing her tightness wide with care.

She began to move of her own accord, tentatively at first, and then felt herself voraciously plundered as the two men began to move inside her, their contrasting skin colours illuminated by the lustrous glow from the candles which filled the room. She let them take her, her exhausted body grateful for the pleasure, her mind giving up responsibility and need so that she was simply a resonant vessel, full of pure pleasure with no thoughts to hinder her.

Turning her head, she could see Valerian. He had drawn the leather throne close and sat in it, half reclining with one leg hooked over the armrest, his left hand stroking the slender length of his rigid cock, while the other cupped and squeezed his own balls. Mesmerised by his hand movements, Lydia watched, the hot rise of her climax harmonious with his.

She felt Conrad jerk his powerful hips upward and Joseph push inexorably downward and abruptly she lost all reason as the rhythmic waves surged through her lower body. She trembled, black shadows flickering at the corners of her senses, almost fainting with the violent force of the sensation that flooded like boiling cream through her body.

Time extended infinitely, then Valerian stood and drew a scarlet robe around his pale nakedness. He looked silently down at the tableau on the bed before him, then curled his top lip upward in distaste.

'So, my dear. Who do you think is lord of all he surveys now?'

Shocked by the sudden change in him, Lydia stared

up and then remembered her own words to him a few days previously. Her face flushed and she struggled free of the muscular tangle of the henchmen's arms and legs.

'You'll never have power over me. Never.'

With as much dignity as her nakedness would allow, she stalked from the room, pausing briefly to scoop up her torn clothes from their sorry pile.

Valerian laughed cruelly and, as she slammed the door, he muttered softly: 'Oh, but I have had, cousin. And will do again.'

Chapter Four

*A*s the autumn sunlight filtered through the dia-
mond-paned windows, Lydia rested her head on
her hand and watched the swirling motes of dust dancing in the warm air. She had been sitting in the low
fireside chair for most of the morning, refusing Valerian's imperious and repeated summonses to come
downstairs.

An embroidery ring lay upside down on the red rug
where she had tossed it, the stitches knotted and poorly
worked. She kicked it, and watched as it flipped up into
the fire, caught behind the fender and slowly burnt at
the edge of the coals. An acrid scent filled the air and
was fanned by a cold draught as the door to her
bedchamber was pushed open.

Angel tapped on the wood panel of the door, bobbed
a curtsy, and then frowned, sniffing the air.

'Why, I can smell – something's burning!' She dashed
forward and twisted the blackened stitchery out of the
fire. She stamped on it with one foot, holding her dark
skirts above her ankles. 'Miss Lydia, your embroidery!
It's ruined!'

'Oh, leave it, Angel. I don't care: I hate stitching. It's
so boring.'

'If you're bored, perhaps you would care to join the

master for dinner now. He's sent me to bring you down: a final request. He says that there is a guest coming.' Angel looked down at Lydia, her fine blonde eyebrows slightly raised. Lydia met her eyes and then looked away, slumping her chin on her hand again.

'Well, the master, as you insist on calling him, will have to greet the guest alone. Tell him I am not coming down.'

'That won't please him. He threw a dish at the wall when you refused earlier.'

'If he chooses to ruin a whole dinner service, the answer will still be the same.' Lydia pursed her lips and stared into the fire, a deep crease between her dark brows.

''Tis an important guest, I believe. I've been asked to air the Blue Room.'

'I don't care! Just go away and leave me alone.'

'Very well.' Tight-lipped, Angel turned to the door.

'Wait!' commanded Lydia, jumping up from her chair and grasping the maid's elbow. 'Give him a message from me. Tell him he has no power to force me to come downstairs for any meal at which I am expected to share the table with him.' Angel reluctantly nodded and made for the door again. 'And Angel, when you have done that, please be so kind as to bring me some cold meats from the kitchen.'

'Certainly, miss. Whatever you say.' There was a trace of sarcasm in the words that made Lydia feel slightly guilty for her sourness. She curled her feet up under her in the chair and hugged her knees, feeling miserable and frustrated.

She stared into the fire for a few moments, then leant forward to grab the poker and give the dying embers a vicious poke. It really needed more fuel, but she knew that she couldn't ask Angel to go and fetch some. The maid would probably refuse after the rudeness she had been subjected to. She bit her lip and decided to be particularly nice to Angel when she came back from the kitchens; she liked the girl and enjoyed her company.

Without warning, the heavy oak door flew open behind her and crashed against the wall, making the mirror rattle in its gilt frame. Lydia jumped, dropping the poker; it fell with a heavy clang and rolled across the rug to lie by the fender.

'What is the meaning of this?' roared Valerian, advancing into the room with long, angry strides. He stood at the other end of the fireplace, a towering monolith radiating fury and impatience, his black hair unruly and his wide mouth set in a hard line. Lydia gazed up at him, swallowing her sudden fear and trying to quell the flicker of excitement which licked her insides. She took a deep breath, stood up, and walked across the crimson rug to stand directly in front of him. She spoke calmly.

'There is no meaning, Valerian, other than that which you surely comprehend. I do not wish to share your table.' She tilted her chin mutinously upward and forced herself to meet his eyes. He stared back at her, spite and lust smouldering in the ebony depths of his anger, as he drew his brows down and narrowed his eyes to impenetrable dark slits. He remained silent for a moment, a muscle flickering in his taut jaw as he sought to maintain control.

'My dear Lydia, your truculence is unbecoming.' He ground the words out through clenched teeth, his voice hard and low. 'You will do as I say. I require your presence at the dinner table immediately. I have a guest arriving and should like you to act as hostess. Accompany me down the stairs this instant!'

'No.'

'What did you say?'

'I said no. I don't want to. You think you have power over me, but you haven't, I do not –.' Her words were swiftly curtailed on a gasp as Valerian slapped her face with the back of his hand. The colour leapt to her cheeks as she raised her hand to cup the burning flesh.

'How dare you!'

'How dare I? Oh, quite easily. Like this!' Her head

54

snapped back as he repeated the slap, this time to her other cheek.

Incensed, she aimed her clawed fingers at his face, but he caught her wrist with ease, laughing malevolently. Then, without warning, he scooped her up and expertly turned her round. He pushed her forward over the nearby chair, throwing her petticoats over her head to reveal the twin ovals of her buttocks.

Lydia shouted, struggling, but it was no help: his iron grip rendered her helpless beneath the heaped skirts which fastened her arms as firmly to her sides as if he had bound her with rope. He applied ten smacks in quick succession to her bare flesh, and her hips jerked with each slap, her anger and indignation gradually replaced by a smarting pleasure.

Furious with Valerian, and angry with herself for succumbing to his treatment of her, she cried out in feigned distress and struggled again as if to free herself. He smacked her buttocks twice more and then firmly stroked the heel of his hand over her exposed sex, causing an involuntary shudder which Lydia sought to conceal by grinding her pelvis forward into the hard chair and pressing her thighs together.

'Since my father's death, you have consistently failed to understand the way things are here. I shall have to punish you for your wilfulness.'

Another resounding slap stung her, and then she felt Valerian's booted foot as he insinuated it between her feet and kicked her legs roughly apart. Biting her lips and pushing her face firmly into the cushions of the chair, Lydia hardly dared to breathe as his fingers harshly kneaded the tender flesh of her inner thigh and then abruptly entered her from below, the knuckles of his two forefingers grazing her as he pushed in. He withdrew slightly and rubbed her fullness with his thumb, then pushed into her and pressed his forefinger against the firm bud which stood slightly proud of her swollen sex.

Lydia moaned and eased herself back against him as

he withdrew, relishing the feel of his fingers as they forced abruptly back in, opening the pliable folds of flesh and delving deeper into her. Stimulation coursed like a fever through her veins; she could see nothing, but sense everything. And what she sensed was pure sexual exhilaration.

As if he could feel her enjoyment, Valerian began to thrust his hand into her more severely, withdrawing and brutally plunging into her again with gradually increasing speed with one hand, while the other continued to apply vicious smacks to her buttocks.

'How dare you disobey me!' His voice resonated with the knowledge of his own power. 'You will do as I say. No more, no less. If I tell you to come downstairs, then you come. Do you hear me?'

'No!' she gasped. 'You don't own me.'

'Oh, but I do. You have nothing, nothing! Everything you eat, everything you wear, comes from me. You belong to me, body and soul.' His mouth was suddenly close to her ear and she could feel the hard length of his body pressing her into the chair, squeezing the breath out of her lungs and almost suffocating her. 'If you don't do as I tell you, then I'll punish you. Do you need to be shown who is master here? Do you?'

'There is no master. Not until Drummond comes home.'

Lydia realised she had hit a raw nerve as she felt fury stiffen his already taut body.

'Why, you little –!' He jerked her upright and held her hair, yanking on it and using it to pull her round, turning her face until she could see his. Her neck was twisted painfully, and her eyes stretched at the corners by the strength of his grip on her hair. She cried out, real fear mingling with her arousal. He was so unpredictable that she was unsure whether he was under control. She tried to break free, but he pushed her roughly back down into the chair. As her chin hit the damask cushion, her cheek caught between her teeth and she could taste the sudden salt of her own hot blood in her mouth. She struggled beneath the heavy folds of her skirts.

'Let me go! Help! No!' She squirmed as he swiftly withdrew his rigid fingers, spanked the bare cheeks of her bottom again, harder this time, with his slickly juiced hand, and then rammed it back between her thighs, introducing a third finger which deliciously stretched her and stilled her struggles. The blood in her mouth tasted foreign, metallic, and she sucked and swallowed, finding the taste of it bittersweet and subtly arousing.

She felt his other hand grasp the back of her gown, and he hauled her into an almost upright position, pushing the layers of petticoats to one side and groping at the tiny fabric-covered buttons at the back of her bodice. Impatiently, he pulled at the fastening, plucking and fumbling until she felt a button give, popping from its mooring to spin across the floor. Unable to master the rest of them with his trembling fingers, he roughly grasped the neckline at the back and, with a single movement, tore the fabric from shoulder to waist, revealing the snowy skin of her back. Encircling her with one arm, he imprisoned her hands at her sides and jerked her backward again until Lydia felt his hot breath on the damp curls at the nape of her neck.

'I will show you who is master here,' he whispered.

Without pause, he sank his teeth into her shoulder and sucked at the pad of flesh there, his sharp teeth contrasting provocatively with the melting heat of his lips.

Lydia moaned and sank back against him, her knees weak and her mind clouded, as he raked his teeth across the sweet skin of her back towards the undulation of her spine. His fingers moved savagely within her: once, twice, and then withdrew to fumble with the fastening of his breeches.

Wondering if this was still part of his punishment, Lydia felt heat emanating from him as the burning head of his unconfined shaft rested briefly between her buttocks. He seized her hips with both hands, and lifted and positioned her with a sudden brutal jerk. Lydia panted, then held her breath as she savoured the hiatus, the waiting, as she was suspended with his hot, silken cock pressing, momentarily denied entry, between the engorged folds of her sex.

Abruptly, his fingers biting into her skin, he moved her hips and his own, sinking deep inside her. He paused for a moment as if to recover from the suddenness of his entry. Lydia tilted her head back so that she could feel the hard muscle of his shoulder beneath her neck, and succumbed to the sensations that built within her. Her scalp tingled and she could feel the down on her forearms lift with arousal and her nipples harden as she relaxed her body against Valerian's thrusting.

He moved inside her with sharp lunges and a barely controlled ferocity, holding her waist tightly in a way which almost impeded her panting breaths. She could feel a febrile sheen beading across her brow, and the edges of her senses tingled. He reached around her and viciously pinched and rubbed her exposed clitoris, sending a shudder quaking through her body.

She could hear his breathing, feel the ragged exhalations as he mouthed her ears and neck, murmuring crudities which inexplicably heightened her own stimulation. As she heard him call her a disobedient slut, she climaxed shudderingly on to him, feeling the echo as his cock jerked in reply. He moved quickly, pumping his hips as he emptied himself into her, and Lydia sagged against him, unable to support her own weight.

She closed her eyes and slowed her breathing as he relinquished his grip on her and lowered her forward until she rested against the chair. She sensed him slip out of her and felt suddenly empty, swollen, and lacking, her desire for him satisfied for the present but not wholly spent.

She wondered if it would ever be wholly spent.

'Tidy yourself, my dear.' His words were flat and coolly spoken, no element of emotion warming his tone.

Lydia turned her head warily to observe him from the slanting corners of her half-closed eyes. 'You're due to play hostess in less than an hour. I will receive my guest in the great hall.'

'And if I refuse?' she enquired.

'I think we both know that you won't do that.'

He buttoned the smooth front of his immaculate breeches and gave her a mocking glance before turning on his heel. His polished boots beat a tattoo upon the uncarpeted expanse of wooden floor as he stalked to the door. Pausing, he hitched his thumbs into the pockets of his long waistcoat and turned to face her once more.

'Oh, and cousin? I have a fancy to see you in red. Wear the scarlet gown that was made for you for the Wilkinson's Ball last winter.' He smiled, his lips hovering between mirth and contempt. 'A scarlet gown for a scarlet woman, how amusing!' With a last insolent stare he left, allowing the heavy door to crash closed behind him.

Lydia remained motionless for a long time, staring with unconcealed hostility at the space where he had stood; then she reached down, picked up the poker from where it had fallen on the hearth-rug and threw it.

The resulting gouge in the door gave her great satisfaction, and she spent the time while she dressed imagining that it had been Valerian's head that the fire-iron had hit.

The commotion in the hall was apparent from the upper floor where Lydia had paused, one hand resting on the dark balustrade, to watch with detached interest as the servants ran this way and that at Valerian's bidding. The huge front doors were wide open, allowing a frosty draught to lick up the stairs towards her. The butler, Anderson, was standing with ramrod erectness just inside, and Lydia could see the smoky huff of his exasperation as his orders were instantly countermanded by his master's.

Two footmen ran across the hall and went through

the door at a trot; they came to a standstill just outside, positioned like a pair of matching guard-dogs on the top step of the entrance, while Valerian snapped peevishly at a servant who was applying bellows without obvious success to the cavernous fireplace on the west wall of the great hall.

If she leant out, Lydia could see the vast dining-table laden with food, gold cutlery, and the best dinner service: a sumptuous array which she had not seen since a long time before Lord William's death. She wondered who the guest was that Valerian held in such obvious high esteem. He had no close friends beyond the hunting members of the local aristocracy and his London club associates, so she could not imagine who he had seen fit to welcome in such an ostentatious manner.

Smoothing the crimson brocade of her full-skirted gown, she glanced down to check her *décolletage*. The low-cut affair had been one that she had insisted on having for last year's ball, after she had seen pictures of ladies of fashion in London wearing wide overdresses which hung loose from the shoulders and fastened in the front with ribbons. Under it she wore a contrasting linen petticoat with the new quilting which kept her legs deliciously warm as the weather grew cooler. Last year, the gown had been a great success, and she had hardly sat out a dance at the Wilkinson's.

Valerian gave a final barking order to Anderson and then stalked to the foot of the stairway to stand with feet firmly apart on the magenta carpet, watching her descend. Unusually for him, he wore a full wig over his own hair and had powdered and patched his face like a town dandy. Azure silk stretched across his wide shoulders and the buckles on his shoes gleamed.

He swept an insolent gaze from her toes up to her face. His dark eyes paused for a long, lascivious moment at the soft skin which swelled enticingly like succulent, forbidden fruit at her neckline, then he extended a pale hand to her and assisted her descent of the last two steps.

'Thank you,' she murmured demurely, the thick lashes of her downcast eyes creating dusky shadows on her cheeks. She found herself unable to meet his sardonic black gaze as memories of their frenzied quarrel and his punishment rose unbidden to the front of her mind.

'Thank *you*,' he replied, apparently enjoying her slight discomfort. 'My memory served me well: that is a marvellous gown. I am sure you will impress our guest.'

'Who is coming, Valerian?'

'A very great friend of mine from London, Madame de Chaillot. She is always very accommodating to me when I stay there, and I wish to return her kindness by offering hospitality here at Hawkesworth. She is newly widowed and desirous of quiet and solitude.' His head turned slightly, listening to the crunching sound of a carriage drawing at a steady pace across the gravel driveway. 'This must be her now.'

There was an unmistakable leap of excitement in his eyes and voice, and Lydia was curious as she watched him stride energetically towards the entrance. He had never been enthusiastic about his father's guests, preferring usually to feign languor and disinterest, and retreat to a corner of the room to scowl. He must be very fond of the old widow: perhaps she had become a mother figure to him during his time in the city. Lydia felt her own interest stir and walked out to see for herself how the dowager had fared on the long journey.

A dark coach drawn by four white horses completed its manoeuvre around the sweeping curve of the drive. It came to rest at the bottom of the golden stone steps just as Lydia stepped out into the weak afternoon sun. The wheels were mud-spattered and filthy, the leather roof pelmet soiled. The timber of the lower part of the coach was painted a beautiful vermilion which could just be seen beneath the grime of the road. Even the brass studs were dirty and dull.

A periwigged coachman reined in the horses and the Hawkesworth footmen dashed forward, one to steady the lead horse's head, the other to swing open the carriage door and position the steps which would help the elderly widow to alight. Two of Madame's own liveried servants hopped down from the back of the coach and came forward to assist.

A hand clad in ivory satin extended from the interior and a footman took it to assist the lady. Lydia glanced at Valerian, who seemed almost to be holding his breath, and when she looked back again, the widow had descended from the coach and was standing at the foot of the steps, looking up at Valerian with coolly smiling hauteur.

Lydia stifled a gasp.

This was no elderly mentor: Madame de Chaillot looked hardly a day over thirty-five. Her face was as pale and smooth as alabaster and her powdered hair swept up and back from her unlined forehead in the most fashionable style; her milky colouring was contrasted beautifully by the lush darkness of a hooded sable pelisse which swept the ground as she advanced. The thinly pencilled arches of her brows raised slightly as she turned to Lydia, who felt instantly gauche in her rustic finery.

Madame de Chaillot narrowed frosty eyes and surveyed her with barely concealed disdain, then extended her hand to be kissed. Lydia dipped her knees briefly and touched the cold satin with her lips, unable to speak.

'Madame. I trust you had a safe and uneventful journey?' Valerian stepped forward, bending his lithe body in a deep bow.

'Thank you, Valerian. We did.' Her voice was low and throbbed with some nameless emotion that Lydia could only guess at. Valerian took Madame by the elbow and led her up into the house, his low words of welcome and his familiar gestures revealing the intimate terms on which they were acquainted.

Lydia glanced towards the coach. A powdered and plump lady's-maid emerged, pulling her luxurious mantle around her ample bosom against the chill of the autumn afternoon. She took the footman's proffered hand, treating him to a lascivious look from beneath her lowered lashes before stepping on to the gravel. Her hand lingered in his a little longer than was necessary, and he flushed, a deep staining red which rose from his immaculate white stock, up over his powdered features to disappear under his wig. Turning, the woman glared at Lydia with open hostility.

'I am Maxine Laurent, Madame de Chaillot's personal maid and companion. Pray arrange to have our baggage sent to our rooms. And I hope the beds are aired!' She shuddered and looked peevishly at her surroundings. 'Clancy, come at once!'

From the interior of the coach sprang a child of maybe six years old, wearing an Eastern-style suit and a turban with an enormous ostrich feather pinned to it. His chubby black face split into a grin and he leapt agilely down from the carriage, ignoring the steps, to land neatly at Lydia's feet and bend into a sweeping, flourishing bow.

'Good afternoon, your ladyship,' he said, carefully enunciating each syllable. He straightened and beamed up at Lydia. 'May I present myself to the lady of the house? I am Clancy: I fetch and carry and tie shoe-laces!'

Lydia laughed; he was so sweet and charming, and obviously had a great sense of his own importance. She felt slightly cheered by his presence and took his tiny hand in hers.

'Pleased to make your acquaintance, Clancy. I am Lydia Hawkesworth,' she said with mock seriousness. Clancy bobbed and chuckled before her for a few moments before being summoned away by the frowning Maxine. He sprang up the steps with enormous vitality and disappeared into the candle-lit interior of the manor house.

Lydia gave a huge sigh and picked up her skirts. A ray of weak sunlight streamed down from the cloudy

63

sky to warm her shoulders briefly before she stepped inside the door to the great hall. The air indoors, despite the huge fire and numerous candelabra, seemed cold, gloomy, and very unwelcoming.

The afternoon passed slowly, with Valerian and Madame laughing and talking together in low, intimate voices at one end of the dining-table, while Lydia hunched at the other end, miserable and sick with something she refused to acknowledge as jealousy, picking at the slices of goose which congealed upon her plate.

Finally she excused herself and went upstairs, sure that the other two had hardly even noticed her departure. Valerian had been engrossed in sliding frosted grapes between Madame's thin, rouged lips, and Madame herself had spared Lydia only a cursory glance before returning her attention to the young man beside her.

In her room, Lydia watched the dark evening draw in: tendrils of mist formed a halo around the crescent-moon and icy beads of moisture clung to the window-panes. Chilled, she undressed hastily by the crackling fire and buried herself beneath the down-filled quilt to fall into a deep and troubled sleep.

Unsure of what had awoken her, Lydia lay for a moment in the dark, straining her ears to catch any sound. The house was silent. Relaxing, she snuggled again into her bed and closed her eyes, but sleep would not come. She turned over, turned back, punched her pillows, and then finally gave up trying to sleep.

Sliding from the bed, she pulled a heavy robe around herself, pushed her feet into thick tapestry slippers and curled herself into the window-seat to watch the stars. Her warm breath melted the crispness of the tiny glass panes and she rubbed with her cuff to clear a circular peephole.

The darkness of the estate was relieved only by the silvery gleam of the crescent moon. Inky shadows cast by trees and bushes lay long on the dark grass, and Lydia thought that it must be somewhere near midnight. A rabbit loped into view just beyond the steep slope which led down to the grassy ride, and she watched as it hopped about and then suddenly took fright at something. It dashed away, its tail a sudden streak of white in the darkness.

A prickle ran suddenly up her neck to her hairline, and Lydia sat up sharply as a dark shape detached itself from one of the trees and moved stealthily across the lawn to a tree nearer the house. Squinting her eyes, she could just about make out a long cloak and a tricorne hat; whoever it was had even masked their face with a dark kerchief over the nose and mouth. She could not see any evidence of a weapon, so he could not be a poacher; besides, they usually came in pairs with sacks and traps dangling from the belts of their short coats.

She waited, curious, for a moment longer, watching the figure in the garden. Then she grabbed her own hat from on top of the wardrobe, wound a velvet stole around her neck, and sped through the dark house to the door which led out into the kitchen-garden. The coolness of the night air closed around her like an icy glove as she pocketed the huge metal key and crept noiselessly around to the front of the house.

Skirting the rose beds, she avoided the noisy gravel and padded across the damp grass to a cluster of elms, careful to keep in the shadow of the big bushes that dotted the informal sweep of lawn. Crouching behind a trunk, ignoring the dampness of the nightgown that clung to her legs, Lydia narrowed her eyes and searched for the cloaked figure. For a moment she thought she had lost him, or alerted him to her presence in some way. Then she spotted a movement as a cloud raced across the moon and she fixed her eyes on his stooped position by the laurels.

Whoever it was seemed to be observing the house, moving gradually closer and watching the windows continuously. She felt a shiver of fear as she wondered whether he was a housebreaker: but then surely he would have an accomplice. Frowning, she decided to creep a little closer and try to identify his face.

As she moved, so did he, and any sound she made was masked by his own movements and the rustle of his heavy cloak. He stepped around the laurels, and Lydia quickly raced to the cover they provided, slipped, lost her footing on the cold, damp grass and skidded into the solid wall of the intruder's back.

Grasping at his cloak to save herself as her feet went out from under her, she stifled a cry and he swept around to grip her wrists, glaring into her eyes.

'You little idiot, what are you doing out here?' he hissed, his eyes filled with anger and impatience above the darkness of the kerchief around his lower face. Lydia twisted her wrists in a vain attempt to free them as she glared at him in silent recognition.

It was the highwayman.

'What are you doing here yourself? I shall raise the alarm this instant!' She opened her mouth wide to scream, but a hard leather-gloved hand instantly gagged her and he pulled her roughly towards him, crushing her arms into her ribs. Momentarily unnerved, Lydia inhaled the masculine scent of him and stared at the face so close to her own.

Her memory was curiously full of him: his smell, the feel of him in her carriage on that day, the strength of his muscled chest as he held her tightly against him. Unable to speak but desperate to communicate, she slid her tongue out between her lips and pressed the tip against the cold leather of his gloves, silently relishing the musty taste. He looked down at her with incomprehension in his eyes, then slowly loosened his grip on her.

'If I take my hand away, will you promise not to scream?'

Lydia nodded. He held her gaze, his eyes searching and a deep frown creasing his brow. The glove slid gently down over her chin, but his eyes remained fixed on hers with searing intensity. As if unable to help himself, he lowered his covered mouth and kissed her through the cloth with a tenderness that almost brought tears to her eyes.

Lydia did not move, her breath tight in her chest and the hardness of her cold nipples pressing into the coarse texture of his cloak. Almost crushing her ribs with a fierce hug, he reached beneath her knees and swept her up into his arms with effortless strength to carry her across the lawns away from the house. She knew his strength and did not struggle, aware that it would do no good. She watched the dark house recede over his shoulder.

'Where are we going?' Lydia breathed, as they ducked beneath a low branch and entered the darkness of the forest edge.

'The folly,' he said simply.

The stone tower had been built as the Hawkesworth hunting-lodge many years ago. It was deep in the heart of the forest, set by the lake which shimmered mysteriously on the edge of the estate: a two-storey folly with a crenellated miniature battlement and a spiral stone staircase. She had often played there as a child, setting up house and clearing away cobwebs, only to cry bitterly when Valerian burst in and spitefully kicked her efforts to pieces before her eyes.

Once, Drummond had challenged him to a fist-fight on her behalf. The two boys had stripped to their breeches and pummelled each other until Valerian had fallen knee-deep into the lake and capitulated with bad grace, scowling his forced apology to her as she hid behind the twelve-year-old Drummond. He had been five years older than she, and her hero from that day forward.

Sighing, she pushed her thoughts away and looked up at her captor's masked face. He gently set her on her feet and untied the horse which was standing patiently by a slender sapling.

They reached the folly within minutes, the horse

trotting sure-footed through the woods, almost as if it knew the route. The highwayman lifted Lydia down, and, holding her hand, bent his head to enter the low doorway set in the side of the little tower. The old wooden door hung on rusty, broken hinges, and the inside of the folly was dark and cold. Worn stone stairs twisted away up to the next floor, and as they climbed several bats took flight, flapping noisily around the ceiling before swooping out of the tiny aperture which served as a window.

The highwayman knelt in front of the fireplace and swept cobwebs away with one gloved hand. He pushed dry twigs into a pile and used his tinderbox. A flicker of orange flame swiftly consumed the pile, and Lydia hurried to gather dry leaves and other pieces of wood from the floor. They knelt together before the little fire until it was truly alight, then the highwayman spread his cloak for them to sit on and turned to Lydia, a serious expression in his eyes.

'There's something I must say to you,' he began, but she silenced him with two fingers laid across his covered mouth. She shook her head.

'You don't have to say anything. What happened that day: I've thought about it. You were very bad to do that, but things have happened since then, things that have changed me. And now, well, I'm glad it happened, and I want it to happen again,' she said softly, caressing him with her eyes as she felt desire quicken in her body. He returned her gaze with equal intensity.

'I wanted to see you again,' he said. 'I want to return this: I can't bear to keep it.' He slid something out of his pocket. The glow from the fire turned it into a golden serpent which lay coiled and still on his outstretched palm. It was her bangle. Lydia felt a rush of pleasure as she quickly took it and slid it on to her arm.

'Oh! Thank you. I've missed this so much. I used to wear it every day, and it feels strange not to have its heavy clank whenever I move or knock it on something.'

'I know you love it,' he said. Pausing imperceptibly,

he continued: 'I remember the day I gave it to you. You kissed both my cheeks and danced around the library.'

Her eyes flew to his face and widened, filled with alarm and disbelief. Before he could stop her, or do it himself, she had reached up and ripped the brown kerchief from his face. As she knelt before him, staring, her heart thudded and her throat became constricted with an emotion that felt like fear, but was something else. She searched his eyes, then placed one finger on his jaw to turn his head from side to side, studying him intently in the firelight.

'It's you,' she murmured, her expression changing gradually from disbelief to incomprehension. 'It really is you. You've changed so!' She could not think what to say, how to speak. Her eyes smarted with unshed tears, but then she felt rage fizz through her veins. 'Why haven't you come to the house? Don't you know that Valerian is ruining things, gambling away all your father's money while you're out here playing highwaymen?'

She leapt to her feet and stood, quivering with fury and cold, staring down at him with unconcealed anger.

'Drummond, what do you think you're doing?' She was suddenly unable to contain herself and slapped at him as hard as she could, her hands stinging as her palms caught repeatedly on the rough fabric of his cloak and on his ears, his cheeks, his neck. Catching sight of his bemused face, she burst into tears and fell on him, holding his broad shoulders and raining kisses on to the parts she had smacked.

'You're back. You're back. Oh, Drummond, everyone said you were dead! Oh, my love, my love.' She wound her arms around his neck and he laughed, holding her away from him momentarily before returning her kisses.

'I'm back, and what a welcome. I thought that you hated me for a moment there. There's so much I have to tell you. Oh, Lydia.' He pulled her face to his and kissed her with a hunger that quickly turned to passion.

Lydia felt him lower her on to the coarseness of his

cloak, tenderly spreading her long hair and holding handfuls of it up to his face to inhale the glorious smell of her. He cupped her face in his bronzed hand and sank his mouth to hers again, his firm lips mobile and questing, his tongue gently probing until Lydia opened her mouth to him. She sucked gently, tasting his salty warmth and feeling her body melt beneath his sure touch.

A roughened palm brushed her nipple, which instantly sprang to granite hardness, and she arched up to meet him, pulling him down until his weight was heavy on her and she could revel in her own breathlessness and feeling of vulnerability.

They kissed for a long time. Finally, as if he could bear it no longer, Drummond lifted himself up from her and pulled the nightgown over her head with one movement. Lydia sucked her breath in as the cool air dimpled her skin. She pressed her knees together and felt the juice of her own arousal damp on her thighs as she anticipated his touch.

As if reading her thoughts, he trailed a hand down her bare body, pausing at the curve of her breast to outline its rounded shape with his fingers, before descending to the dark curls which shadowed the pale skin between her legs.

'Move your leg,' he murmured. The infinitesimal pressure of his warm hand separated her thighs, and he slid his fingers between, entwining his forefinger in the velvet mound as Lydia tilted her pelvis and raised her hips towards his hand. He slid his fingers into her moistness, and Lydia gave a mew of pleasure, drooping her eyelids like a cat that had found a sunny spot. She sighed and curved her body up towards his hands.

Drummond moved between her legs, bending his head and placing his mouth on her, inhaling the lingering scent of her muskiness and tentatively pushing his tongue on to the swollen bud which pressed out at him, the width and colour of his little fingertip. He licked, gently at first, then with increasing fervour. Her slick

70

juice rimed his lips, nose, and chin, lubricating his face as he pushed deliciously at her tenderest parts. Lydia twisted her fingers in his unruly brown hair and gasped, pushing herself up to meet him, widening her legs and pulling his head and face into her as if she would devour him with her sex.

Slowly, he moved up her body to kiss her long and deep on the mouth, his tongue probing the very depths of her throat and his body pressing urgently on top of hers. She could feel his cock like a steel ridge in his breeches and yearned to feel it, to see it, and hold its length in her hands.

'Let me undo you,' she whispered. He smiled and she moved her fingers to the buttons of his flat-fronted breeches. Together they unbuttoned and slid off his clothes until he was as naked as she was.

Lydia knelt beside him, gazing down at his outstretched body and feasting her eyes on the muscular limbs and chest. He was sun-kissed and athletic, the distribution of his colouring indicating the long hours he had worked, stripped to the waist, on a ship's deck; his broad shoulders tapered to narrow hips and long legs with well-developed thighs.

Lydia thought how differently his body had developed to that of his brother, who rarely exercised and whose pale skin indicated his preference for indoor pursuits. Drummond's body was a glorious celebration of manhood, lightly sprinkled with glowing, golden-brown hairs which gave him an earthy, masculine, hungry look; Valerian, by contrast, was lightly muscled but with a predatory strength and a mean streak which Lydia, against her better nature, found electrifying.

'You're so big.' She shivered as she spoke. 'Hold me. Tell me this is real.'

'It is real. You can't imagine how often I've dreamt of this.' Drummond opened his eyes and gazed at her for a few seconds, then, smiling, pulled her down to lie along his body. The warmth of him permeated her skin

71

and she felt a feverish shudder which began at her toes and rippled upward to engulf her completely.

She slid her hands across the silken skin of his shoulders, up across his throat to his jaw, sensing the roughness of his unshaven chin beneath her fingers. Aroused by this evidence of his masculinity, she dropped her mouth to his and devoured his lips with her own, holding his chin with one hand while the other delved into the tumbled mass of his hair and gripped him, controlled him, moved his head to her rhythm. Biting his lips with a sudden fervour, she groaned and moved her face, rubbing her soft cheek against the sandy texture of his beard and simultaneously sliding her legs apart, curving her back until she was sitting upright and astride. She pressed herself insistently on his hardness.

Drummond seemed driven almost to a frenzy by her movements, by the rocking motion of her hips, and she felt him reach around her waist to grip her and raise her above him. Their kiss fragmented and broke as she was lifted, and Lydia pressed her hands flat against the muscle of his chest to help him.

They paused a moment, surveying each other in the coppery glow from the fire, before moving in harmony: Lydia sank her weight down on to him as Drummond eased himself up and guided the hot, straining head of his cock into her.

Both paused, then exhaled as one and Lydia rode down, down on to the hard shaft which thrust into her so deliciously, filling her, pushing into every crevice and corner of her being until she thought she would scream with the fullness of it.

She raised and then lowered herself, feeling herself unfurl as his width and length pressed her and then withdrew, almost to the shining hot tip, before she engulfed him again, and again, and again. Repeatedly, without conscious thought, they enjoyed each other and the blissful sensations, until Lydia began to tire and move more slowly. Her thighs ached from the burden of her own weight and the chill of the night air that settled around her shoulders.

'Here, let me: come down here by me. Does that feel nice?' Drummond drew her face down and kissed her mouth, pressing his soft, warm tongue between her lips and imbuing her with his own strength.

He slowly rolled them both until they lay side by side on his cloak, noses touching and lips brushing. He cradled her leg with his arm and raised it around his hip, almost at the level of his elbow, and continued to plunge into her, grinding himself against her and sucking her tongue with a delirious intensity.

Lydia felt a tightening which began somewhere beneath her eyelids and tingled through her body, pushing her awareness to an almost dream-like pitch. She jerked her mouth from his and cried out, unable to maintain any sort of control as her climax slipped over her, wavering and silky. She stiffened, her back arched and her body rigid, digging her nails into the firm flesh of Drummond's back.

He gasped, crying her name and burying his face into the tangled damp hair which wound around her neck, breathing heavily and crushing her against him. He thrust into her until she felt him come, hot and hard, and she bit into the muscle of his shoulder.

They lay motionless. Lydia felt that her limbs were too heavy to move, and Drummond seemed exhausted and unwilling to surrender his hold on the body that, for so long, had been no more than a drowsing fantasy.

The fire, now barely more than a few smouldering sticks, flared and then subsided, leaving an inky darkness and a chill which began to permeate the air around them. Lydia, half dozing, turned her head and watched the tiny amber glow in the old hearth. The smell of Drummond's skin, and her drowsy recall of their lovemaking made her loath to move, but the cool night was beginning to chill the side of her which was furthest from the fire. She could feel, by stroking her hand lazily down Drummond's flank, that he was growing cold too.

'We should get dressed,' she whispered, moving her lips tenderly against his ear. He lifted his head and smiled at her, his pleasure in their shared climax bright in his eyes.

In silence they felt about the floor, bumping heads and hands in the dark, their touches reluctantly parting and then rejoining as if their bodies would not let them separate for more than a few moments. Finally, fully clothed, they leant together and kissed, Lydia straining her breasts against the thick leather of Drummond's brown jerkin as he reached around her to fasten his cloak under her chin.

'There, that'll keep the dawn mists out.' He smiled and kissed the cold tip of her nose.

'Drummond, when will you come home?' she asked, scanning his shadowed face. 'Valerian has taken control of everything at Hawkesworth. We need you.'

Drummond kissed her forehead and then rested his chin on her head, inhaling the perfume of her hair and holding her tightly against him.

'My love. My dearest Lydia. You know that I want to do that more than anything in the world. I haven't spent months travelling home just to skulk in the woods like an outlaw; but if I declare myself now, there's a risk that Valerian will make another attempt on my life, just as he did before I left. I'd be poisoned, or something similar, and my death passed off as the result of some tropical disease. I have to come back legitimately, with my father's will, and discredit my brother, enough to force him to leave and make a life for himself elsewhere. It has to be done properly.'

Drummond held her away from him, looking into her eyes and searching their clear depths. 'Will you tell no one of our meeting? No one at all? Please, trust me and wait for me. It's all that I ask of you at present.'

Reluctantly, Lydia nodded. She held tightly to him as they rode back through the forest, thinking of all the ways she could help him, trying to remember long-forgotten conversations with her uncle and recalling significant visits from his solicitor, Mr Lavendale.

When they reached the edge of the wide sweep of lawns, she slipped from the back of the horse and wordlessly they kissed, their lips lingering and hands clasped. Then Lydia turned and ran quickly away, her slippers leaving tiny dark marks on the silvery grass as she sprinted, silent and fleet of foot, to the house.

Chapter Five

*L*ydia closed the heavy kitchen door and returned the key to the hook behind the pantry door. The cold of the marble shelves chilled her fingers as she broke a piece of bread from a loaf that lay on a wooden board and twinned it with some crumbly cheese made in the Hawkesworth dairy. It tasted delicious and she swallowed it quickly before foraging for more.

A low sound from the kitchen made her start guiltily, and she slid the carving knife back on to the breadboard as quietly as she could. Thinking that Cook was making a very early start, Lydia wiped the crumbs from her mouth with the back of her hand before going to the open door of the pantry.

What she saw made her stop abruptly and pull back into the shadows of the little whitewashed room. Maxine Laurent sashayed into the kitchens wearing little more than her petticoat and corset, her ample breasts spilling over the top of the tightly laced garment like over-ripe gourds. Behind her, his face reddened and coarse with ale, lurched one of the footmen, obviously very drunk. Lydia recognised him as the one to whom Maxine had given that lascivious flutter of eyelashes on arrival that afternoon. Lydia could see that they had been together for some time by the familiar way they laughed together, and the manner in which Maxine drew him into the kitchen by grasping his breech-clad loins.

'Oh, Harry, come and play with me,' wheedled Maxine, her accent growing more pronounced as she became newly aroused. 'Come: you have seen what I like. Give me more, *mon cheri*.'

Harry grasped her left breast and squeezed it roughly with his hand, then fell upon it, gorging with his mouth as if he had not eaten for a week. Maxine leant her hips against the wooden table in the centre of the kitchen, and Lydia watched with fascination as Madame's maid tipped her auburn head back and groaned with pleasure, her hands cupping her own bosom and proffering it to Harry, who sucked with greed upon her large, brown nipple.

His hands gripped her waist and lifted her up so that she sat on the table. He hitched up her petticoats and then took her knees, clad in slightly wrinkled stockings, and spread them suddenly wide. Fumbling a little, he unbuttoned himself and pulled his cock free of its constraints, pausing to stroke its glistening, veined length.

Lydia swallowed, feeling herself begin to moisten at the sight of it. Bigger, possibly, than Valerian's or Drummond's, it was thick and crude, like a tool, but with a shiny texture to its reddened skin. Lydia reached involuntarily down to the soft, crumpled linen of her nightgown and pressed through the fabric on to her own throbbing sex, fingering herself lightly at first but with increasing pressure and pleasure as she watched through the half-open door.

Maxine lowered herself back on to the table until she lay full-length upon the rough, scrubbed surface, her buttocks poised at the edge. She spread her legs impossibly wide and carefully placed her stockinged feet to grip the edge of the surface. Harry reached between her thighs, scooped a generous fingerful of her juices and liberally doused himself with it, stroking and coaxing his own flesh to even more rigidity. When he placed the gleaming head on to her, Maxine quivered in anticipation, opening around him like a rose about to bloom, and Lydia could see the glistening pink of her sex as she spread herself with her fingers.

Harry reached forward and roughly massaged her breasts, his cock lying ramrod stiff across her sex, then he took his prick in one hand and sharply slapped her, making her gasp with the unexpected pleasure. Lydia firmly pressed her own finger up under her nightgown and into herself, her eyes fixed on the actions of the footman. She clenched herself on to her own deeply probing finger as Harry continued to smack himself against Maxine. He laughed and muttered, manipulating his cock with one hand and kneading her breast firmly with the other.

Maxine arched her back, offering herself up to him, her arms splaying wide and grasping at the surface of the table as she cast around for something to hold on to. Her face was pink in the glow from the range, and her eyes closed, her mouth loose and open: the picture of sensual abandon. Harry also watched her for a time, then ceased his slapping and placed his thumbs at either side of her entrance, holding her pink folds wide like wings before plunging suddenly and ramming himself into her with a guttural cry.

He gripped her fleshy thighs with firm hands, moving her on to his cock while simultaneously working his buttocks back and forth. Lydia watched, enthralled, as his muscular arse, liberally sprinkled with coarse black hairs, contracted and thrust, like one of the stable-yard stallions covering a mare at full speed.

Unable to support her own weight with her trembling knees, Lydia leant against the door jamb and held her chemise high with one hand, working at her sex with the other. Her long fingers rode firmly over herself, alternately pressing and stroking, occasionally plunging in to bury themselves knuckle-deep inside. A liberal flow of cream wet her hand and the silken skin at the tops of her thighs. Glancing down, she could see the silvery trail and smell the gorgeous dark scent of her own arousal.

Maxine cried out in the full flush of her climax and Harry shuddered, groaned, and fell on to her, panting and burying his face in the tumbled mass of her Titian curls, his hips suddenly still.

Harry recovered first and murmured into Maxine's ear. Despite straining her ears, Lydia could not hear his words and had to content herself with leaning close to the open door, pressing her eye to the crack to see what the footman did as he moved about the kitchen. For one heart-stopping moment she thought he would enter the pantry, for he seemed to be gathering items for a meal, but he simply wandered about the main kitchen, lifting lids and peering into stone jars, removing vegetables from the basket by the door and cream from the cooler.

Maxine, meanwhile, arranged herself decoratively upon the table, one leg hooked up and over the horizontal pole intended for bunches of drying herbs. Harry set his ingredients on the wooden surface beside her, and together they perused the items. Maxine delved a long forefinger into the cream and licked the thick curds from her hands, with a suggestiveness that made Lydia tingle with anticipation. It also seemed to communicate an idea to Harry, for he took the bowl and stood over the prostrate Maxine, frowning with lecherous intent.

After tearing her own clothing from her body, Maxine massaged her breasts and giggled her approval as Harry began to spread the cream over her ample form. Unable to contain himself, he began to lick and suck at every inch of her body, beginning with her breasts, but moving swiftly to her shoulders, back to her breasts, down her arms, lingering in the warm crease of her armpit. He trailed his broad tongue down between her bosoms and lapped at the swelling curve of her belly, before thrusting his nose between her thighs.

Lydia watched Maxine wriggling beneath his face and mirrored his actions with her own hands; her fingers traced a light pattern over her nipples, arms, and belly, and she shuddered, feeling her blood begin a heated throbbing. Harry continued his feast down thighs which were lathered with the heavy cream, nibbling at the backs of Maxine's knees until she begged him to stop.

Finally he turned her over and anointed the ivory cheeks of her behind, before falling carnivorously upon them as if he would actually devour her flesh. She squirmed and squealed beneath him, the skin of her buttocks quivering and rippling as she thrust herself out to him, her movements becoming quickly more frenzied as he applied a handful of the buttery curds to the neat puckered rose of her anus. He rubbed around it, circling with his thumb and forefinger, and then dipping his head to rim her with his stiffened tongue.

'Oh, Harry, *c'est bon*,' muttered Maxine, her hands extending and gripping the opposite edge of the table. Harry straightened and rubbed the heel of his hand up her spine, watching her arch under his hard caress.

He reached towards the pile of food that he had gathered earlier, and Lydia watched with increasing excitement and disbelief as he selected a thin, under-ripe baby marrow and gently worked it into the opening flower of Maxine's rear, to the accompaniment of groans of pleasure and encouragement gasped in her native tongue.

He was leisurely, and spent a long time inching it in and then easing it out again, waiting to hear her tiny gasps, then pressing further in until most of the six inches had disappeared between her pink buttocks. Next, he chose a long, thick carrot and pushed it slowly into her swollen sex, twisting and pulling it back before pressing it in to its full, hard length.

Lydia stared through the narrow crack of the pantry door and concentrated on Maxine's reaction to this double plundering with the hard vegetables. She could just see the side of the maid's face, partly obscured by the tumble of her dark coppery hair, Maxine's eyes were closed, and her cheeks flushed with a sexual glow; her lips were parted and her neck arched back to reveal her snowy throat and the pulse which beat just below her jaw-line.

Behind her, Harry ravished her with a gradually increasing and insistent rhythm, until she cried out and he reached around to silence her with one strong hand to stop her alerting the household of their nocturnal activities. His hand disappeared from Lydia's view, but there was silence; then he leant back, groaning, the tendons on his thick neck standing out in coarse relief as he pumped his cock with one fist and jerked his thick come across Maxine's naked back.

Lydia trembled in the pantry: her sex felt thick and heavy to her own fingers, and she bit her lips with frustration, unable to achieve her own orgasm for fear that the suddenly silent couple would hear her.

Removing the carrot slowly from Maxine's swollen sex, Harry casually bit the end off and crunched it with big square teeth.

'Same time tomorrow?' he enquired. Maxine reached up and gripped his semi-erect penis, squeezing it gently.

'*Mon cher*, I will expect you in my room soon after midnight. I think that being stuck here in the country may have its benefits after all.' She slid her arm around his neck and drew his mouth down to hers, and, as Lydia watched, their tongues twisted and entwined while Maxine massaged Harry's balls with her cupped hand.

The maid and the footman left the kitchen, abandoning the food for Cook to imagine what she wished in the morning. Lydia counted silently to one hundred before stealing along the darkened passageway into the main house, avoiding floorboards she knew to be creaky. The clock on the half-landing chimed four as she passed it, making her jump and hurry up the last few stairs to the warmly carpeted gallery that led to the sanctuary of her own room.

The softness under her bare feet felt warm and comforting after the chilly stone of the pantry, and Lydia paused for a moment, one hand placed flat on the wall, as she savoured the sensuous luxury beneath her toes. She pressed her tender soles downward into the close-textured cushioning, and momentarily closed her eyes in the inky darkness.

When she opened them again, she could see that a golden glow of light had appeared which lit the darkness a little further along the corridor. Someone had opened a door. Not wishing to be discovered prowling through the house at dawn, Lydia shrank back against the dark wall and held her breath.

The door swung wider, and she could see into the room, where a huge, blue-draped four-poster bed could be seen in disarray: the bolster tossed to the floor, the sheets crumpled and pushed into ruched humps as if the occupant of the bed had writhed in a feverish convulsion. The Blue Room was part of a suite that Valerian had allocated to Madame de Chaillot for the duration of her visit, so Lydia, thinking that Madame must be ill or in need of assistance, started forward to go to her aid.

Almost instantly, Lydia jumped back and pressed herself against the wall behind her. A dark shape had appeared in the lighted doorway, too tall to be the diminutive Madame. As she watched, the figure turned and the glow from a taper in the room fell upon the smooth planes of Valerian's face as he leant forward to kiss the naked woman who stood just inside the room.

Lydia caught her breath and her eyes widened as Madame, serpent-like, slid her pale, slender arms around his neck, and drew his head down to receive her returning kiss. Their tongues were visible as their lips drew slightly apart and Lydia watched as Madame sank her sharp teeth into Valerian's fleshy bottom lip.

Expecting him to be angered by this, Lydia was surprised to hear the low rumble of laughter and his tender whisper as he slipped his mouth along Madame's cheek to the slender stem of her neck. He raked his teeth across the smooth porcelain of her skin there and bit down hard on to the curve of her shoulder. Madame groaned and arched herself against him, like a cat luxuriating and rubbing itself on its master's leg. Her nipples hardened and lengthened, cork-like and ruby red, and Lydia watched with fascination mixed with revulsion as the woman reached down to the growing bulge at the front of Valerian's loose white shirt. He laughed and stayed her hand, and, reluctantly it seemed, they parted.

As the door closed gently, Valerian stepped away into the dawn shadows.

Lydia darted forward.

'How dare you?' she hissed. 'You're disgusting. How can you stoop so low as to bring your – your – whore into this house?'

He swore, then there was a flare and she saw him light the candle in the wall sconce above her head. In the soft light she saw him raise an eyebrow, and his mouth widened in a sardonic smile. He seemed completely at ease, and not at all surprised to see her.

'Good morning, cousin Lydia. What brings you here at this hour?'

Momentarily caught off guard, Lydia hesitated before replying.

'I was hungry; I went down to the kitchens for some food.'

'Indeed. Have you given your maid the night off? Really, Lydia, you must utilise the servants, or they will become redundant and I shall get rid of them.' He casually examined his nails in the dim light. 'Staff are a needless expense if you persist in doing their work yourself.'

'I didn't wish to wake Angel for such a simple task,' she whispered.

'Your generosity is commendable, dear coz. Perhaps you will extend the same consideration towards my so-called whore and refer to her by name. Either that or refrain from meddling in affairs which do not concern you.' Valerian moved closer, and Lydia could smell the feral scent of his masculine sweat mingled with a darker, mysterious odour which caught at her senses.

She stepped back carefully and he advanced again, as if they were performing some slow and ritualistic dance movement. As he moved forward, Lydia felt the cool pressure of the wall behind her, the stone chilling her shoulders through the fabric of her nightgown. Curiously, it did not make her feel cold, but merely intensified the warmth which stole through her body at his proximity, a feverish heat which tingled along her taut limbs and caused her to inhale a little more deeply, as if out of breath from a sudden exertion.

'Affair is just the word, Valerian. And, as you say, it certainly is not my affair but quite patently yours. I don't care what relations you enjoy with this French woman, but I do care that you sully our name by conducting yourself so shamelessly.' She glared up at him through angrily narrowed eyes, just able to make out the darkened curve of his jaw in the shadow of the candlelight. Valerian gave a low, malevolent laugh.

'I do believe you're jealous,' he whispered, stepping even closer so that their bodies almost touched, and Lydia could feel the warmth which emanated from beneath his loose white shirt. A burning flush rushed to her cheeks and she shook her head in denial, hardly trusting herself to speak. Valerian's eyes fixed on hers in the dim light, his hooded gaze intense and probing; Lydia dropped her eyelids, afraid of betraying herself.

She prepared to push him away, fight him if need be, and was surprised when his hand moved tenderly up her forearm to her elbow, where his thumb stroked her skin before moving downward in a sensuous trail to her wrist. His fingers interlaced with her own, gripping her. He lifted her hand firmly, sliding up the cold smoothness of the wall until she was stretching upward, lifted almost on tiptoe, her arm extended high above her head and her breast thrust up and out. She gasped, just in time, as his pliant mouth found hers, and he kissed her with a breathtaking intensity, his lips soft yet hard, his tongue tip just touching hers before he withdrew to bury his face in the mass of shining hair which tumbled freely over one shoulder.

'Aah, Lydia, so fragrant and fresh. You smell of the crisp dawn breezes which drift through the gardens. I could swear that you have been outside.'

He inhaled again, and then kissed the softness of her cheek and the curve of her jaw before mouthing gently at the sensitive lobe of her ear. Lydia felt herself melt beneath the unexpected restraint and passivity of his caresses, and she tipped her head back to reveal the innocent arc of her neck. Valerian kissed her there, lingering at the pulsing beat which thrummed through the taut skin. He placed the tip of his tongue on the camber of her throat, and drew a line slowly upward to the pointed tip of her chin, teasing her with light bites from his gentle teeth before claiming her lips once more.

As his mouth skilfully seduced her, so his hands tempted and toyed. His fingers played idly at her waist for several moments, then stole up to weigh the firmness of one breast in the palm of his hand. His thumb brushed lightly over her already firm nipple, and Lydia felt herself tighten as he rolled it between his first two fingers, pulling lazily, squashing and kneading her in his large and powerful grasp. His thigh pressed insistently on to hers, and Lydia shifted her leg a little to allow his to press between her trembling knees. She could feel the masculine rigidity of his cock pressing against the bony curve of her hip, and the pressure of its potent strength excited her almost beyond control.

She raised her hands to his face, and drew him down so that his mouth grazed hers as she pushed him towards her breast. His hands grasped the linen of her nightgown, pulling downward and sideways to reveal the rosiness of her flesh. When he fastened his lips at last to her nipple, she pushed desperately against him, feeling him suck and draw with his lips, tonguing at the puckered flesh which rose to a peak beneath his mouth.

One of his hands cupped her proffered breast, while the other slid firmly down the line of her belly to the soft down at the top of her thighs. The springy curls pushed at him through the cotton fabric as she tilted her sex towards him, and he groaned, stepped back away from her and stared at her from beneath lowered brows.

'God, Lydia, I swear –!'

Without finishing, he pulled her to him once more, and Lydia pulled at the nightgown with him, lifting the hem high around her waist. She reached for the loose folds of his own oversized shirt, and pulled at it, eager to see and feel him against her again, revelling in the gradual exposure of his lean hips and the rampant stiffness which reared out towards her from the tangle of black hair.

Valerian grasped her waist, lifted her, and turned, propping her buttocks on to the polished timber of the balustrade. Lydia sensed the steep drop behind her, but the slight frisson of fear was quickly overtaken by another, far more urgent, sensation, as he spread her with one hand. She caught her breath and closed her eyes as he slid his cock, ramrod stiff, into her creamed and ready sex. She arched her head back, her inky black hair tumbling behind in waves as it merged with the darkness of the stairwell behind her.

Suspended in time and space for an eternal moment, Lydia was roughly pulled back to earth as Valerian jerked out of her and grasped her neck with his hand.

'Why, you're as wet as a tuppenny whore after a whole troop of soldiers!' he hissed, thrusting his fingers deep into her moistness. He withdrew and lifted his hand to his face, widening his nostrils as he inhaled the scent which clung to his forefinger.

'You slut! You stink like a bitch in heat! Who else have you had?' He shook her by the neck until she thought that she would fall backward over the banister and be cast to certain death on the stone flags far below. 'Tell me, you strumpet. Where have you been? You've been fucked as surely as Madame has, but it's not my seed that perfumes your inner parts, by God!'

Lydia pressed her lips together. Meeting his penetrating gaze, she shook her head and twisted her neck beneath his firm grasp.

'I'll be damned if I tell you. If you have to be angry then I am your target.'

'Angry? Angry? Livid is the word. I am livid that my cousin sees fit to squander her most precious commodity and sneaks around in the dead of night to do so. You cheap little trollop, did you think I would never find out? To think that for one moment I thought – I really felt as if – as if there was something more between us than kinship.' He shook her again and she wriggled forward, trying to slide off the banister and on to the safety of the landing, but he held her fast with an iron fist. 'I'll find who you've been with if I have to torture all the men in this household to do so! I am the master here. I will be obeyed and respected! By deceiving me, you have lost all claim on being treated as one of the family. Henceforth, you will be locked in your room without privileges unless I feel inclined to bestow them.'

He took her hair in his steely grip and yanked her harshly down from the banister. As she fell, Lydia tried to stand, but he quickly jerked her head downward so that she could do little but crawl behind him, holding her own hair slightly above his hand to ease the pain in her scalp, as he used it like a leash to drag her along the hallway. Her knees grazed the carpet, which felt no longer like velvet, but coarse hemp beneath her, and she struggled along behind him, her eyes smarting at the pain of her tender head.

As they neared Madame's doorway, Lydia held her breath for fear that the occupant would hear the scuffling in the corridor and emerge to investigate, but everything remained dark, and Valerian continued to drag her along until they reached her own bedchamber.

'You will remain in here until I decree that you may be released,' he muttered, tightening the cords with which he had leashed her wrists to the bedpost. 'Don't imagine that struggling will loosen your bonds. I'll also tie this around your mouth: I don't wish the household to be disturbed by your calling or crying.'

Lydia jerked her head to one side, but Valerian caught her expertly and fastened a leather belt across her mouth, buckling it firmly at the back of her neck so that she could feel the bite of the hard leather around the soft skin of her face. He stood back to admire his own handiwork: Lydia's slender body was upright against the carved wooden post with her arms lashed behind her, another wide leather belt encircled her waist and held her tight to the bedpost, while a third bound her bare thighs. Her hair tangled over her shoulders and covered her breasts like a dark mantle, while her eyes above the gag were wide and full of fear.

Valerian narrowed his eyes, and then leant forward, his lips curved in a malevolent smile as he roughly tore her thin cotton nightgown from her body and kicked it to one side. She wilted, but found herself held fast by her bonds, and he raked his eyes over the exposed ivory skin and tender curves.

'My, what a pretty sight,' he murmured. 'If another had not had you so recently, I think I would indulge myself by spreading your legs wide and taking you there. To have you bound and delivered up to my mercy is an appealing temptation.' He stepped closer and slid his hand down her hip, his mouth so close to her ear that she could feel the humidity of his breath on her cheek.

'You may demur, but I think you enjoy my touch more than you care to admit. Perhaps your nakedness in this chill morning will cause your appetites to cool and your head to clear. Pray, do tell your maid if you decide to advise me of your lover's name.'

Then he was gone, the door closing softly behind him, and Lydia was left alone to shiver in the gloom. She closed her eyes and rested her head on the smooth wooden curve of the bedpost behind her, swallowing angry, frustrated tears as she prepared to wait for Angel's first visit.

Angel started slightly at the harsh sound of the summoning bell. Glancing at the board, she saw that she was required in the study. That will be Master Valerian then, she thought grimly, smoothing her muslin apron and tucking an escaped wisp of gold into the plaited coil at her nape. She hurried up the three flights of stairs from the basement, and knocked gently on the oak panelling of the study door.

'Come!' The demand was compelling, and she felt her legs carry her into the room as if they had a will of their own.

Dropping a deep curtsy, she studied the edge of the vast Aubusson rug, not daring to raise her eyes to her master.

Eventually, the silence was such that she began to imagine that she had entered the wrong room by mistake, and flicked her eyes upward, quickly, to see Lord Hawkesworth lounging on the other side of a wide, beautifully varnished desk. One polished black shoe was propped on the gleaming surface where he rested his leg; the muscles of his shapely calf stretched the taut fabric of his leaf-green hose, and the underside of his knee was clearly reflected in the mirror-like gleam of the timber. Angel felt her pulse begin to race as her gaze followed the line of his leg relentlessly upward. The master was obviously at ease with himself and with the world: a careless insouciance seemed to emanate from the soft fabric of his olive-green coat and the gentle folds of pure white cotton which frilled beneath his smooth cravat.

Angel's eyes continued their ascent, observing with deepening interest the swarthiness of his cheek, the dark shadow which cast a masculine pall across his finely chiselled jaw, the long straight nose, the sweep of raven lashes. Her heart leapt to her mouth and she tucked her head down swiftly. The penetrating look in those hooded eyes was intense and searing; Angel swallowed her sudden irrational fear and willed herself to meet his commanding face. His top lip raised contemptuously as if he sensed her fear and despised her for it, and Angel tipped her head up proudly, pulling her shoulders back and throwing him a challenging stare.

'Did you require something, milord, or did I mishear the bell?'.

'You heard correctly, Angel. I wish to discuss your mistress and the punishment I have deemed fit for her to endure.'

'Punishment?' Angel stared at him, her faintly drawn eyebrows raised. 'Why is Miss Lydia to be punished?'

'Her crime is not your concern. Her care is. I have decided that she will be locked in her room for a period of – oh – four days,' he announced arbitrarily. 'During that time she is to receive no visitors, her meals are to consist of bread and water, and she is allowed no fire in her room. Do I make myself clear?'

'But, milord, it grows so chill at this time of year. If Miss Lydia is not allowed a fire, her room will be uncomfortably cold.'

'Do I make myself clear?' Valerian wrenched his leg from the desktop and sat suddenly upright, banging his clenched fist on the timber as he did so.

Angel jumped and nodded, determining then and there that her mistress would have the choicest morsels from the kitchen smuggled to her room, whatever her crime. She watched Valerian rise to his formidable height and rest his knuckles on the desk, leaning forward as if to create an air of greater authority. Boldly, she met his eyes and flinched a little, but did not drop her gaze. She bobbed a small curtsy, deep enough to acknowledge his superiority, but shallow enough to suggest a distinct lack of servility.

'Yes, milord. It's very clear. Will that be all?'

'Get out.' His lips curled in a sneer and he waved an imperious hand.

She backed away across the rug, and turned as her

soft pumps sensed the edge of the rug. Instantly she froze. There, just to one side of the study door, and until now hidden from view, sat Madame de Chaillot. Her slender form was perched on a gilded salon chair, her blue silk gown arranged artfully around her shapely legs, so that the fabric appeared at once to reveal and yet conceal. Her back was ramrod stiff and her thin hands were folded neatly in her lap.

Angel thought for a moment that she was relaxed and careless, hardly listening, but the whiteness of her knuckles showed her tension, and as the maid glanced up she saw the woman's cold eyes fixed on her with a pale intensity. Angel interpreted the look as anger, but as she moved towards the door and came close to Madame de Chaillot, she saw that the other woman appeared consumed with a predatory hunger as her gaze remained fixed on Angel's waist. Feeling the flush which warmly stained her own cheeks, Angel paused slightly as she reached the door.

Madame remained motionless, her body rigid, but her eyes mobile and devouring as they roamed over the younger woman's body, as if memorising the details of her curving hips and the small, pointed breasts which pushed at the fabric of her dress.

Angel composed her features into a mask of distaste. Slanting her gaze sideways, she gave Madame an insolent stare before she left the room, leaning briefly against the door to steady herself as she closed it behind her.

Chapter Six

*L*ydia had been imprisoned for three days. Cold and hunger had not bothered her as much as Valerian had planned, for Angel had visited at intervals bringing hard bread and jugs of water, but with her apron pockets covertly filled with pieces of capon or goose. Warm bricks wrapped in flannel had kept the bed aired, and frequent nips of cognac from a bottle Angel smuggled into her room kept dismal spirits at bay.

At first Lydia had thought that boredom would defeat her, and had sat in the window for long hours gazing out at the colours of autumn. Slowly the leaves on the trees changed from darkest green to curling browns and reds. Angel's visits gradually took on a significance of their own, and the tiniest sound at the door would send a flicker of excitement coursing through Lydia's veins, and set butterflies fluttering in the pit of her stomach.

When she first attended her mistress, Angel had been shocked, and gently ministered to her by untying her bindings, washing and soothing her body, dabbing cologne at her temples, and helping her to dress. They did not speak of Valerian or his cruelty.

On the second evening, Angel's hands had softened as she unlaced Lydia's stays, and a smooth finger had crept inside the stiff fabric to lie on the flushed skin around Lydia's ribs. Lydia had become very still and held her breath as the fingers began stroking the flesh beneath her breasts, while the other girl's tiny exhalation warmed her shoulder. Finally, Lydia had shuddered with desire and the spell had been broken, the hands removed, and Angel had reached for the linen night-gown before helping Lydia into bed. When the covers were pulled up, Lydia watched Angel's face, hoping to meet her eye and give her a sign of encouragement; but the maid had kept her lashes modestly downcast, and bid Lydia goodnight in a low voice before leaving.

On the third day, Lydia laid in bed until she heard the grandfather clock strike midday deep in the interior of the house. Angel usually woke her with breakfast, but she had failed to arrive that morning. Lydia rolled on to her stomach and tried to ignore the hunger pangs which rumbled around her insides. Where was Angel? She was just beginning to feel bad-tempered when there came the familiar sound of a key scratching in the lock and she sat up, composing her features into an expression of deliberate petulance.

'Where have you been? It's noon, and you've usually been to see me by this time!' As she spoke, Lydia realised the strange dependency she had come to feel on seeing her maid, her absolute reliance on this contact, and it made her feel even more fractious. 'Have you brought me anything to eat? I'm ravenous.'

'Here. It's baking day and I've brought you some fresh bread. It's still warm.' Angel smiled and perched on the edge of the bed, as she broke the loaf and passed fragrant handfuls to her mistress. 'I couldn't come up earlier. The master has had me running around all over the house preparing for the ball. It's like a madhouse downstairs!'

'A ball?' queried Lydia, between mouthfuls. 'Is there to be a ball?'

'Only a small affair. He decided yesterday, and I think Madame had a lot to do with it. He wants her to be hostess, would you believe! Lord William must be turning in his grave to see his son's whore parading around Hawkesworth as if she were the lady of the manor.'

'Tell me about the ball.'

'Well, invitations have gone out to ten local families: the usual county set, I believe, and two or three of Master Valerian's friends from his club in London. The great hall is being decorated today. Oh, I wish you could see it,' she added, laughing. 'Anderson is directing them, and the footmen are all up on ladders with sprigs of –'

'Am I to be released?' demanded Lydia. Angel paused, glancing sideways at Lydia, then shook her head.

'The master says you're to stay here for another day.'

'I will not! Angel, give me that key!'

'I can't, you know how much trouble I'd be in if –'

'And you know how much trouble you'd be in if Valerian found out that you'd been feeding me. Now give me that key!'

'You wouldn't tell him!'

'I would! And I will unless you give me that key.' She changed her tone to a wheedle, sensing Angel's reluctance to be bullied. 'I won't use it until later, when the ball is in full swing. Please, Angel. I'll go mad if I have to stay in here while people dance and be merry without me. I'll only watch: no one will see me.'

'I can't let you. He'll know that I gave it to you. I'll be in terrible trouble, and you know what he's like if he gets angry.'

'He shall not know. If he does find out then I'll tell him that I stole it from you while you were dusting or something. Please, Angel.'

Lydia sensed that the other girl was weakening, and she reached out and stroked her fingertip lightly down Angel's forearm, raising the fine golden hairs which downed her skin. The other girl shivered and sighed, a frown creasing her brow. She raised her eyes and looked

94

into Lydia's face, one hand clamping suddenly on to Lydia's forefinger and trapping it against her own arm.

'All right, but you'd better not get me into trouble,' she whispered.

'Thank you.' Lydia found that her own voice had sunk to a whisper too.

With her free hand she reached up and tucked a stray strand of Angel's flaxen hair behind her ear, stroking the silken skein until it joined the coiled plait at the nape of Angel's neck. The other girl remained motionless, but somehow taut, expectant, and Lydia moistened her own lips with her tongue, hesitant and wondering.

As if she sensed Lydia's indecision, Angel turned her face and leant forward a little to kiss Lydia on the lips. Her mouth was mobile and gentle and oh, so soft: Lydia thought that her own mouth would explode just from the touch of the girl's lips. Her experience of kissing had, until now, been limited to men. Their lips were so male: hard, hungry, and devouring, leaving her breathless and incandescent with excitement and arousal at the predatory masculinity of their searching mouths. She had never considered another girl's lips, or felt them, apart from that time when Angel's mouth had given her an unrepeated pleasure. The memory of that stolen afternoon made her feel languorous and trembling with a weakness which began somewhere behind her knees and stole up the trembling muscle of her thighs, to create a hot and feverish anticipation in her belly and below. She reached up and held Angel's face between her hands, returning her kiss now, tasting the salty rose-petal of her tongue and feeling the tiny, sharp teeth just behind.

Angel took Lydia's hand and pressed it firmly to her own breast; Lydia squeezed gently, feeling the button-hard nipples which pressed against the thin fabric. She sensed, rather than consciously felt, Angel's fingers find the puckered tips of her own and pushed herself forward against the girl's hand. Gradually, she lowered Angel to the bed until the girl lay full-length on the slippery violet satin of the coverlet; then she lay her own body over her, their mouths still conjoined, their lips still gently questing.

Lydia felt an arousal as strong as any she had felt with the men she had recently experienced, and the discovery of her own limitless capacity for sexual pleasure made her groan and thrust her tongue deep into Angel's throat, sucking and biting with a sudden frenzy of sensual need. She pulled at the other girl's skirts until her stockinged legs were revealed to the hip, and then she knelt between them, gazing down and feasting her eyes on the exposed thighs and her pearly moistness.

Angel bent her knees up either side of Lydia, and tilted her pelvis upward as if inviting Lydia to do more than look.

Lydia, at once fearful but desperate to indulge her own desires, placed her two pale hands on the skin of Angel's thighs; they were already damp with a milky viscidity, and Lydia slid her thumbs over the slippery curve of flesh and tentatively pressed. Angel drew in a sharp breath, and Lydia watched her as she drooped her eyelids and seemed to disappear into herself, her cheeks flushed and her face soft and relaxed. Her mouth fell slightly open, and the fleshy pink pad of her generous bottom lip reminded Lydia of the swollen flesh beneath her thumbs. She pressed slowly, sliding across the ruched flesh, noting the tiny shell up near the tips of her thumbnails, which seemed to beg for her attention. She lightly ran the pad of her forefinger over it and saw that it was as responsive as her own.

She applied a little pressure. It enlarged. She applied a little more. It swelled. Rubbing repeatedly, she watched with fascination as Angel became wetter and wetter, and the tiny shell-like bud became longer and more engorged, like a delicious barley-sugar that begged to be sucked. Lydia bent her head and licked. Angel tasted sweet: darker and more delectable than any marchpane Lydia had ever eaten. She rubbed with the rough surface of her tongue, while Angel arched her back above her and made delicate sounds of pleasure. Suddenly, she grasped Lydia's head with her hands and pulled Lydia on to her. Lydia thought momentarily she would suffocate, but then her tongue entered Angel and she felt the girl come on to her mouth, jerking and shaking and wetting Lydia's lips with the cream of her arousal.

Afterward, she lay her head on Angel's milky thigh and savoured the musky scent which emanated from the other girl's wet, springy curls, lazily stroking and curling a lock around her forefinger.

'I suppose you'll be wanting that key now, then?' Angel raised herself and propped her head on one hand, looking down at Lydia's flushed face, her expression of interest tinged with cynicism. Lydia stared up at her indignantly.

'Do you really think that, well, that I only did that just to obtain the key? Angel, I didn't.' She reached up and grasped the maid's fingers tightly between her own.

'It doesn't matter, I'll give it to you either way. I just wanted to be sure that you meant it.'

'I meant it.' Lydia stood and leant over Angel, holding her little pointed chin in the cup of her hand. Angel tilted her head back and closed her eyes as Lydia gently kissed her mouth before releasing her and taking the proffered key.

'Maxine, pass me the little box of velvet patches.'

Madame de Chaillot turned her head first to one side and then to the other as she examined her reflection in the gilt mirror. A gloating smile lifted the corners of her carefully painted lips, as she leant closer to correct a smudge of the black powder that elongated her eyes. Taking the lacquered box from her maid, she sighed and picked over the contents with a slender forefinger.

'Which shape were they wearing in town?' she asked.

'I think the moons, Madame.'

She checked her reflection again before selecting a

tiny heart-shaped velvet patch which she placed high on her cheekbone, then a crescent moon was added just to the left of her scarlet mouth.

'You look wonderful, Madame.' The maid's voice was low and full of admiration. 'That blue gown is like a waterfall. Master Valerian will not be able to resist you.'

'He never can.' Madame stuck a last pearl bodkin into her coiffure, and smoothed her beautifully piled-up curls. The silvery powder that shimmered over her hair complemented her translucent complexion, accentuating her porcelain skin and setting off the cold blue of her eyes.

She rose from the low stool and strolled across the velvet carpet to the full-length looking-glass, stroking her hands over her waist and stomach. Her body was taut, narrow like a boy's, and her gown hung perfectly straight, almost undisturbed by breasts or hips. The front of the bodice clung to her narrow form with slippery ease, while the back – cascading loose from her shoulders to the floor – was almost like a negligee. It was fastened from breastbone to hem with tiny jet ribbons, and beneath it she wore a sheer black petticoat through which careful observers would see that she was naked but for stockings and sumptuously jewelled garters.

Placing her feet into high-heeled black mules, she watched herself as she stroked her hands over her breasts, pinching her already taut nipples and pulling them to prominence. Now her small breasts looked as though they would pierce through the diaphanous fabric, her areolas darkened circlets beneath the midnight colours. Madame shivered: sexual arousal was never far away, but tonight she anticipated something very special from the repressed local aristocracy.

She reached for her bottle of perfume, and then paused. As she lifted her gown, she rubbed a finger lightly over her sex, which swelled a little, warm and inviting. She was ready now, but there would not be time for even the quickest satisfaction. First wetting her

98

finger with her own cassolette, she then touched the fragrant cream to her pulse points: each wrist, behind her ears, and finally into the shallow scoop of her cleavage.

'Resistance would be futile,' she murmured. Maxine smiled and held out an ornate feathered fan.

A thrill of feverish anticipation rushed through Madame's veins as she paused at the top of the staircase, one hand on the smooth banister. Her excitement was mirrored on several of the upturned faces, and she recognised some of the young libertines who, with Valerian, frequented the Avernus Gentlemen's Club in Piccadilly. Later, when the older and more staid members of the county set had made their way home in their horse-drawn coaches and carriages, Madame would preside over a private gathering of these men and a select group of the younger, more promising local inhabitants.

Anticipation was a fine aphrodisiac, she thought, as she felt the quicksilver pull of arousal and the throb of the hot blood which raced through her veins. The libertines were well known to her; they were handsome young men, fit and muscular with the stamina of youth, but the dissolute experience of older men.

She caught the eye of one of her favourites, Andreas. He smiled up at her, and she saw the gleam of his pure white teeth, saw him slide his hand slowly over the front of his tight breeches in a discreet but clear gesture of sexual promise. Madame coolly ignored him, composing her features into the customary, expressionless mask as she descended the stairs. Valerian materialised at her side and swept his dark eyes over her body with silent appreciation. She met his look with an imperious tilt of one thinly pencilled eyebrow, and together they stepped into the great hall.

The wainscoting had been polished to a sheen which reflected the glow of hundreds of lighted tapers; the chinaware that usually rested in the recesses had been replaced with huge candelabra and vases of fragrant greenery. Against one wall, a long table bowed under the weight of platters of sweetmeats, roast swan, jellied fruits, and a centrepiece of suckling pig, while a well-stoked fire roared beneath the ornate mantelpiece.

The warm smell of food and fifty perfumed bodies assailed her, and Madame flared her nostrils as she took a glass of syllabub from a passing footman. Valerian held his own glass to his lips and surveyed the hall.

'What do you think?' he enquired.

'So many people at such short notice,' murmured Madame, fluttering her fan in front of her chin. 'A sign of acceptance of your place in society. Would you agree?'

'Indeed.' Valerian smiled and bowed at an elderly gentleman who passed by. 'The only obstacle now is to have my departed brother declared legally dead.'

'Have you spoken to Lavendale recently?'

'The man urges caution. He insists that Drummond must be missing for seven years.' His cheeks flushed with irritation. 'Then, Claudine my love, I can take my rightful place, but for now I am merely the unofficial Lord Hawkesworth. Everyone knows he must be dead. All attempts to trace him have failed, and between you and I, my dear, if by some miracle he sent word of his continued existence I'd burn any letter before it became public.'

'What if he should come in person?'

'Then God help him. I'd rather see him at the bottom of the deepest lake on the estate than renounce my claim!' Valerian felt the cool pressure of Madame's warning fingers on his arm.

'Let's begin the dancing,' she suggested, smiling up at him. He held out his hand and they moved into the centre of the hall.

As she moved among the throng, Madame silently appraised the younger guests, and tried to memorise the faces of those who showed most promise: romping nearby was the energetic Lord Irving, a young aristocrat whose muscular thighs and broad shoulders made her heart jump. Then she passed a sweet-faced girl of maybe seventeen years, who looked incorruptible and therefore truly challenging. Later she offered a dish of comfits to a blushing priest, whose habit of wearing his long, pale hair bound with a scarlet ribbon belied his air of humble seriousness. As it neared midnight, she exchanged smiles with a pretty matron whose smooth bosom swelled longingly out of her tightly laced busk.

Finally, she noticed a flash of chartreuse velvet which moved at intervals in the minstrel's gallery far above: Lydia. She pretended to ignore the partly hidden figure who knelt behind the balustrade. Smiling across the crowded room at Valerian, she savoured thoughts of a suitable punishment for his cousin, and quivered with amusement at the thought of the innocent girl's shock when she witnessed the spectacle that Madame planned for later.

'I think the evening has been a success, *mon petit*,' Madame murmured to Valerian. A cool night breeze lifted several loose strands of her hair as the couple stood in the main doorway bidding farewell to the last of the gentry. Valerian turned with an enigmatic smile and steered her indoors.

'The evening, my dear, is still young, and I anticipate even greater success. As I am sure you do.'

'Indeed. I thought you did particularly well persuading Squire Matthews that his wife would be escorted safely home. Thank you.'

'My pleasure. What do you plan for her?'

'Aaah, you must anticipate a little longer.'

She strode ahead of Valerian, back to the hall. The food lay ransacked on the table and the tapers had burnt low, throwing long shadows across the floor. Near the imposing fireplace, the young men of Valerian's acquaintance filled their goblets with claret and ensured that the remaining guests were equally replenished.

Madame glanced around, wondering where to start. Excitement stirred her, and she felt a fluttering in her breast as she wavered between the blond priest who sipped his claret, and Lord Irving, who stood alone and remote on the far side of the room.

Making a sudden choice, she approached the priest and spoke softly. He smelled pleasantly of soap and beeswax, and she moved closer, relishing the look of surprise that widened his deep grey eyes. He blushed as her hand slid teasingly down his black garb to linger at his groin. Pleased with what she felt there, Madame rose on to tiptoes and kissed him fully on the mouth, pressing her thin lips to his and insinuating her serpent-like tongue between his teeth. He stepped back, but she leant closer, massaging him with an insistent hand until she heard his low groan of defeat.

Behind her, she heard Squire Matthew's young wife, Sophie, gasp as one of the libertines mirrored Madame's performance with his own kiss and caress. Initially, Sophie seemed reluctant, but the wine she had consumed – and the inattention of her overweight husband since their marriage – made her respond with growing passion to the young man's overture. Another young man joined the first, and soon any observer would have found it hard to distinguish between the three bodies and their exploring hands and mouths.

Madame watched as Sophie savoured the ecstasy of having one man suck on the swell of her bosom while another nibbled at her exposed and extended neck. She had obviously never experienced such ecstatic sensations, and appeared almost to swoon from sheer erotic pleasure.

One of the young men encircled her with muscular arms and lowered her back on to the scarlet couch behind her. At once she was surrounded by Valerian's entourage who tended her feet, hands, and legs. One cherub-faced boy with wildly curling ringlets slipped her satin shoes from her feet and sensuously rubbed her toes with the fleshy pads of his thumbs; another slid her bracelets from her arms and fastened his questing mouth to the tender inner curve of her elbow. A blond

Adonis began the task of unlacing her bodice to free her bosom and waist, while Andreas, a youth with the colouring and fierceness of a Romany, lifted her petticoats and began to knead the pale softness of her thighs.

As she continued to entwine herself around the increasingly ardent priest, Madame noticed Lord Irving standing in a shadowed recess near the fireplace. He was watching Sophie Matthews intently, and had unbuttoned his breeches to stroke himself, but his attention seemed caught by something else, for his eyes widened, sliding along the length of their prostrate bodies and lifting to a higher level.

Madame twisted a little to follow his gaze, loosening her hold on the priest's cock and watching Valerian approach the cherubic youth from behind. He unbuttoned himself with practised ease, spread the young man's plump buttocks, and spat on his own fingers before moistening the youth with saliva. With a swift contraction of his lean hips, Valerian entered the boy and rode smoothly back and forth, sensual enjoyment playing across his face as he closed his eyes. The cherub gave a moan of pleasure and bent forward to accommodate his friend, pressing his arse back and arching himself keenly. His face brushed against the side of Sophie's foot, and he turned slightly to slip his mouth over her largest toe, engulfing it with his pink lips.

Madame stared in fascination as the lad's rounded cheeks curved inward with the strength of his sucking. She heard Sophie gasp at the intensity of the sensation, but the sound was swiftly silenced as another man bent to kiss her with bruising passion, before straightening and holding his swollen cock to her mouth. At first she seemed to hesitate, her eyes round and wondering, but then she opened her lips to the straining shaft and began to pull with a vigorous thirst.

Madame glanced back at Irving: his muscular body was taut and expectant, his eyes closed. She abandoned the priest and darted to him, soundlessly reaching out to grip his cock tightly between her thumb and forefinger. His eyes flicked open in surprise as he found his climax abruptly halted.

She held the forefinger of her other hand to her lips in a silencing gesture, before running that same oval-tipped digit down over the ivory flatness of her chest to the first ribbon which fastened her gown. She pulled smoothly and slipped it free before placing it between her lips. Holding one end, she slid the ribbon across her tongue, and Irving stared as if hypnotised as the narrow sliver of black satin was finely coated with saliva. Her other hand sought his swollen balls and freed them from his breeches, then she wound the wet ribbon tightly around him until he was firmly trussed.

He was completely harnessed, unable either to subside or ejaculate.

Madame's eyes remained fastened upon his as she slowly bent forward and wrapped her lips around him. She sucked once and withdrew, sucked again, then delved the point of her tongue into the little slit that opened the top. Irving groaned above her, and she smiled before sliding her tongue under the cuff of his foreskin and riding around it. She played like that for a few moments before she gave him a final hard suck, then straightened up with a flick of her tongue over rouged lips.

Taking his hand, she led him into the centre of the candle-lit room and pushed him into a straight-backed chair, before striding away and stepping up on to the dais at the far end of the room. Lord Irving gave her a beseeching look, which she cruelly ignored as she took her seat on a carved throne. She could feel the skirt of her gown dampen beneath her, treacle-thick and warm, as she looked at the bodies below her.

Joseph and Conrad, Valerian's faithful henchmen, stepped forward to help her remove the diaphanous garments which clung to her slender form, and she sat erect, naked but for her stockings and jewelled garters, her feet tipped on her impossibly high black mules. She stayed very still, imperiously surveying the tableau.

Below her, Sophie, surrounded with libertines and plundered by their probing tongues and cocks, came shudderingly as her various attendants climaxed almost simultaneously into her mouth and hands. The cherub bit down hard on her toe, as Valerian stiffened and spasmed behind him, and Sophie quickly jerked her foot away from the sharp teeth. Almost immediately, she was lifted upright by a team of muscular arms and shepherded to a chair beside Lord Irving. Others grouped around, the cherub leaning over the back of Sophie's chair, with his hand lazily squeezing one of her breasts.

There was a silent expectancy in the hall.

'My friends.' Madame stood and stretched herself to her full height, her nakedness glowing in the soft light cast by the flames from the fire. She paused for a long time before speaking again, ensuring that she had undivided attention, aware of the many eyes that devoured her body. 'You are all here tonight by your own free will. Each of you has, by now, deduced the manner of our revelry, and if any should wish to leave, then I suggest that you do so at this moment.'

There was a long silence. No one moved, and finally she smiled, inclining her head slightly as if to acknowledge their choice. 'Then let us feast.'

She stepped back and sat in the throne once more, her legs crossed and her back ramrod straight. Her posture thrust her ribs forward and her small breasts stood proud. Admiring her own body, she stroked her hands over herself, pinching her ruby-red nipples, pulling them out to hard lengths which she rolled between her fingers. When she was satisfied with their shape and position, she stretched her slender arms elegantly out, and Joseph and Conrad moved towards her. She grasped their naked cocks, one in each fist, and gripped them tightly.

Her predatory gaze circled the room, until she lit upon the priest who sat, still fully clothed, on one end of the semicircle of acolytes.

'Father Clarence, please rise. You appear flushed. Could it be that you are warm? Undress yourself, I pray.' As the priest fumbled to obey, she continued: 'But wait: leave your clerical collar on. I wish to see you wear it as you break your vow of celibacy.' Her hands continued to work at Joseph and Conrad as she surveyed the others present. 'Little Miss Madeleine.' She smiled benignly at the young maiden who was perched, hands demurely folded, on a low footstool at Valerian's feet. 'Your education should be started by a man of the cloth, I think.' The girl dipped her eyes virtuously, her sweet face blushing and her bottom lip trembling. 'Come, my dear, these gentlemen shall make you a bed with their bodies, and we will see how the priest excels with his tongue.'

At her words, three of the libertines moved forward from the shadows and lay side by side upon the woven carpet. Madeleine remained where she was, her knuckles showing white on her folded hands. Valerian, behind her, raised his eyebrows and smiled with satisfaction as if he enjoyed her reticence. Madame sighed.

'Oh dear. Little Madeleine has become shy. Valerian, my love, persuade her.'

She watched, holding her breath, as Valerian reached down and grasped the girl's chin. He twisted her face upward and Madame swallowed as he bent to crush Madeleine's lips with his own. As he feasted on her mouth, one hand slid into her bodice, and Madame could see the outline of his fingers as he squeezed the girl's breast, rubbing his thumb firmly over her nipple. Madeleine struggled, but at a signal from Madame, the cherub and the Adonis grabbed her arms and twisted them behind her back, holding her captive. Valerian finished his kiss and stood up straight, his eyes catching Madame's and a cruel smile twisting his lips.

'Bring her,' commanded Madame.

The two libertines dragged the now vigorously struggling girl to where the bed of men lay. She stood between them, her chin tilted defiantly up, and Madame felt her heart skip a beat: the fighters were always so much more thrilling, she thought. Madeleine's dark eyes burnt into hers, and then, as if the girl could read her mind and knew how to win, she slumped between the two men, her body soft and passive, the fight gone from her limbs. Madame ground her teeth, her lips pursed and angry. She glared at the girl through eyes which became two narrow slits of glittering fury.

'Get on to the bed!' she spat.

Madeleine slowly advanced until she stood by the head of the nearest prostrate man. Unsure of how to proceed, she paused to throw Madame an appealing glance.

'Mistress Sophie, please help her undress.' Madame squeezed the cocks in her hands as she spoke, but neither Joseph nor Conrad showed any reaction. Sophie Matthews went to Madeleine's assistance and removed her silky garments until Madeleine's perfect young body was bare.

Several of those watching inhaled audibly, for the girl was a veritable Venus, with high, creamy breasts and an auburn thatch which curled shyly between her shapely legs. The thought that she was also as yet untouched caused Lord Irving to shift in his chair and finger the ribbon which laced his swollen genitals.

Sophie took both Madeleine's hands in hers and gently eased her back until the girl lay upon the bed of men. The one upon whose chest her head rested reached up and gripped one of her wrists in his fist; the other arm he pinned to the ground with his strong thigh so that she was displayed like a butterfly, her wings out-stretched and imprisoned for all to see and feast upon.

Under Madame's instruction, the priest advanced and knelt between her raised knees.

'Kiss her, Father.'

He feasted his eyes momentarily on the exposed body before him, drinking in the sight of her. His cock leapt and jerked, straining outward as if it would go to her even if its master wished otherwise, which he obviously did not. He leant forward, pressing his tongue between her parted thighs, and Madeleine squirmed beneath his mouth and cried out, trying to close her legs and deny him entry. His hands were heavy on her thighs as he prised them apart again, his thumbs leaving a white imprint on her flesh, and she sobbed a little but then seemed to relax under the pressure of his tongue. Father Clarence spread her knees further and buried his face in her scented flesh, lapping thirstily.

Madame watched with intense interest, leaning forward slightly and pausing in her masturbation of the henchmen. She called to one of the libertines.

'Andreas, come to me.'

He broke away from the group in the shadows and stepped lithely up on to the dais. He seemed to know what she wanted without having to hear her words, for he dropped to his knees before the throne and placed his hands on Madame's rigid thighs. Delving with firm thumbs, he held open the swelling of her sex to reveal a thick golden loop: a ring which entered the skin at one side and disappeared deep into her labia before glittering in the light where it protruded. Andreas licked it once and then leant forward to place his stiffly held tongue on the finger-like protrusion of her unusually large clitoris.

Madame closed her eyes momentarily, savouring the sensation as he licked and sucked, her hands closed tightly on the rigid cocks she clasped. Joseph, the more well-endowed of the two, gasped and shuddered, the muscles of his ebony belly contracting in spasms as he tried to control himself.

Madame's ice-blue eyes snapped open, and she stared fixedly at Mistress Matthews.

'Sophie, I wish you to lie upon Madeleine. Lie on your back atop her, and allow her to reach around you and squeeze your breasts. She will oblige or she will know the consequences. Father Clarence will enter you, and Madeleine will receive every sensation of being fucked, but without the loss of her maidenhead. That's right: now, Father – that's it. Tup her well, Father, and allow young Madeleine to feel every thrust that you make. Every plunge of your sword, every slap of your balls, will thrill her parts until she imagines that it is she, not Mistress Matthews, who feels the divinity of your cock. Oh, Father, I would that you could see yourself, fulfilling the aims of God's creation and teaching a maiden the ways of heavenly pleasure.'

Madame became still as Andreas plunged two rigid fingers deep inside her, and she was thrust into an engulfing climax that seemed to burn and tear at her flesh. She gasped and her long eyelids fluttered, casting deep shadows over her cheeks as her hands tightened on their twin handles.

Joseph and Conrad quivered and groaned deeply as they climaxed on to the pale skin of her shoulders and neck. Father Clarence drove into Sophie Matthews with a final ferocity while Madeleine moaned beneath them on her bed of men; there was a strangulated cry as Lord Irving tore the ribbon from himself, and cradled his aching cock in his palm as he spurted viscous seed on to the timber floor. Then he slumped, sobbing, in his chair.

There was a silent pause as all lay spent.

Madame, rubbing her sticky neck with a leisurely hand, stood and pushed her three attendants aside. She stepped down from the platform and strode to the tightly woven bodies on the scarlet carpet. The exhausted priest had buried his face into Sophie's abundant hair, and Madame bent to stroke his head with an almost maternal tenderness.

Kneeling, she slipped her hand between his muscular thighs to stroke her forefinger over Madeleine's dewy parts. Lifting her hand to her nose, she inhaled the delicate virgin scent before gliding that same finger into Sophie's soft mouth. The sensation of the other woman unexpectedly sucking the juices from her moist digit caused a welcome thrill of sensuality and power to flood feverishly through her, and she stood to survey them all for a long moment.

'Who would like the virgin?' Her gaze swept the men present, and she met Valerian's eye with a slight upward twist of her thin lips. 'I give her to you. But it must not show. Leave her maidenhead intact.'

Madeleine struggled as Madame grasped her wrist and jerked her to a sitting position. Her face was pale and her eyes wide, entreating the merciless Madame.

'No, please. Don't hurt me,' she pleaded.

'You have no choice,' murmured Madame, bending so that her lips were almost touching the girl's ear. 'I know you want to. I saw the look in your eyes when you felt the priest take Mistress Sophie. I saw envy! Now turn over.'

'No.'

'Turn over, or I'll have them make you.'

Madeleine glanced around at the faces that surrounded her in the candlelight. Her eyes were still wide, but the hint of fear that had shadowed them before had been replaced by interest as she studied Valerian. She pouted.

'No.' She seemed almost to be challenging them. Madame felt a thrill of desire as she stared at the girl and wondered whether it was too late to change the plan and have her to herself; then she remembered Lydia upstairs and smiled, her pulse skipping as she anticipated possessing her. She took a step back and gestured to Valerian.

'Turn her over.' Her voice was taut and the libertines obeyed immediately. They grasped Madeleine's arms and legs and twisted her, expertly flipping her so that she lay face down on the floor. One of them reached for a padded footstool and slid his hand under her waist, lifting her and positioning her over it so that her face was pressed into the carpet and her plump little bottom was raised and open.

She struggled, tiny whimpers coming out from under the cloud of auburn hair, and they all bent over her, stroking her back and limbs while Valerian knelt behind her and smoothed her buttocks with his soft palms.

'Madeleine, I shan't hurt you,' he murmured. 'And I shall not disturb your maidenhead. That will be left for your husband, whoever he may be. Enjoy this now, feel it, savour it, for it is certain that any husband your father provides you with will never have the imagination to repeat the experience for you.'

Her body relaxed under the caresses, her tight muscles softening as she listened. The cherub lifted up her curtain of hair and bent to kiss her cheeks and then her lips.

'She is smiling, my lord,' he said softly. Valerian nodded, then bent to examine her sex. He gestured to the others and several of them clustered around him, their eyes intent, their breeches bulging as they observed his long fingers sweeping across the folds of tender skin. She was very aroused, and a slick of warm cream came away on Valerian's forefinger; she seemed to press herself out towards them, encouraging them. In turn, they each slid their fingers over her, lightly touching but not entering. When he judged that she was ready, Valerian steadied her with one hand, his fingers long and pale across the pinkness of her bottom, then he slid his forefinger into her anus.

She bucked in surprise, then held herself still, rigid, as she waited for his next move. He eased his finger in, pushing as far into her as he could so that his knuckle was pressed up against the flesh of her behind. The room was silent: no one moved, or breathed. Valerian slipped his finger out and bent to press his tongue to her, moistening her.

'Madeleine, you will feel me enter you.' He spoke softly, his hand stroking the length of her spine. 'Ready yourself, make yourself open for me, and it will hurt less.'

The others watched as he pressed forward, the cherub kissing her face and several others gripping her when she struggled suddenly as he broached the virgin

111

entrance. Her initial cry of alarm was silenced by a deep kiss from the cherub, his tongue sliding easily into the mouth she had opened to scream, and others grasped her breasts from below and massaged them firmly until her struggles subsided and she submitted to Valerian.

He took a long time, his movements very slow and leisurely. Madame came to kneel near Madeleine's head, her eyes holding his, and when he moved gradually faster, he stared almost unseeing into the glass-pale depths.

'She likes it,' murmured one of the libertines. 'By God, she's lubricating him.'

Madame leant forward and smiled as she saw that Valerian's plunging cock had been anointed with a mysterious cream from deep within Madeleine's body. She heard him groan and she leant up to kiss him deeply as he gave a final thrust and became still, his thighs taut and rigid as he came.

'Who shall be next?' Her voice was low and amused as the libertines moved forward, each vying with the other to be the one to fill Valerian's place. She heard Madeleine sigh, and felt a swell of heat deep inside her own body. She held out her hand.

'Valerian. I need you now, my love. Let us retire to my chamber, alone.'

Arm in arm, Valerian and Madame left the debauchery, their bodies taut with the anticipation of private revels still to come. Halfway up the curving sweep of stair they paused, and Valerian kissed his mistress with the depth and passion of a man possessed. Impatiently he bent and swept her slight form into his arms and ran up the remaining steps. There came the sudden, echoing thud of the bedchamber door as it slammed shut behind them.

Then silence.

Chapter Seven

*T*he darkness was complete. Velvety and thick, it was like a cloak around her as she raised her head from her arms and blinked to dispel the sleep. The only sound was the low and constant ticking of the great clock on the landing. Lydia moved slightly, easing her cramped legs and listening for other movement. Nothing stirred.

Below her she could just make out the distant glow from the dying embers of the fire, but the light was only enough to give a gilded hue to the fender and slate hearth, and the solitary, unidentifiable body which curled, sleeping, on the hearth-rug.

Wondering how long she had been asleep, and what had caused her to wake, Lydia sat up and stretched her arms wide to ease the life back into their numbness. At once her heart was in her mouth and she gasped, dread filling her limbs as her fingers felt the hard flesh of another.

'Who's that?' She patted the shape beneath her hands and wondered at its smooth hairlessness. 'Angel?'

'You'd like that, wouldn't you?' The low reply had a slightly mocking lilt, and Lydia recognised the hardness of Madame de Chaillot's lightly accented voice. 'But it is I. My dear, I cannot sleep and wish for company: pray come to my room.' Her fingers grasped Lydia's

113

wrist in a bony circlet, and Lydia found herself being pulled to her feet with a strength that belied Madame's delicate frame. Reluctantly, she stepped after Madame and walked the short distance from the minstrel's gallery to the guest suite.

The salon was lit by numerous creamy church candles set in black and silver candelabra. The dark oak wood of an enormous four-poster bed glowed softly, and the blue sheen of the hangings invited the fingers to stroke and the hand to caress. As Lydia advanced, guided by the coolness of Madame's hand in the small of her back, she felt an almost overwhelming urge to sink into the cerulean sea of the quilt which covered the bed.

She had all but obeyed her impulse, when she saw that the tumbled sheets already possessed an occupant. Black hair lay in stark contrast to the snowiness of the white pillow. His face relaxed in sleep, Valerian gave the tiniest of snores as he dreamt. Lydia stopped, turned almost to stone. Glancing at Madame, she saw the other woman quickly veil her triumph with a look of tender concern.

'But my dear Lydia, I was certain that you knew: Valerian and I have been lovers for years.'

'Of course. You've left no room for doubt.'

'There can be no doubt.' As she spoke, her fingers caressed the curve of Lydia's elbow. 'We first met in London when Valerian was just a boy of sixteen. He was fresh from the country, sent up by his father for tutorials with the Jesuits; but one of those irrepressible fathers took him to the Avernus Club, gathering place of rakes and libertines, and from then on he needed very little guidance. His hell-raising quickly became legendary in certain circles, and I engineered a meeting between us. I was a full ten years older than him, but it soon became apparent that we were two of a kind, two faces of the same coin, and we have been inseparable in town ever since. You have no idea how boring this provincial little place has become for him; he needs every diversion he can obtain while he is here.'

114

Lydia's cheeks burnt as she inferred that she, and indeed everything at Hawkesworth, was little more than a 'diversion' for a bored philanderer. Her chin went up in defiance and her eyes flashed at Madame.

'You may think that he is in need of every diversion, Madame, but I assure you that Valerian is always very well provided for here. He lacks for nothing. You forget that before your arrival my cousin was nobility and you were nothing but a common *putain*.'

'*Touché*, my dear. I had no idea you were conversant with my native tongue. However, I must correct you. A *putain* fucks for money; I fuck for the gratification of my own desires. But, when you have tasted all that I have, the palate becomes somewhat jaded and is enlivened only by the most piquant of dishes. Valerian and I explore the full menu together. Perhaps in time you will understand: at present I understand that you are still a virgin.'

'Well, you understand incorrectly.'

Too late, Lydia saw that she had been led into a trap, teased and gently reeled in like a small fish on the end of a very dangerous line. Madame's eyes burnt with a near zealous fanaticism as she moved towards Lydia. A slender hand pushed between her legs, pressing through the velvet of Lydia's gown.

'Indeed.' The hiss was sibilant, hypnotic. 'What a bad girl you are. I think that you're lying.'

Lydia stepped back, aroused in spite of herself by the firm pressure of the older woman's fingers against the heaviness of her skirts. A primitive thrill fizzled through her as the pressure increased, and she found herself almost unconsciously pushing herself forward. Madame arched one thinly plucked eyebrow and curved her lips in a predatory smile.

'Despite my earlier feast,' she murmured, 'I find that I am still hungry. Would you care to sup with us, Lydia?' Her eyes penetrated Lydia. 'I see that you would, in spite of yourself.'

She placed her hand flat against Lydia's chest and

pushed her back until the buttoned leather edge of a couch pressed behind her knees. Lydia, finding her legs were weak and tremulous beneath her, sat down abruptly and allowed Madame to twist her into a reclining position. Madame's fingers moved across the fastenings of the chartreuse velvet gown, and Lydia's breath came more quickly as she was made naked. Madame delved suddenly, viciously, between the tenderness of Lydia's rounded thighs.

'So, you did not lie. How interesting. The little virgin is actually as much of a *putain* as any common little streetwalker! Oh, no! Don't try to get up! If you are going to be difficult I will have to bind you.' She raised one eyebrow. 'I see in your eyes that the idea does not revolt you. Come, give me your wrists. And, I think your ankles: no, not your ankles. I want your legs free for the moment. We may wish to have access to you when we are done with each other.'

Lydia made little struggles, more for show than with any real desire to escape. Madame swiftly tied her wrists, and slid her cool hands smoothly down Lydia's naked arms to the warm curves of her armpits, then inexorably to her breasts. As she watched, the painted fingernails raked the camber of her tender skin which puckered and goosebumped. When Madame bent her head and flicked the rosy nipples with her narrow tongue, Lydia cried out, arching her back and closing her eyes. She was incredibly aroused: the thought of Valerian sleeping only feet away, and the memory of the sights on which she had spied earlier, made her feel wanton and shameless. She pressed the warmth of her shoulder-blades on to the cool leather of the couch, surrendering to sensation.

Suddenly her eyes snapped open.

Valerian towered over them, his face stern. 'Claudine, you infernal slut. What are you doing?'

'What, my darling, do you think?' Madame stood and pressed herself against him, wrapping her arms around his neck. 'She claims not to be a virgin, and I wanted to verify her words. It is in your interests, Valerian. You do realise that you'll have to give her a larger dowry if she has lost her maidenhead?'

'An ample dowry was set aside by my father. I know she's not intact: some dog has sniffed around her skirts once too often, but she refuses to tell me who.'

'Well, for now, my sweet, we have nothing to lose by sharing in his good fortune! Wouldn't you like her as a dessert?' Madame's pale blue eyes bored into Valerian's, and her hunger was reflected in his face. A cruel smile curled the corner of his mouth, and he glanced over his mistress's shoulder, feasting his eyes on Lydia's bound nakedness. Lydia writhed and widened her eyes as he pushed Madame aside and strode to where she lay.

'Dessert. Oh, indeed, but she should not be able to call for help.'

He lifted one of Lydia's own discarded stockings from the floor and tied the emerald-coloured silk swiftly around her lower face, gagging her with the diaphanous fabric before she could protest. Lydia could feel the warmth between her legs become a searing heat as he towered above her, vulpine and predatory. She waited for him to touch her, her sex pouting and anticipating the pressure of his long fingers, but he abruptly turned on the bare pad of his heel and strode to Madame.

Lydia watched, surprised, as he bent in supplication to kiss her tiny feet. He applied his tongue to the arch of her foot, licking and polishing her feet and ankles with his mouth.

'You worthless creature,' Madame snarled. 'You cannot even protect the innocence of a girl placed in your care. You shall be punished for that.'

Lydia was astounded at the way Valerian, usually so dominant, bowed his head and humbly stroked Madame's calves. She could just see the tiny smile that played around his handsome mouth, and the shiver of pleasurable anticipation which rippled his skin. At first she felt repulsed that her omnipotent cousin should display such submissiveness, but gradually, as she observed the exchange between Valerian and Madame, she realised that their game had the delicate intricacy of a complicated dance with a long-established routine.

Madame was fully in control.

'What happens to people who need to be punished?'

'Madame, I know not.'

'I think you do.'

'Please. No.'

'Oh yes, milord. Approach the bed.'

'Madame! No!' Valerian cried out, but his eyes told a story of tormented desire as Madame opened the carved chest at the foot of her bed. From it she extracted a long and beautifully plaited horsewhip. She gently caressed the shining leather, her hand gliding over the chestnut sheen while a ruthless smile curved the corners of her lips.

'Assume the position, milord.'

Valerian moved to the bed and stood near the side of it, his feet half-hidden in the pool of azure silk which drifted down the side of the mattress. Madame buckled his wrists with thick leather manacles. Lydia saw that the cuffs were lined with a soft padding of amethyst-coloured fur, and she noticed that Valerian shuddered as his arms were imprisoned and pulled wide before Madame fastened him to the bedposts. His pale body hung between the two uprights, the muscles taut under his ivory skin, and Lydia felt her breath come in ragged gasps as she stared at him. He was so beautiful, suspended there like a crucified man, awaiting his punishment.

The first lash licked his flesh with lightning speed, and Lydia leapt simultaneously with Valerian. Fascinated, she watched as a cruel red weal snaked across his back. Madame, impassive, flayed him again. This time he yelped, and a second crimson mark glowed parallel to the first.

Lydia watched the chastisement, her own arousal becoming ever stronger as the marks on Valerian's body gradually crept lower towards the hard crescent of his buttocks. She was desperate to touch him, to kiss the scarlet lines and lick his pained flesh, but her own bindings held firm, and she could only observe in a storm of desire and wonder as he received his castigation.

'Have you been very bad?' Madame's hiss cut through Lydia's dream-like state, and she glanced at the woman who stood only two paces away. Madame's eyes were narrowed to thin slits and the light which shone from under her lashes gleamed with pure savagery. Her small breasts rose and fell with the effort of her exertions, and through the light fabric of her negligee Lydia could see her arousal in the hard nipples which pressed out through the fabric like jewelled bottle-stops. As she moved, her gown parted and revealed the pearly skin of her thighs, showing the tiny dewdrops which had glazed the smooth flesh there.

Lydia felt the blood in her veins rage and swirl, leaving her faint as if she were in a state of fever; her own sex became suffused and almost liquid as she drank in the other woman's power. She tried to cry out, to attract Madame's attention to herself, but the murmur which sounded from behind the gag served only to irritate Madame, who, without looking round, savagely flicked the whip in Lydia's direction. The tip caught the girl's tight nipple and a shock of exquisite pain licked her senses.

'Answer me! Have you protected this girl's virginity?'

'I have not,' came the gasping reply. A further application of the whip was greeted by a tortured groan, and Valerian sagged, kept upright only by his cuffed wrists.

Madame threw the horsewhip to the ground and stood directly behind Valerian, leaning forward so that her small body moulded to his and her chest was pressed to the wounds she had just inflicted. He flinched away at the contact, but she gripped his hips and jerked him on to her so that his weals were covered by her belly and breasts.

'Oh, you naughty, naughty boy. I think I have just the thing for you.'

Her fingers sinuously slid on to the polished surface of the bedside table and grasped the string of polished topaz beads which lay coiled there. She weighed them in her hand, a sly smile curving her mouth, then she scooped the handful to her lips and toyed with them, the tip of her pointed tongue lapping at the pearlescent droplets and the silken string between. She slid downward, knelt behind Valerian and smoothed her hand up the hairiness of his leg to reach under and cup the crepey sac of his balls. His buttocks convulsed at her touch, and she gripped his scrotum, twisting slightly until he moaned. Her nose was level with the underside of his left buttock, and she rubbed against the skin there, inhaling and savouring his scent, tickling him with her exhaled breath.

Her tongue, red and moist, flicked out and licked the crease which ran from his thigh up to the hollow at the base of his long spine. Placing both her hands on the twin curves of Valerian's arse, she pulled the cheeks apart to reveal the tender pucker which nestled there. Her tongue shot out and rimmed it suddenly, completing a full circle before pushing inside.

The man above her sighed and pressed out towards her as she withdrew her tongue, circled the place once more, then again pressed back in. When she was satisfied that he was lubricated, she lifted the handful of topaz beads to her mouth and drew them slowly in, until her mouth was crammed full of them and only one on the silken string remained outside. Then she pressed her nose into the crease of his buttocks and worked the necklace into him with her tongue and fingers.

At last she stood back to admire her handiwork. All the beads had been pushed in except for a tiny length, just enough for her to grasp with her fingers. Valerian, obviously stimulated beyond control, rocked his pelvis back and forth as if begging her for release. She walked around the bed and stood on the opposite side from him, staring into his eyes before dropping her negligee to the floor and mounting the bed.

When she was in front of him, almost touching, she took his swollen cock in her hand and stroked him, watching him grow to greater length and thickness, while she caressed herself with a stiffened forefinger. She held his stare as she lay across the bed and hooked her legs around his hips and waist. With a sudden jerk, she impaled herself upon him and Valerian cried out, perspiration beading his body in a glistening sheen as her agile body moved on his.

He thrust with her, until, with a trembling in his legs and a sudden stillness of his clenched thighs, he came to his peak. Madame, continuing to work her hips on him, reached around him and jerked her wrist to quickly withdraw the topaz beads from his anus. He cried out, almost as if in pain, as he climaxed into the depths of her demanding body.

Lydia lay stunned. She wanted nothing more than for Valerian to turn and take her too. Now. Here on the dark hide of the couch while Madame watched. She pressed her thighs together and bent her knees up to her chest, aware that the bindings and gag she wore made her an appealing sight. The flower of her sex, engorged and full, swelled between her enfolded thighs like a juicy fig, dark and moist with a luscious, edible centre.

Madame, involved in unbuckling Valerian's manacles, noticed nothing, but Valerian had twisted around to gaze at the effect their hedonism had had on his untameable cousin. Seeing her sex framed by the paleness of her milky thighs, his softened cock leapt in response and he jerked impatiently at his cuffs.

'Wait. You shall have her in good time.' Madame took him by the hand and led him to a gilded chair set near Lydia's feet.

'Sit,' she commanded. 'You may observe as I ready her for your delectation.'

She stalked the room, lighting more candles, gathering armfuls of fluffy blue towels and pouring water from the ewer into a large porcelain bowl. When everything had been arranged to her satisfaction, she knelt on the rug next to where Lydia lay and smiled at the girl.

'My dear. You are superb, but I wish to make you exquisite.'

Soapy fingers trailed down over Lydia's belly and delved into the soft curls at the join of her thighs. She lathered and rubbed, while Lydia tried to lie as still as possible. She watched curiously as Madame lifted a small brown leather case and opened it.

Then the woman withdrew the cut-throat gleam of a long razor.

Lydia gasped beneath her silken gag and struggled, pulling at her wrist bindings, thrashing her legs and bucking her foam-soaked hips. She could feel the fear fizzing through her veins, and perspiration sprang to her forehead as she begged for mercy with her widened eyes.

Madame, observing her with interest, gave a slow, thin smile which failed to extend as far as her eyes. She deliberately ran her fingertip along the silver blade until it beaded with crimson blood, then slipped it between her lips. There was a long pause while she sucked.

'Are you afraid, my dear? There is really no need. You see, I have no intention of holding this implement to your beautiful throat as you seem to imagine. No. Watch. And be still. Do not even flinch, for you have seen how sharp I keep this. When I say I wish to make you exquisite, that is precisely what I mean. Hairless. Sensitive. Exquisite.' Her smile broadened and she leant forward so that her lips almost touched Lydia's, and the girl could smell the delicate scent of her breath. 'So much more hygienic, don't you think?'

She glided down Lydia's body, and her face became a pale mask of concentration as she trimmed the dark curls which covered Lydia's mound. Fluffy clouds gradually gathered in vibrant clusters on the floor and in scattered wisps on Lydia's widely spread thighs. Lydia raised her head and watched, absorbed in the glittering flash as she was pared to the bare skin. She was fascinated by the movement of Madame's fingers over her undulations and the change in her own appearance as the crisp hairs were scythed from her body.

Soon she was smooth and denuded, the skin cool and bare. Madame lifted a small crystal bottle and poured a sweet-smelling unguent on to Lydia, who quivered as tiny rivulets ran from her belly down into her creases. Madame's fingers kneaded her flesh, massaging the sticky oil into the shaven folds, dwelling on the grooves between the naked lips. When she was satisfied with the results of her labours, she arranged the blushing flesh to her satisfaction and sat back on her heels, admiring the newly depilated aperture.

Lydia felt strange. The hairlessness made her feel exposed and very vulnerable, but she was titillated by the sensation of her own flesh sliding over other parts of herself without the dulling of a layer of hair. The moistness of the perfumed oil, combined with the cream of her own arousal, made everything feel slick: somehow larger, more important. She opened her legs wide until her knees touched the surface of the couch either side and looked up at Valerian, clear invitation in the depths of her liquid green eyes.

He remained motionless but somehow taut, expectant almost, while Madame moved her hands once more to the little case. She drew out a long length of black cord, knotted at equal intervals, which she held in one hand. With a firm pressure, she pushed Lydia's legs together and wound the cord around her thighs, midway between her knees and her hips. It was tight and the knots cut into her flesh. Madame smiled and urged her legs upward, so that her knees rested on her breasts and Lydia could feel her oiled shaven sex protruding between her thighs. Valerian's eyes were fixed intently upon Madame's hands.

The cord was wound twice around her ankles, and then a length taken around and slipped between her legs so that a large knot pressed on to her clitoris. The rope snaked over her sex and down to cut between her buttocks. Finally, Madame passed the end around Lydia's waist and tied it firmly to itself, ensuring that there was a good tension on the rope and that it held Lydia in position. The knots were hard against her flesh, making it feel sore but stimulated. She knew that her sex, creamy and plump, was swelling either side of the thick black knot that pressed there.

Madame bent to the case again. She took out a phallus-shaped object made from glossy, dark leather. It was some seven inches in length, and its thickness was that of a well-endowed man. Madame caressed it lovingly, a secret smile curving her lips. Then she lifted it and slid it into her mouth, moving it in and out until the supple leather gleamed with her saliva.

Wordlessly, she placed it on to Lydia's neck and stroked her with it, dragging it slowly over her breastbone and then to one nipple, which contracted tightly. The other nipple also puckered in response as the dildo was slid over it, and Madame smiled, guiding the firm leather baton down and around until it rested on the plumpness of her shaven sex. Lydia waited, hardly daring to breathe, marvelling at the toy. She could feel herself melting and unfurling in anticipation, while the hardness rested purposefully between her legs.

Then Madame, with a leisurely action, held the pink folds apart with the fingers of one hand, easing the thick rope aside. She pushed the dildo and Lydia felt it glide sleekly in. It was surprisingly hard. And cool. And quite unlike her experience of men.

'Does that feel good?' Madame moved it firmly, easing it out and smiling at the slick sound of Lydia's wetness. Then she plunged it back in, a little further this time, and Lydia could feel the firm nose opening her deepest recesses. Her knees were almost up to her chin, and she could feel the dildo probing her body more deeply than anything had ever penetrated before. She gasped and let her head drop back, arching herself and focussing totally on the long strokes of Madame's device within her, concentrating on the heat and liquid between her legs and the pleasure that was released there. Her body turned to pulp and she could feel a beat throbbing in her temples, while a thousand tiny bubbles seemed to fizz inside her head as the first waves of orgasm trembled through her.

The promised release was sublime but short-lived.

Madame withdrew the dildo and waited. When she was sure that the crisis was passed, she gently pushed it back and slowly pulsed and twisted it until Lydia once more found herself teetering on the brink of delicious rapture.

Again it was removed.

Lydia, unable to move her hands or speak for her bindings, made a mute appeal with her eyes, but Madame simply waited and gazed back at her. When this happened for the third time, Lydia felt helpless and began to cry, tiny salt tears trickling across her cheeks.

Madame seemed pleased by this and stood up, gesturing to Valerian to take her place. His satanic features were suffused with lust as he knelt beside the couch and filled her emptiness with two long fingers, his thumb giving extra pressure to the knot that crushed her clitoris. She clenched herself on to him and silently begged him to finish her orgasm, but he also withdrew, although more reluctantly than Madame.

Lydia watched as Valerian moved along the couch and raised himself up on his knees beside her. The animal smell of his proffered cock served as an added stimulus. It swayed above her face and she inhaled the scent of sex, musky and feral, while Valerian untied the stocking which gagged her. She twisted her head and took him between her lips, momentarily surprised by the taste of Madame which silvered the hard flesh. He moved closer and slid easily to the back of her throat as she opened her mouth wide to accommodate as much of him as possible.

She was vaguely aware of the emptiness between her

legs being filled once more and she curved her buttocks upward in response. She felt herself being swept up and carried along on a tide of ecstasy, as her long-denied orgasm built within her. Glancing down the length of her shins, she marvelled at the sight of Madame nestling at the end of the couch, moving the leather cock not with her hands as before, but with her mouth. Her lips were stretched wide around the end of it, her teeth gripping the black leather, and she slid it back and forth while spreading her hands wide on the softness of Lydia's thighs, her forefingers dipping ever closer to the slightly open pucker of her anus.

When she felt Madame's fingers enter her bottom and stretch her as wide as the dildo was stretching her sex, Lydia was instantly tipped over the brink and into glorious orgasm, the culmination of everything she had seen and experienced that night erupting and burning through her folded body until she gave an almighty shudder and screamed her release against Valerian. Madame gave the dildo one final push, pressing it far into her silky depths as Valerian jerked himself free, pumping his hot, gushing climax on to Lydia's hair and eyelids.

Later, as she drowsed in the aftermath, Lydia was aware of unhurried fingers releasing her bindings, and then the soft weight of a sable cloak covering her nakedness. She saw Madame and Valerian sink into the ocean of the vast blue bed with their limbs intertwined, then there was welcome blackness as she surrendered to the opiate heaviness of sleep.

Chapter Eight

The Chequers Inn was almost full. Situated on the northbound road, it caught most of the passing trade on market-day; farmers and traders clustered at the rough wooden bar, lifting tankards to thirsty mouths, while the staff threaded through the heaving mass bearing platters of capon and enormous flagons of ale.

The inn was dark, the only light being a flicker of orange from the crackling grate and a few guttering tallow candles, but the man who stood alone at the bar could see well enough. His hooded gaze was fixed on a table near the chimney breast where a small man of skinny build sat nursing his third tankard of ale. His greasy hair was combed thinly over a pale head and his long nose had the bruised ruddiness of a long-term drinker.

Drummond had heard that this man, the notary Silas Peake, could be found at the Chequers most nights, and his informer had added that Silas's unguarded tongue could easily be loosened with the local brew. Swallowing the last of his own ale, Drummond banged his tankard on the counter.

'Fill this up, would you? And I'll have one of whatever he drinks.' He jerked his head to indicate the notary. He wound his way through the throng and sat opposite Silas Peake. The other man glanced with interest at the tumblers in front of Drummond.

'You thirsty?'

'Are you?'

'A man is always thirsty after an honest day's work.'

'What line of work would that be?'

Silas Peake squinted up through tiny dark eyes. He swayed slightly and then sniggered.

'You'd be a stranger to these parts, but I'm thinking that I know your face.'

The tallow on the table flickered and Drummond wondered whether he could shift it unobtrusively to prevent Peake from recognising him. On the pretext of moving his own drink, he pushed his forearm against the candle-holder and slid it to the edge of the table where it could not light his face so effectively.

'No, my friend, you wouldn't know me. I'm a traveller, passing through. If you're thirsty, take this second tankard. My own thirst is not so sharp now that I've started on this one.'

Peake needed no further encouragement. He tossed back the dregs of his own and started eagerly on the fresh one. Halfway down the tumbler he paused for breath, smearing the foam from his lips with the back of his hand before nodding thanks to Drummond.

'So you're a notary?'

'Did I say that?' Peake frowned, confused for a moment, then his brow cleared. 'Aye, we were talking about the thirsty work. Oh yes. That's me.'

'I suppose you handle all the work for the family up at the big house, then.'

'Sometimes, sometimes.' He nodded sagely, swallowing his ale. 'Mostly Mr Lavendale deals with them, but I am his personal clerk. Oh yes. The Hawkesworths need people they can trust.'

'Well, you certainly look like a man they could trust. I imagine you're privy to all of old Lord Hawkesworth's documents.' Drummond tipped his weight back casually, the image of a man in careless conversation. He surveyed the crowd at the bar: the smell of roast meat made his stomach growl.

'I was. Oh yes. Mind you, stranger, old Lord William is no more. No, he's been dead more than a six-month, now.'

'Indeed? My sympathies for the family. Would you care for a refill?' Drummond indicated the near-empty cup. As a girl passed nearby with a pewter flagon in each hand he nodded at her, and she hastened to refill their tankards. Drummond, admiring her tiny waist and sumptuous hips, smiled lazily into her eyes and she blushed, bending lower to their table to afford him an improved view of her firmly buttressed cleavage.

'What's your name, lass?'

'Molly, sir.' She smiled broadly and, having poured, she rested one of the flagons on the curve of her hip.

'Molly, what's the food like in this inn?'

'Very good, sir. Plenty of juicy meat and fresh vegetables on market-day, and very attentive maid-servants.' Her honey-soft eyes promised far more than her words, and Drummond found himself smiling at her forwardness.

'Well, then. I think I shall dine here later; perhaps you could reserve a private room for me.'

'Certainly, sir. Will you be requiring a maid to serve you, then?'

Drummond considered her for a long moment, then nodded. Molly arched one dark eyebrow and told him that she would see to it personally, then turned with an exaggerated sway of her hips and returned to the bar.

Drummond turned back to Peake, and caught a look of naked lechery in the weaselly little man's eyes as he watched her retreating bottom.

'Oh, yes. You have a way with the wenches, stranger. Perhaps you'd care to leave me your pickings when you've done?' His narrow tongue flickered out to touch the crusty corners of his mouth. Drummond fought an overwhelming urge to push him off his chair.

'Perhaps, friend. But first, finish what you were telling me about Lord William's will.'

'The will? Ha. I copied it myself, earlier this year. Oh, yes. I had it for some weeks and then Lord William gave it –'

His chin suddenly dropped to his chest, then he gave a start and tried to focus on Drummond's face. 'What's that, stranger? Oh, I remember not. I care not.' He waved his hand and leant forward to rest his head on the table-top. Drummond heard him belch and then snort. Staring in disbelief, he realised that Peake had fallen into a drunken stupor from which he would not easily be roused. He shook the other man's bony shoulder.

'What? Oh, let me be. Tired – I'm tired, stranger.'

'What did Lord William do with the will?' Drummond hissed at him, impatience fermenting in his limbs. To come so close, to be so successful in getting the man drunk, only to be thwarted at the last moment by the demon sleep! He shook Peake again, this time more roughly.

'He took it to . . .'

The words dissolved into a long snore, and Drummond threw himself back in his chair with barely controlled anger. Damn the man! Getting the notary to talk had been his best plan. He couldn't stroll into Lavendale's plush office and ask the same questions without alerting Valerian to his presence in the town. He couldn't go up to the house; he couldn't claim his rightful place. He could do nothing without the will. Draining his ale, he reached for the half-full tankard that Peake had left and gulped that down too. The warm glow in his gullet and belly comforted him, and he stood, thinking he would return to the bar.

'Whoa there, young fellow! The Chequers ale is stronger than you think!' A plump, ruddy-faced farmer eased Drummond back to standing, and he realised that he must have fallen.

'Sweet Jesus, what do they do, lace it with gin?' he asked.

'Nay, but it's famous in these parts. I see old Silas has wound up early tonight!' The farmer had a hearty laugh and a friendly face, and Drummond decided to risk a query.

'Yes. He was just telling me an interesting story about the old Lord and his will. Shame he didn't get to the end. Now I shall never know how the story goes.'

'That old tale. There b'ain't no ending to it, son. Lord William died without naming an heir. The elder son is missing and the younger is waiting to take his place. Far as anyone knows, the will be lost. But between you and me, I think young Master Valerian destroyed it himself.' His huge hand, like an enormous piece of ham, almost felled Drummond as he clapped him on the shoulder and gave a loud guffaw. 'But it don't matter, do it? Because he's the only surviving son anyway.'

'Not if I have anything to do with it,' muttered Drummond, lurching away and wondering whether he should go outside to be sick. As he headed for the door, he caught sight of a pretty face smiling at him from behind the bar, and all at once remembered why the drink had gone to his head, and legs, so quickly: food. He needed food. And Molly was going to serve it to him. His heart swelled and he made his way over to her, trying to appear sober and dignified.

'My!' She giggled, two dimples puckering her cheeks. 'You've obviously not tried our ale before. Come and soak it up with some rabbit and roast potatoes. I've laid up a room just above the bar. Come through here.'

She lifted a hinged section of the wooden bar and led him along a narrow, dim corridor which stank of warm beer and sweet wine, the dregs of which he could feel underfoot as he walked. He followed Molly's swaying curves up a staircase which opened out into a wide landing with several doors leading off.

The room she gestured for him to enter was simply furnished with a clean table and chairs, a cushioned window-seat, and a welcoming fire which crackled and popped in the small grate. Drummond sank into the comfortable haven in the window and peered out through the smoke-stained lattice. Below him, outside, it was dark and quiet: a few horses snickered in the ostler's yard, and the revelry in the tavern echoed unevenly against the walls of the stone outhouses. The cool panes soothed his hot head, and Drummond felt sobriety stealing slowly back into his limbs.

'Would you like to eat straight away? I can ask the kitchen maid to come and help me serve when she has finished in the next room.'

'You seem busy here tonight.' Drummond was hungry, but his desire for company made him reluctant to send her below stairs immediately.

'Market-day is always like this: most people do their business in the town and then come here to slake their thirst. It gets quite rowdy, sometimes.' She stepped a little nearer. 'You aren't from round here, are you?'

Drummond turned from the window, relishing the chill of the damp night-dark panes through the cotton of his shirt. 'Not exactly,' he replied, smiling. 'But I know my way around. Are you local?'

'Yes, I am. My Pa farms some land here. I've got plans for a better life, though. If I work here for long enough, maybe a gentleman will pass through and fall madly in love with me and carry me off!'

'Well, make sure he puts a ring on your finger first. These gentlemen can be quite ungentlemanly at times.' Drummond gave a wry grin. Molly's eyes widened with mock innocence.

'Well, I'm not sure I know what you mean, sir. Perhaps you'll have to show me this ungentlemanly behaviour so's I can watch out for it in future.'

'I'd be happy to show you.' Drummond's mouth widened with good humour and a stirring of lust as he reached for her. The girl moved forward into his arms, and he propped her on his knee as he explored the laces at the neckline of her simple white chemise. Her head dropped comfortably on to his shoulder, and their fingers entwined slightly as she reached up to help him.

Beneath her top, Drummond was excited to find that Molly was wearing a beautifully boned red and black corset, which nipped her already tiny waist into handspan proportions. Above it, her breasts were pushed upward and spilled over the top like ripe fruit tumbling from an overfull basket. He grasped one strawberry nipple between thumb and forefinger, and rolled it, savouring the pertness and the increasing rigidity of the muscular button beneath his hand. His mouth quickly followed his fingers. He sucked thirstily at her breast, and heard her gasp as his teeth gently grazed her erect flesh.

Her fingers delved into the unruly tow of his hair, and she cradled his head to her bosom, breathing heavily and pushing her ribs outward to offer his mouth the maximum amount of her peachy skin. Beneath her soft thighs, Drummond could feel his cock stirring and pushing in his breeches, a bulging rod with an independent spirit which pushed at his fly and insinuated itself against the cushion of her skirts. He shifted his position a little, and Molly pulled away slightly to stare into his eyes, her own soft chestnut depths framed by the sooty smudge of dark lashes. An unspoken question hung in the air between them for a long moment, then she stood and stepped back a little.

'Wait.' Drummond reached for her again, but she evaded him with a sway of her sumptuous hips, a smile curling the corners of her full lips.

'No. You wait,' she said simply.

Obediently, he waited and watched, his tension growing as the girl loosened the chemise from where it had fallen around her waist. She lifted it over her head, and Drummond watched in fascination as her breasts rose, lifted by the movement of her arms as she slid the cotton top up over her face and dropped it on to the floor beside her. Next, she unbuttoned her skirt and let it fall in a pool of blue serge at her feet, where the creamy drift of her petticoats soon joined it.

Drummond held his breath, afraid to move, for the aching in his groin had now become a merciless burn. Molly stroked one hand over her breasts and met his eyes. She looked beautiful: tall and curvaceous, her pale skin gilded by the glow from the fire behind her. The scarlet and black corset hugged her body and moulded it into a perfect hourglass shape, and the long, opaque stockings which skimmed her legs to just above the knee gave her an elegance more suited to a French courtesan than a country barmaid.

Smiling, Molly began to unbraid her honey-toned hair, and said, 'I can see you wondering. This corset was a present from another ungentlemanly gentleman.' Her cheeks dimpled and her fingers moved rapidly over her lustrous tresses, parting and spreading them over her shoulders where they lay gleaming, burnished by the light from the single candle on the table. She delicately sidestepped her discarded garments. 'So if you are one of those who suffer from guilt, please don't. Guilt-free loving is my speciality.' With that, she came towards him and Drummond forgot everything, immersed in sensation.

She released him from the prison of his breeches with expert hands, her fingers finding and gripping the shaft of his firm cock before she moved her mouth on to his hot flesh. Exquisite ripples of pleasure quaked through him as the plump satin of her lips fastened on to him. She found the slit at the top, which opened beneath the pressure of her pointed tongue, and he leant back against the cold window, his mind spiralling into the abyss of pleasure as she alternately sucked and probed, fucking him with the tip of her tongue, while her hands kneaded his balls and he felt his sap rise unexpectedly quickly within him.

His climax came suddenly, erupting with great force, like molten lava flowing through his loins and along his cock, and shooting into the back of her throat as she swallowed around him, arching her long neck to accommodate his heady pulsing. Drummond groaned as she licked his manhood, sucking the sticky residue from every inch of his silken length, and polishing his swollen glans to a varnished sheen with her lips.

Amused, he lifted her chin and smiled into her satisfied face.

'You're like a little cat, lapping a bowl of cream. I don't think I've ever seen a girl enjoy the taste of a man so much.' His forefinger stroked a pearl from the corner of her mouth, and he slid it between her pouting lips. The feel of her mouth as she sucked his finger created a tingling arousal in him once more, and he knew then that he would be ready again before very much longer.

Bending, he kissed her salty lips, and was surprised to find that the taste of himself upon her was not as unpleasant as he had supposed. Probing with his tongue, he searched the depths of her mouth, plumbing the moist recesses and running across the hard ivory of her teeth. She fastened on to him, sucking and drawing on his tongue, pulling it into her until he felt a tautness at its root and he pulled back slightly, his hands roaming from her waist to the fleshy roundness of her bare buttocks as he pulled her astride his lap. She settled on to him, stretching her legs wide either side of his hips, until he felt the soft pliability of her sex resting over the renewed hardness of his prick.

Drummond's hands caressed the taut curves of her figure, gradually moving forward and down until his thumbs lightly stroked the triangle of hair which nestled plushly at the base of her corsetted stomach. She shuddered beneath his grazing fingers and pressed herself on to his thighs, her mouth still fastened to his, her hips rocking as she wordlessly urged him to continue.

Drummond could feel the heat that rose from her, the humidity of sweet arousal, and he delved further, parting her moistness with his thumbs and burrowing into her folds. The knuckle of his right hand brushed the protruding bead of her clitoris, and she bucked above him, her mouth momentarily breaking contact with his as she reached down to push his finger firmly on to the stiff jewel. Drummond obediently curved his hand under her, fitting it to her and rubbing her quickly until she squealed for mercy, biting at his neck and pressing against him.

'Do it now,' she whispered. 'I want to feel you all the way up inside me.'

He lifted her with both hands firm on her waist until she was poised above him, and stared into the depths of her eyes, seeing his own flushed reflection in the pools of her dilated pupils. Then he thrust into her, plunging himself upward with a strong jerk of his lean hips as he brought her firmly down on to his hardness. Crying aloud, they moved together with abandoned sensuality, she arching and falling while he moved his rhythm beneath her, the sinews on his bronzed forearms standing up with his exertion as he pumped in and out of her.

'Oh! Sweet Jesus! You feel so good!' he cried.

When they came it was a simultaneous crescendo, intoxicating and exhausting. They collapsed on to each other, and Drummond leant back against the window; the heat of their ardour seemed to melt the ice on the panes, and a coolness trickled down Drummond's back, soaking his shirt and mingling with the sweat of his animal passion.

'Molly, you're gorgeous.' He cupped her face in his hands, kissing her lightly. 'I'm so hungry now. I bet you do this to make us poor fools spend more on feasting!'

'Indeed!' She frowned up at him, pretending to take offence. 'Well, you'd better not disappoint me by refusing your food, now.'

'I could eat a horse,' he confessed, as she moved away to pick up her abandoned clothing from the floor. The sight of the twin crescents of her luscious behind stirred him again, and Drummond stood, reaching for her and pulling her backward into the curve of his waist.

'But I could eat you, too.' He nuzzled her ear, nibbling

and sucking at the plump lobe through the scented cloud of her hair. Laughing, she pushed back against him, pressing herself into his belly and causing his cock to stir against her naked flesh. He slid a finger into her from behind, revelling in her warm readiness and the clinging velvet of her sex as she tensed on to his probing hand.

'I believe you'd do it again, if I let you,' he murmured.

'Let me? I doubt if you'd be able to quite so quickly.'

'Try me.'

He turned her quickly and sat her up on the table. Her face registered her surprise when she saw the ramrod stiffness of him as he moved towards her. Jerking her legs apart, he entered her with a sudden thrust of his hips, gripping her thighs with his strong hands until white marks paled around his fingertips. He plunged deep into her and she gasped at his sudden ferocity, sinking back on to the table and hooking her legs tightly around his waist.

'Oh! Oh, yes. Do it hard. Do it harder!' She bucked and writhed beneath him as he ruthlessly rammed her with every stroke of his throbbing cock until he felt the waves of her orgasm shudder on to him. Her taut body undulated, and she gave a loud cry, arching her neck and tipping her chin up towards the ceiling. The sight and feel of her pleasure tipped him over the edge and he too came in a torrent. Hot flames licked through him and he collapsed, panting, on to her prone body.

'Well, not many of my gentlemen would be ready again so quickly,' she murmured, her mouth soft against his ear. 'You're a regular stallion. Will you be staying long in the town?'

'Long enough.' Drummond raised himself from her and smiled down at her curvaceous form spread on the table beneath him. She was gorgeous and vital, but he was reluctant to encourage her hopes. Commitment was something he had never been enthusiastic for, although the prospect of repeat visits held a certain appeal.

137

He ran a long forefinger down her body and buried his hand in the soft down between her thighs.

'But don't get any ideas about rings from me. You keep looking out for a real gentleman. One will come along soon enough.'

Molly pouted and looked vaguely offended. She slid off the table and picked up her clothes.

'That wasn't quite what I meant,' she said firmly. 'I know you're not for me: but there's no harm in us getting together sometimes, is there? Guilt-free I said, and that's what I meant.'

'Here, let me help you.' Drummond turned her and began buttoning her skirts from behind. 'If I'm ever in need of company, I assure you that this is one of the first places I'll come. Now, where's that rabbit and potatoes? A man needs food as well as love.' He gave her padded bottom a resounding smack as she headed for the door.

The food she served was excellent, and Drummond ate slowly, washing his meal down with a sweeter and less potent ale than that which he had taken at the bar. He sat in the window-seat for a long time after, gazing out at the darkness, but absorbed in his own thoughts.

When he took his horse from the ostler's lad, he gave him a coin and turned to lead the mare out. A sleek horse in the next stall, a sixteen-hand stallion with perfect palomino colouring, caught his eye and he stopped to give the velvety muzzle a gentle stroke.

'You're a beauty; what's your name?'

The horse's breath warmed his hand, and Drummond smiled in the half-dark, glancing at the saddle which adorned the animal's back. The Spanish leather surface was polished and well cared for, and the initials of his owner were tooled neatly into the flap near the stirrup length: V OH.

Valerian Olivier Hawkesworth.

It could be no other. The thought that his brother was at the inn made his blood chill, and he suppressed a shudder. Had he been seen? It was almost impossible to tell. He gave a low whistle and waited.

'Jake. Did you see the owner of this horse arrive?' The ostler's son, a relation of Jim Handfast, was a lad he had come to know well since his homecoming.

'Yes. He came here almost an hour since. He always takes a meal with Molly, one of the serving wenches, and then tries his luck at cards or dice with one of the other gentlemen.'

Drummond nodded. He was wryly amused that his brother's taste in wenches could be so similar to his own, and wondered whether he was the gentlemanly donor of the red and black corset.

'Jake, do you remember we discussed you helping me sometimes? Well, if you have a need for a sovereign or two, then I can give you a job to earn it.'

The man and the youth spoke quietly for several minutes, then Drummond mounted his horse and trotted swiftly away into the darkness of the night.

Valerian leant back in his chair, drew on his cheroot and surveyed the other man across the card table. The private gaming room of the Chequers Inn was small and lit by guttering tapers which added to the dark smokiness of the atmosphere. The pile of gold and silver pieces before him glittered; not an hour since, he had been losing badly, and Madame's words about the dowry he would have to pay out for Lydia played repeatedly through his mind. His quick exchange of the dice-box for a specially painted false box had enabled him to throw winning numbers on the three ivory dice and reclaim much of what he had lost.

'You have the devil's luck tonight, Hawkesworth.' The opponent, Squire Aldridge, slumped dejectedly in his chair. 'I can't let you take all my gold, so I think I'll retire gracefully. Until the next time, what?'

'It's your decision.' Valerian nodded graciously, and stabbed his cheroot into a plate of half-eaten food. He scooped the coins from the table-top and tipped them, clinking, into a large hide pouch which he slipped into his breast pocket. The weight was reassuring against his chest, and he leant forward to shake hands with Aldridge.

'Until next time, as you say.' His hand moved rapidly over the baize surface as, with a sleight of hand worthy of a magician, he replaced the false dice-box with the true one before standing and draining his tankard.

When he reached the darkened stables, there was no sign of the ostler's lad and no one to help him mount; he muttered with displeasure as he swung his polished black boot over the stallion's hindquarters. The route was dark, and the path which wound out of town towards Hawkesworth land had few other travellers. When he reached the wooded copse which signified the eastern reaches of the estate, a fine drizzling rain began to fall, and he shrugged his cloak higher around his cheeks, muffling his ears. The horse beneath him shied a little, ears flickering.

'Come on,' snarled Valerian. 'Let's get home before an infernal storm sets in.'

The stallion took a few reluctant steps forward and then halted. The swirling clouds had partially blocked the waxing moon, and the darkness around man and horse was almost complete. A dry stick cracked somewhere to Valerian's left, and he urged his mount onward with a jab of his spurs. The steed flared its nostrils and bridled sideways, shaking its huge head and prancing in the middle of the path.

'Come on, damn you!' Valerian was impatient now, and pulled the reins in tightly to give him greater control, but the horse continued to pull sideways, both eyes rolling and shining white in the darkness. Valerian felt the first flicker of unease and squinted, straining to see the road ahead.

It was empty and silent. There was nothing to fear. He dug his heels in and the stallion reared, almost unseating him. He swore viciously. At that moment the ragged clouds parted and the scene was brilliantly lit with silver moonlight.

Where the road had been empty, there stood a large ebony horse with a solitary rider, motionless, some ten yards ahead, blackly silhouetted against the pewter shingle of the hill behind. Valerian saw with a quickening of his heart that the rider held a cocked pistol, and, beneath his tricorne hat, a mask occluded his features.

'Get out of my way!' The brave words sounded hollow even to himself, and he could feel a nervous twitch start in the muscle of his jaw. The highwayman remained motionless. 'Get out of my way, damn you! I am Lord Hawkesworth, and if you dare to touch me I'll have you strung up from the nearest gibbet by sundown tomorrow!'

There was still no movement or reply, and he felt fear turn his bowels to water as the shingle on the path behind him crunched loudly. Twisting in his saddle, he saw the dimly lit shadow of another horseman blocking his retreat. Slowly the dark figures advanced until they were only feet from him, fencing him in fore and aft. But still they did not speak. The rider in front leant forward and grasped Valerian's bridle, jerking it out of his hands and pulling the nervous stallion in close.

'My dear Lord Hawkesworth.' The formal address was spoken with withering sarcasm, and Valerian flinched as the other man brought his pistol up and held it against his throbbing temple. 'I believe you have been possessed of good fortune at the gaming table tonight. There are people who need that money more desperately than you, and I intend to give it to them. So, my dear sir, it's your money, or your life.'

Valerian, frozen with fear, had no thought other than to save his own skin. He lifted his hands in a gesture of surrender, and the pistol was moved fractionally away from him.

'I have money: here, take it. There is near on a hundred gold pieces in this pouch. Will that satisfy you?' He thrust the jingling pouch at the highwayman, and saw a brief gleam of white teeth as the other smiled.

'Indeed it does. I am very satisfied. For now.' The pouch disappeared beneath the thick, dark cloak that the highwayman wore. 'It's a shame that you choose to give us no sport by putting up a fight. But of course your vanity will have you tell everyone at the manor that you bravely fought your assailants, so we'd better give you proof of your valour.'

Swiftly, before Valerian had even absorbed the significance of his words, the man had drawn a thin blade and flashed it across Valerian's cheek. The wound was shallow and only an inch in length, but the pain and shock made Valerian wince and hold his hand up to his face. His ivory kid glove slowly stained with crimson blood, and he gave a choking sob and fumbled for his silk kerchief.

The highwayman gave a roar of mirth which echoed against the trees, and Valerian's head shot up. There had been something familiar in that laughter. He mopped at his wounded cheek, and the two men released his horse.

'Good night! And thank you, *Lord* Hawkesworth!'

And they were gone, their shadows flitting into the blackness of the night and dissolving into the trees at the side of the path.

He was alone.

The rain came in earnest then, lashing out of the clouded sky with needlepoint sharpness. Valerian steered his skittish horse for home, a slow rage smouldering in the pit of his belly.

Chapter Nine

The morning sun streamed in through the window-panes, warming the corners of the library and making the newly made fire in the grate almost unnecessary.

Lydia was curled in the corner of a well-padded sofa, a copy of *Roxana* propped on her lap. She had devoured the salacious *Moll Flanders* during her imprisonment, and found Mr Defoe's vivid narrative entertaining as well as educational. She nibbled her thumb as she read, totally absorbed in the story which unfolded on the coarsely cut parchment pages.

There was a sudden distant pounding from the hallway of the main house which startled her. Slipping an embroidered marker into her book, she set it aside, rose, and tiptoed towards the door. The library lay off the west corridor leading from the great hall, and she could hear one of the footmen welcome a visitor. Gently, and as silently as possible, she eased open the library door and pressed her eye against the gap.

She almost expired with shock as Valerian, not two feet away, strode into her field of vision, and she shrank back, catching her breath and trying to steady her hammering pulse, silently praying that he had not seen her. But Valerian continued along the corridor and shouted a command to the visitor.

'Enter, my good sir! We will discuss the matter in my study.'

Lydia was consumed with curiosity, but she knew that the route to Valerian's study would take them both right past the library door. She pushed it closed and leant back against the carved wood surface, straining her ears for every footfall.

As soon as she heard them pass, she opened the door wide and recklessly stuck her head out, craning round the jamb to see Valerian, followed by the taller, but slightly stooped, figure of Mr Lavendale, the lawyer. She moved back inside the room and softly closed the door.

She wondered what purpose Valerian could have in asking Mr Lavendale to the house. It must have something to do with the inheritance, but she could not imagine why he had called a meeting with the lawyer. She had not seen her cousin all day, although she knew that he had returned late the previous night and stormed straight up to Madame's room, shouting about brigands and slamming all the doors in his wake. She thought of Drummond, out in the forest somewhere, unable to come home, and her heart ached for him. She decided to waylay Lavendale on his way out and try to extract information which could be of some use.

A floorboard creaked and a door banged somewhere in the depths of the house. Lydia jumped up out of the sofa. Delving into her work bag, she rummaged amongst the knotted threads and jumbled wool until she found a small bottle of eau de Cologne. She dabbed some on her temples and throat, smoothed her hair and, as an afterthought, lifted her skirts and applied a smear of the scent to her thighs. Throwing the little bottle back, she pinched her cheeks and bit her lips to make them attractively red before hurrying to the door. If she timed it just right, she could swing the door wide and innocently step out right into Mr Lavendale's path.

She pressed her ear to the door. There was silence.

Her heart thudded in her chest as she waited impatiently for the solicitor to pass. No one approached. To pass the time she checked her *décolletage*, pulling the lace-edged neckline lower and plumping her breasts up a little. At once, she heard a shuffle and footsteps outside the door, took a deep breath, and pulled the door wide.

'Why, Mr Lavendale! How lovely to see you. If I had known that we had guests, I would have arranged for a tray of tea.'

'Good morning, Miss Lydia. How kind.' The lawyer was nearing sixty, with silky white hair and a hawk-like nose. His penetrating grey eyes fixed on her cleavage, and Lydia felt almost embarrassed. Steeling herself, she gave a coquettish smile and folded her hands demurely before her.

'I trust that my cousin has looked after you. Have you taken refreshment?'

'No, Miss Lydia. He offered some brandy, but I fear that it is too early in the day for me.'

'Perhaps you would care to join me for tea? I was just about to ring for some. Please stay awhile. I am often starved of company.' She smiled, dipping her chin and looking up at him from the corners of her wide eyes. He seemed to hesitate, and then nodded.

'Very well: it would be my pleasure. It isn't often that an old man like me can take tea with a pretty young thing like yourself.' His eyes ran boldly down her body.

Lydia pretended to simper at his compliment, holding the door wide and gesturing for him to enter.

'Oh, Mr Lavendale. You're hardly an old man! You look remarkably strong and vital.'

Having summoned a servant for a tray of tea, Lydia sat on a low stool at Lavendale's feet, a position in which she hoped to give an effective view of her cleavage. Folding her hands around her knees, she smiled at his air of distraction.

'Would you like milk and sugar?' she asked.

'What? Oh – ah, yes. I mean no – no, thank you. Just tea.'

As they sipped, Lydia filled the silence with inconsequential chatter about the weather, the view from the library window, the fashion for taking tea with lemon, and anything else she could think of. Lavendale grew progressively more uncomfortable as she warmed to her task. He loosened his cravat twice; he fidgeted with his watch-chain; he rubbed the edge of his nose. Finally he knocked his half-empty cup from the saucer and spilt tea on the pale blue fabric of his hose.

'Oh, Mr Lavendale! Let me help you: it will stain. Here, let me rub it with the lemon. Oh, your poor leg!' Lydia could hardly believe her luck as she rubbed back and forth on the solicitor's calf: she could feel him leaning closer and closer down to her. She decided to catch him off guard.

'Mr Lavendale, do you know what happened to my uncle's will?'

'Heavens, my dear, what a strange thought to enter your head. Master Valerian was just discussing the exact same subject. Although that is confidential, you understand.'

'Of course. I know he is anxious lest it disturb his claim.'

'Well.' Mr Lavendale patted her hand, obviously mistaking her concern. 'Have no fears on that score. He will be declared Lord in good time. Perhaps you will marry then? I know it was Lord William's fondest wish to see you safely settled.'

'Really?' Lydia lowered her eyelids thoughtfully. 'So, do you have any idea what Uncle William would have done with such a precious document?'

'Put it in a safe place and forgotten all about it, I expect.' Mr Lavendale moistened his lips and moved to the edge of his seat. 'But it is of no concern. With only one surviving son, there is no cause to worry.'

'So you don't have it?'

'My dear young lady! What are you suggesting?'

'Nothing at all. Forgive me, I'm being fanciful.' Lydia smiled and stood up, moving away to stand near the desk. 'Thank you for taking tea with me. Shall I call for your horse?'

'There is no hurry. I would rather venture abroad when my hose is drier.'

Standing, Lavendale smoothed his waistcoat over his chest and stomach, appearing to admire his reflection in the mirror above the fireplace. Lydia watched him, wondering about his wife, a notorious nag. He was really quite a fine figure of a man, despite a slight tendency to stoop, but she supposed that was due to his extraordinary height. She tried to imagine him achieving conjugal relations with his nagging wife, but decided it was simply too awful to contemplate.

Lydia saw that the book she had been reading earlier was caught under a cushion, its pages creased, and she leant over to retrieve it, smoothing the pages with one hand. She slid open a desk drawer and stowed *Roxana* inside, only half aware of Lavendale moving soundlessly across the room to hover at her elbow.

'Aaah, Defoe. You are familiar with such literature? I am surprised your reading habits are not kept under tighter rein.' Lavendale seemed visibly to adjust his opinion of her, and stared into her face, one silky white brow raised.

'I have always had free rein in the library.'

'Disgusting. Improper.' He leant close and inhaled as if to draw in the odour of decadence. 'If Lord William were alive, he would have had such books thrown from the house.'

'Indeed?' Lydia studied the flaring of his nostrils with distaste. 'I think you would have found that Lord William was very enlightened in such matters. It was he, after all, who allowed me to attend lessons with the boys and gain an education.'

'To what end, Miss Lydia? A lady has no need of any knowledge other than sewing and instructing servants.

147

If one wishes to make conversation, then one seeks the company of gentlemen over port.'

'How dull.'

'Give a woman an education and see civilisation on the road to corruption.'

'Really, Mr Lavendale, that seems a little excessive. What can you mean?'

'Sin, my dear.' He took a step closer to her, and she could smell the scented powder on his hair and periwig. 'There are women in this world who, having read the works you have, would seek to avail themselves of the same experiences as, say, Moll Flanders. Soon you, too, may seek to taste the pleasures of the flesh. Disgusting though they may be.'

'If they are so disgusting, why are they called the pleasures of the flesh?' Lydia found her hip pressed against the edge of the desk, as the lawyer advanced inch by inch and she correspondingly eased herself backward. She was not sure that she liked the way the conversation was progressing. Their talk seemed to have wandered from the location of the will and uncomfortably close to a lecture on carnal knowledge. She stared up into his face, and noticed the gleam in his eyes as well as the tiny hairs which protruded from his flaring nostrils.

She was taken by surprise when he sprang forward, imprisoning her against the desk, and grasping one of her breasts in his large, bony hand. Her sudden instinctive struggle seemed to inflame him further, for he leant his body weight on to her, bending her backward, while his free hand reached up to grasp her ringletted hair and twist it up to his face. He gave a groaning exhalation.

'You wanton temptress. Do you think I don't know why you invited me in here? I know your sort, you educated women: you seek to tempt and tease a man with trickery learned from vile books. You know very well why they are called the pleasures of the flesh. I can imagine you, writhing on that sofa with your hand

148

under your petticoats, expecting a man to stay sane and pass the time of day.'

Lydia strained her hands against the embroidery of his waistcoat. With a strength that belied his years, Lavendale swept her up and deftly laid her on the polished surface of the desk, simultaneously catching the hem of her skirts and pushing them up to expose her pale thighs. Like a man possessed, he fell upon her in a frenzy, feverishly pulling at her and parting her legs until she could feel the steeliness of his fingers on her sex.

She gasped and struggled to sit up, but he abruptly twisted and the weight of his body came down across her, pinning her helplessly, his head diving suddenly between her thighs, until, before she could draw breath to cry out, his mouth was fastened on to her.

'Stop it!' she gasped. 'Mr Lavendale, stop it this instant. I shall call for help.'

He did not reply, but simply pressed his long hard tongue into her moistness with a skill that surprised her and made her hesitate. She gave a last feeble wriggle as he probed and licked, sending the first flickers of sensual pleasure through her body. His tongue was long and hard, and he used it with consummate skill. Lydia let her body soften under his caress, and wondered whether she could use this encounter to her own advantage. With his knowledge of the workings of the law he could be a useful ally, and the enthusiastic application of his tongue excited and inflamed her.

'Wait! Please wait one moment, kind sir. We may be disturbed. If we are to proceed, let me at least lock the door.'

He hesitated momentarily, then stood to watch her slide off the desk and hurry to the door. When she rejoined him, he seemed to hesitate, his features flushed and his eyes uncertain.

'I beg your pardon,' he murmured, his usually resonant voice quiet. 'Miss Lydia, I have behaved abominably. Will you excuse me and forget that this happened?

149

I mean you no harm, it is simply that your beauty, and your knowing eyes, led me astray.'

Lydia watched him straighten his silk coat and prepare to leave. She was surprised at his humility and sudden change of heart; she felt a little worm of displeased vanity stir inside her.

'Mr Lavendale, do not be so hasty. I admit that I was at first shocked by your advances, but on calm reflection I think I would like you to continue. Your touch is not repulsive to me, and you leave me wanting more. Come now, the door is locked. We shall not be disturbed.'

She perched on the edge of the desk again, this time lifting her skirts herself and revealing the pouting, newly depilated sex which swelled and throbbed under his intense scrutiny. The lawyer seemed to fight, and lose, an inner battle, for he breathed heavily and tried to drag his gaze away, but the sight of her partial nudity proved irresistible, as Lydia had hoped it would, and he advanced slowly to place his hands on her spread thighs.

Lydia watched in fascination as he tentatively pushed his tongue on to her, stiffened it and applied pressure. She gasped and leant back on one hand as an exquisite warmth engulfed her senses and she allowed her eyelids to droop, her head reeling and sending images of other seductions to her mind's eye. The solicitor's expert mouth became Drummond's, and she remembered the night in the folly and could feel trembling waves shiver at the edges of her senses.

Sliding her hand down to grip Lavendale's soft white hair, she recalled the first time that Angel had played her, using her tongue like a musical instrument, then Valerian with his unique brand of ferocity and devouring barbarity. Suddenly the sensuous images came quickly, one hardly finishing before being superseded by another, each more erotic than the last, until her voluptuous mind was reeling and swooning from the blissful pleasure of the lawyer's tongue and her own delectable imaginings.

She could feel his hand easing along the yielding skin of her thigh, and sensed the firmness of his finger as he entered her. The pressure he applied drove her over the edge, and she moved her hips in a rhythmic impulse, silently demanding that he fulfil her need. She felt his lips close around the sweetness of her sex, and moaned as he pressed another finger in, then another until it seemed that his whole hand would ease into her. He plunged inward, stretching her and filling her rapacious body as she climaxed suddenly and sweetly, feeling the waves break over her as he sucked and plumbed her depths. She felt the pulsing of her sex and the shivering ripples of her skin as she came, and heard him groan as he became still. She realised that he had been rubbing himself with one hand, and had achieved his own satisfaction along with her.

'Do you still desire the company of gentlemen, with their port and cigars?' A smile curved her lips as she surveyed him from the lofty height of the desk. He fell to his knees, cradling his groin in one hand as a slowly spreading stain darkened the pale fabric of his knee-breeches.

'Miss Lydia, I am completely in your thrall. Your company has infinitely more appeal.' His hands, slightly trembling, helped her to rearrange her garments. 'If I can ever be of service to you, you have only to ask.'

'Thank you.' Lydia demurely slid down from the desk. 'I shall bear that in mind.'

Outside, she watched him mount his grey mare and carefully arrange his full-skirted coat about his lap. He saluted her and rode away. Musing on his potential uses as an ally, as well as on his surprising sexual prowess, she wandered slowly back up the steps and into the house.

In the library, she ran her fingers over the smooth surface of the desk and smiled, her body still humming and warm. She wondered where Drummond could be; she felt a strong desire to see him again. If he were looking for help or a place to hide, then she imagined that Jim Handfast's bothy would be the first place he would go.

As the trees ahead of her thinned out, Lydia could see the ramshackle cottage set in a clearing. The glow of the low sun touched the walls with a golden hue which made the little building seem more appealing than it actually was. As she drew nearer, she saw that several slates had dropped from the sloping roof, and the wooden lintel was rotten and split.

She found them at the rear of the cottage. Jim was perched on a felled tree stump sucking on a foul-smelling pipe, while Drummond – stripped to the waist and gleaming with fresh sweat – rested on the handle of a long axe. A pile of chopped logs lay near his booted feet.

Lydia paused, unobserved, a shiver running through her as she stood motionless in the shadow of the eaves and admired his wiry masculinity. His bare skin shone cinnamon-brown in the late afternoon sun, and the bulging muscles beneath stood in burnished relief around his long bones, his biceps corded and pumped up with his recent labours.

Lydia breathed gently, afraid to disturb him and wanting to revel for a moment in his semi-nakedness. She felt aroused and allured by the delicious thrill which pulled at her and caused a fiery juice to swell and moisten her sex. Pressing her thighs together to prolong the silky pressure, she wondered how she could get him alone.

Her mind played tricks as she imagined what she would do to him, and he to her, when they were together in some lonely part of the forest. She could almost feel that burnished skin puckering under her tongue, as she slid her mouth in a perfect arc over the flatness of his belly to his navel, there to dip and lap until he grasped the back of her head and pushed her further down to nestle her nose and mouth against the straining buttons of his breeches.

As if he could sense her presence and the force of her thoughts, Drummond raised his head and looked straight at her, his eyes burning into hers and a slow smile curving his mouth.

'Lydia. How did you find me?'

'Oh, I followed my nose and it led me here.' She stepped forward, out of the shadows, and strolled across the clearing, leaves crackling under her feet. Jim stood up and gave a small bow.

'Evening, Miss Lydia.' He glanced at Drummond. 'I'll go inside and put that soup on the stove.'

They watched him go, and then Lydia turned back, gazing up at Drummond.

'Do you mind me coming? I had to see you and this was the obvious place to find you.'

'If it was obvious to you, then it will be obvious to others if they become suspicious.' His shoulders heaved as he swung the axe, embedding it deep into a convenient log, and stepped forward. His proximity and the musky smell of his hot body made her tremble inside and feel helplessly sensual as well as ravenous for him. She fixed her eyes on his nipples, seeing the coppery smoothness of the outer edge and the rigid peak which rose from the centre. Her own seemed to tighten under her stiff bodice as if in response, and she felt a coolness flush across her scalp in spite of the warmth of the evening.

'Are you certain no one followed you?'

She shook her head, unable to drag her gaze away from the curves of his chest.

'Did you tell anyone that you were going out?' Impatiently, his hand came under her chin and tilted her face up to his, forcing her to meet his questing eyes.

'No, I let myself out of the kitchen door and cut behind the stables. I'm sure nobody saw me and they won't miss me for hours, now.'

'How can you be sure?'

'Valerian and Madame have gone to the Spa. They won't be back until tomorrow.' She was unable to stop herself as her fingers stole to the smoothness of his chest, and she stroked the satin skin, her nails curving under the crisp golden hair. 'Listen, Drummond, I spoke to Mr Lavendale earlier. He seemed to think that you were on the verge of being declared legally dead, and that – that Uncle William wanted me to marry Valerian.'

To her surprise, Drummond threw back his head and laughed. Arching one eyebrow, she stared up at him.

'But that's not funny, it's horrible! I can't possibly marry him. He's disgusting, and so cruel.'

'Don't fret. You don't have to marry anyone that you don't want to. Father planned a decent dowry for you, and you'll have your pick of the best suitors for miles around.' For some reason, this did not reassure her. She was left wondering, as he grabbed her hand and led her towards the cottage, whether he included himself in the list of eligible bachelors.

Jim had scrubbed the wooden table and propped a sliver of wood under one leg to stop it rocking. The floor had been hastily swept and three earthenware bowls set to warm on the stove. Lydia curled her legs up as she sat in the only chair, her hunger sharpening at the smell of thick broth and the sight of the game pie which had been set on a chopping board.

'I take it you'll eat with us, miss?' Jim lifted the iron cauldron from the stove and set it on the table. Lydia nodded, leaning forward to sniff appreciatively as he removed the blackened lid.

'It smells delicious. I'd love some.'

Jim ladled the stew and carved chunks of game pie. When they had eaten, Lydia snuggled further into the depths of the chair, resting her chin on her hand as she watched the men smoke and drink small cups of dark liquor. She felt deliciously full, warm and relaxed. Her eyelids drooped sleepily.

'I'd better walk you home.' Drummond's voice cut across her drowsing thoughts and she sat up, smiling at him.

'I can find my own way back.'

'No, you can't: it'll be dark in less than an hour. I'm coming with you.' His tone brooked no refusal, so she thanked Jim Handfast and wound her cloak around her shoulders before following Drummond to the door. He lifted a dark, full-skirted coat from a hook and shrugged himself into it, leaving the brassy buttons open over his linen shirt.

'I'll see you later, Jim. Don't wait up.'

They walked in companionable silence at first, Lydia trying to match her steps to his long-legged, rangy strides. Glancing sideways at her, he grinned and slowed down, catching her hand and tucking it into the crook of his elbow.

'I'm glad you came to find me,' he said. 'It was the best surprise I've had for a long time, to turn and see you standing there.'

'Good.'

'When you spoke to Lavendale, did you think he was honest?'

'Honest? Well, I suppose so.' She thought for a moment. 'Do you think he may not be?'

'Well, you know what my brother's like. He can sniff out the corrupt at twenty paces. If he thought he could turn a situation to his advantage, he'd have no hesitation in blackmailing someone to work for him.'

Lydia walked in silence for a few minutes, holding tightly to Drummond's sleeve and thinking of her encounter with Lavendale. Was he corrupt? Was Valerian bribing him? It was possible, she supposed. But surely he would have more to lose – his reputation and profession – if he were found out. Or maybe he had done something to compromise those things; perhaps Valerian knew and had threatened to reveal it. The memory of the lawyer's practised tongue made her shiver, and she considered the possibility that he made a habit of employing it on others. If he did, and Valerian knew, then blackmail was a strong probability.

'I really don't know,' she said. 'It's possible. Do you think he has the will, but is pretending that it's lost?'

'I don't know. I don't trust anyone at the moment, except you, of course. And Jim. I think I should come to the house. If I show myself, even if there is no will, then I inherit. I am the eldest: it's simple.' He stopped, as if suddenly struck by a new thought. 'Unless Valerian tries to say that I'm an impostor. It's been five years since anyone saw me, so he could throw doubt on my identity quite easily.'

'No! I would stand up for you. Nobody would believe him!'

'They would if Lavendale concurred with him and not you. You're only a woman.'

Troubled, and slightly angry with his dismissal of her, she stared up at him, thinking how handsome he was despite the narrow white scar which marred his cheek. Reaching up, she slid her hand to the back of his neck, where a thin leather thong secured his unruly hair, and pulled his face down to hers.

The first light touch of his lips reawakened slumbering urges. An image of his flat stomach sprang unbidden to her mind, and she quivered inside at the memory of the line of crisp hair that passed between his nipples down into his waistband. Her mouth opened and a flame of pure pleasure shot through her at his touch; his lips were so firm on hers, his tongue so delicate as it rubbed against the ivory hardness of her teeth.

She let him be gentle at first, revelling in the softness of his touch, kissing him with small movements, entwining her fingers in his hair, enjoying the smell of his skin and the feel of the light stubble that roughened her cheek as he rubbed against her. Gradually, she felt her pulse quicken with need and she pushed against him, seeking the resistance of his belly and hips as she rose on to tiptoes and arched against him. She wanted to feel the promise of his arousal, needed to have the granite hardness of his cock pressed against her.

Responding eagerly, he took her waist in his hands and crushed her tightly on to him, tilting his pelvis and grinding into her. His tongue sought and found hers, his kiss so urgent and forceful that her lips tingled and she gasped against his mouth.

'Please, take me here. I need to feel you. I want you inside me.'

'I'm going to fuck you so hard you'll beg me to stop.'

'No, I won't. You'll beg *me* to stop.'

Her hands grasped the lapels of the thick black coat and jerked him closer, her mouth grinding on his and her knee forcing between his thighs. Taken by surprise by her forthrightness, he paused, then held her elbows and thrust her roughly backward.

She felt the roughness of tree bark behind her as he pushed. The breath slammed out of her lungs as she hit the trunk, and the bones of her spine protested. Catching her breath raggedly as he lifted her, she instinctively raised one leg and wrapped it around his waist, her fingers sliding down his shirt-front to grapple with the buttons of his breeches.

He did not speak, merely stared into her eyes as his fingers stole between their straining bodies and pulled at the ribbon-fastening of her skirts, jerking her clothing free. A coolness chilled her bare legs and hips, complementing the lush heat between her thighs, and she felt herself tremble as sexual need exploded through her body. Her hands fumbled at his waistband.

'Here, let me.' His fingers joined hers and unbuttoned the front panel of his breeches until her thumbs could part the fabric. She sensed the energy which emanated from him, could feel his hardness as she slid her hands inside.

Suddenly impatient, she grasped the waistband and thrust it down, catching and gripping him in her fist, pulling him to her. He was rock-hard and dark with lust, his cock rearing from the pale fabric almost to his navel. She stroked his length, briefly savouring the satin glide of skin over solid muscle before guiding him towards her, silently demanding fulfilment.

'Lydia,' Drummond murmured, his face buried in her hair. Kissing his way round her neck, he licked her throat with tiny sensual movements of his tongue as if tasting her; then his lips widened and he sucked hard, pulling her skin into his mouth and biting, as if he would devour her. This rough caress intensified the sensations which curled around her hairline to the nape of her neck and tingled down her spine, making her shiver and search for his mouth with her own.

Holding her buttocks in his hands, Drummond lifted her a little further and she felt the rasping bark against her naked hips. Curling her other leg up and around him as he supported her weight, she moved her hips, searching for him. They moved together, and she felt the luxuriant parting of her swollen sex as his hard length pressed against her, then pushed in: only a little at first, but then more, further in, until she was full of him and her breathing came in ragged gasps as she clung to his broad shoulders.

He held her so that she was hard against the tree with her buttocks stretched wide beneath his fingers. She moved slightly against him and he drew imperceptibly out of her before ramming himself home, once, twice, then faster and harder, until Lydia closed her eyes, her head tipping back and her fingers clutching at the thick lapels of his long coat. She absorbed his rhythm, pulling him fiercely into her.

His thrusting became more urgent, and violence replaced tenderness. Her back slammed against the mossy bark and her hair suddenly loosened, tumbling over one shoulder. Drummond caught her neck with one large hand, and jerked free the narrow ribbon which secured her hair. As he grasped handfuls of her curling locks, he twisted them up to his face, inhaling her scent before winding a thick hank of it around the back of his own neck so that their faces were pulled tightly together and she could no longer move of her own volition. All her movements were his now, every gasp smothered by the tense curve of his neck, every vigorous thrust he made echoed through her taut body.

She clung to him, her legs scratched by the rough

texture of his heavy coat, her arms tight around his shoulders. Her skin felt tinglingly alive, and tiny shivers oscillated along the length of her spine and around her ribs until she thought she would be unable to catch her breath. The smell of his neck, just by her nose, and the feel of his muscular buttocks clenching repeatedly beneath her entwined ankles made her lose herself and she came suddenly and violently, shuddering against him.

He paused momentarily, as if surprised by her quick response, and then pumped his lean hips into her ever faster until he reached his own climax as hers subsided. As she felt the tautness of him, sensed the abrupt stillness of his body and heard his harsh groan, Lydia felt a second wave of ecstasy thicken inside her and throb on to him. She squeezed her legs tightly around his back to prolong the blissful sensations and the delicious heat which curled inside her.

She clung there, limpet-like, breathing heavily and listening to the sound of his heart hammering against hers.

'Let me put my legs down,' she murmured, her arms still wound tightly around his strong neck.

'I'm sorry, did I hurt you?' Breathing hard, he eased her away from the tree and smoothed his hands over her bare legs. Reaching up, she kissed him softly on the mouth, her hand sliding around his hard jaw and up to his forehead, wiping the beaded perspiration there. The look on his face touched her, and she felt a swell of love for him.

'You don't ever hurt me. I like what you did. I like what we did together.'

His mouth descended on to hers. His kiss was gentle and soft as he pulled her to him and cradled her. His voice was low and caressing.

'I wanted you so much. Every time I see you I get hard, and I have to have you. The tree seemed a good place.'

'It was a good place. Although the foliage in my hair

may raise my maid's eyebrows.' She smiled, retrieving her ribbon and swiftly bunching her hair into it. She knelt before Drummond, pushing his breeches up. Just before covering him, she gave his softened cock a long lick from root to head. It jerked in response and he laughed, tilting her chin up so that her eyes met his.

'Not just yet,' he said. 'Let's walk on a while first.'

Chapter Ten

*T*hey broke away from the path to circle the lake, which was just visible through the last line of trees.

'It'll be dark soon. The days are getting short now and I suppose winter will be upon us before long.' He narrowed his eyes against the glare that set the glittering black water of the lake to flame. The sun had just dropped below the trees, and the sky above them was beginning to change to the enveloping blue of night.

'At least it's still warm. When the cold weather comes it won't be a good time for you to be camping out at Jim's and holding up carriages on the road. You'd better decide what you want to do before very much longer.'

He walked on a little further, the toes of his boots scuffing the dry leaves on the path. Lydia thought for a moment that he had not heard her. When he finally spoke, his voice was low and tense.

'I don't know. I really don't know. If I knew Lavendale was honest then I'd go straight to his chambers, but – oh, damn! I wish there was someone to tell me what to do! If my father was alive –'

Lydia suddenly felt irritated.

'Well, he's not!' she cried.

Drummond, even during his absence, had been someone she had always felt she could depend on, the one person who could sort out the mess at Hawkesworth. Her anger at the delay since he had come home suddenly got the better of her, and she quickened her pace, swinging round to face him and slapping her hands against the lapels of his coat. Her temper flushed her cheeks and made her eyes sparkle dangerously.

'He's dead and there's no one to tell you what to do! It's up to you now. You're the head of the family, Drummond, so act like it. Make a decision and stand by it.' She softened her tone a little as she caught the look of surprise and hurt on his face. 'Look. I'll do all I can to help you and so will many others, but we can't wait forever while you make up your mind.' As he returned her stare, she saw the confusion and doubt edged away by something steely and resolute: his eyes held a focus and strength which had not been there before.

Grasping her wrists, he held her still.

'You're right.' He stared over her head as if he could see something in the far distance. 'You're right. There's only me now.'

He dropped her arms, twisted on his heel and strode ahead, leaving Lydia to run after him as he dodged between the thinning trees. He skirted the shore of the dark lake, his stride determined and his face closed and thoughtful.

'Wait! Wait for me,' she called, almost losing sight of his broad, retreating back. His pace did not lessen and she was soon left alone. Exasperated, she kicked at a stone on the path. It hit a tree and rebounded, cracking painfully against her ankle, and she winced, kicked it again, and then trudged on along the path.

Out from the cover of the trees the darkness seemed less dense. The sky was a warm pinky-blue low over the lake, deepening to twilight overhead. There was a sprinkle of tiny silver stars, and the reflection of the moon glittered on the lake. In the distance she could see the stone folly casting a long shadow, and under it, hunched on a large rock at the water's edge, sat Drummond.

162

As she approached, he looked up and held out a hand. She came close, standing at his side, then placed her hand in his. He sighed.

'We used to come here so often as children. I wonder if Valerian ever remembers those times, when he's gambling the family fortune away?'

'I doubt it,' said Lydia. 'He seems to have no memory of times past. Or if he has, he never says.'

Drummond interlaced his fingers with hers and she looked down at his hand, stirred by the sight of his long fingers squeezed between her pale ones, her arousal pricked by the tiny golden hairs which roughened the back of his hand and disappeared under the stark white of his linen cuff. Her thumb stole up and round to rub the pad of it over his wrist: she enjoyed the calm throb of his pulse which she felt quicken slightly at her touch.

'Do you remember swimming here? Valerian threw me in once and you dived from this rock to save me.' She chuckled. 'You didn't know that old Starchy had been teaching me to swim. Your face was a picture when I calmly struck out for the opposite shore!'

Laughing, he caught her waist and pulled her to him.

'Yes. Explain to me just how that old witch got you down here and swimming without anyone knowing.'

'It was no secret. We would finish conjugating verbs and then she'd suggest a walk, while you two were still struggling over the multiplication she'd set you the previous day.' As she spoke, Lydia kicked off her shoes and tucked her long hair up on to the top of her head. 'We'd run down here and strip, like this –' she let her skirt drift in a soft pile to her ankles and began to unbutton the fastenings at the front of her bodice '– and then my swimming lesson would begin.'

She stretched before him, enjoying the look of dark lust on his features as he took in the length of her bare legs, the nip of her waist, and the upturned curve of her full breasts. He slid off the rock and reached for her, but she was too quick, evading his grasping hand as she skipped to the water's edge.

'Catch me if you can!' She sprinted into the shallows, steeling herself for the inevitable chill on her warm skin. The touch of ice bristled and she could feel her whole body shudder and tingle with the autumn freshness of the lake. Looking down, she saw her pale feet tinged green with the cool water which lapped at her knees. Her hand stroked up over her waist and she lightly touched one hard nipple, watching the tip tighten further with her cold fingers. She scooped water in her cupped hands and trickled it over herself, shivering as the rivulets ran like icy fingers over her breasts and belly.

Turning, she scooped both hands together and sloshed water back at Drummond, who hopped on one foot on the shore, struggling to pull off his heavy boots.

'Damn, that's cold!' he cried. 'I hope you don't want me to come in there and get you.'

'Of course not!' she mocked him. 'You mustn't get your poor self wet and cold.'

She panted a few times, steeling her nerves for the plunge, then threw herself forward into the water, diving under and coming up gasping and spluttering. The top few inches had been warmed by the day's sun, but under that the water was glacial; her scalp felt as if it had shrunk on to her head, and her nipples were as hard as acorns. Desperate to get her blood moving, she struck out vigorously for the centre of the lake, her feet kicking through the weed in the shallows until she reached clearer water.

'Don't go too deep! You might get cramp and then I'd have to save you!' Drummond yelled.

Lydia turned on to her back to float and watched him between her toes. He had flung all his clothes on to the shingle beach and climbed up on to the rock, his rangy form poised at the overhanging edge as he prepared to dive. His body hit the water and sliced it with knife-like precision, then he disappeared with a sharp kick of his legs. Lydia waited for him to surface. He stayed under for a long time, then burst up a few feet away from where she floated, snorting and shouting at the freezing temperature.

He stood chest-deep and swiped his hair back from his eyes, blinking and grinning at Lydia. She thought how little he had changed since boyhood: his exuberance was undimmed, despite the difficulties he faced with his brother.

'This is the coldest water I've been in since I swam in a lake in Acadia,' he gasped, sinking into the water and swimming over to where Lydia calmly floated with her toes wriggling above the surface.

'Where's Acadia?' she asked.

'In the Americas,' he replied. 'It's the New World. Everything is so big over there: the trees here would look like knee-high stumps in comparison.'

Lydia glanced at the tall trees which shaded the lake and smiled with disbelief. Then she dipped her head back and gazed up at the rapidly darkening sky. She could feel the lapping of tiny wavelets as Drummond swam closer, then the warmth of his breath on her ear as he moved behind her. His legs came up beneath hers and he slid one arm around her, under her breasts, and moulded his body to hers in the cold of the lake.

They floated like that for some time, then Drummond shifted under her and she could feel the hardness of his cock pressing against the curve of her buttock. It felt smaller in the water, kept thin by the cold, and she wriggled against it, letting the solid head bounce against the crease of her buttocks.

'The water's too deep here: let's swim into the shallows,' he whispered.

When they were in only a few inches of water, he lay back on the sandiest part of the beach and pulled Lydia on to him so that she lay nose to nose with him, her legs slightly apart and her toes resting in the water. Their lips bumped and then joined, and she felt herself being pulled into his warm embrace, her chilled body gently heated by his vitality and her own anticipation. She raised herself slightly and reached for his cock, but his firm hand stilled her.

'Wait,' he said. 'We can do something better.'

He whispered in her ear and Lydia giggled.

'That won't work.'

'Believe me, it does.'

'Stay still, then.' She raised herself above him and used the shallow water as a lubricant to smooth her passage as she swept her body up and down him, the plumpness of her sex brushing his muscular lower abdomen and rubbing the underside of his cock as it hardened towards his navel. She moved faster, the water easing her movements, and she felt him jerk to rock-hard proportions under the sweeping glide of her body. The gradual pressure of his rigid length on her mons aroused her in a very subtle way, and she moved faster and harder, grinding herself down on him, watching the changing expressions on his face below her. The sight of his pleasure increased her own, and when she felt him jerk between the compression of their bellies, she cried out triumphantly. He gripped the back of her neck, pulling her down for an open-mouthed kiss, their bellies sliding slightly on the hot pool of come.

'Where did you learn how to do that?' she asked, sitting up and easing her legs astride.

He smiled and shook his head, then rolled her over until she was underneath him, her body shadowed by his and her back pressed into the wet sand. He scooped handfuls of water and trickled it over her, making her arch up as she felt her skin prickle and her nipples extend with the cold. He then picked up a handful of smooth round pebbles and began to arrange them on her body: one on each of her nipples, one in her navel, a line between her breasts which snaked down to her bare sex. He trailed a stone lightly over her there.

'Where's your hair?' he asked. Lydia felt herself blush; her whole body became hot and embarrassed as her mind considered various explanations. Glancing up at him, she saw enquiry and amusement in equal measures in the depths of his golden-brown eyes. She thought of the question she had just asked him, then mimicked his reaction by smiling and shaking her head.

He laughed, then bent his head to her mouth and plunged his seeking tongue between her lips. She sucked him in, and, when she felt his hand press her thighs, she let her legs fall open. She felt a cold, hard pressure as he placed a stone there, and she froze for a moment, but pleasure soon overcame her reluctance and she let her limbs fall heavy and loose, allowing him do as he would.

He filled her with smooth stones, each one the size and shape of an egg. Then he made her tighten herself on to the stones repeatedly, while he flicked the roughened edge of his thumb over her clitoris until it swelled and she could feel her whole body begging for release. She relaxed under his hands and he played with her, smoothing her sex then squeezing the flesh until it pouted, glossy and engorged. He coaxed, cajoled, and finally put his mouth to her, until she capitulated and shuddered on to him, calling his name and gasping with the intensity of her climax and the muscles that oscillated on the cold hard stones inside.

'What are you doing sitting there in the dark? You made me jump.' Lydia leant against the cool timber of the door and held her hand to her throat, her heart thumping and forehead prickling with fear. Angel rose from the low stool by the fire and advanced across the darkened room.

'I was waiting for you,' she said. 'You've been gone for hours.'

'Since when has it been any concern of yours? I'll go where I want, when I want. I get enough of this from Valerian, so don't you start telling me what to do.' Her voice was harder than she meant it to be. Part of her mind had told her that the dark shadow awaiting her was Valerian, back early, and it was only when Angel had lit a candle that the relief had flooded through her.

'I was just worried, that's all.' Angel's voice was now low and soothing: she stood close to Lydia and laid one hand on her arm. 'You're freezing, and your hair is wet! What's happened to you? Are you hurt?' Her firm hand drew Lydia into the room and closer to the warmth of the glowing grate. 'There are thieves in this region, did you know? The master was set upon late the other night: that's why he has that cut on his cheek. And two masked men were seen at the gates yesterday. I've heard that they only steal to give money to the poor, but they wouldn't hesitate to do something worse to you. It would be too tempting. Miss Lydia, have you been set upon?'

Although her words were gentle and sympathetic, Lydia could detect the frisson of excitement and vicarious pleasure in Angel's voice. She caught the girl's hand and pushed her back down on to the stool.

'Oh, it was terrible! They chased me through the woods and –'

Angel's hands flew to her mouth, her eyes wide and bright above them.

'How many?' she gasped.

'Three,' said Lydia, beginning to enjoy herself. 'They all wore dark masks so that I couldn't see their faces, and cloaks with golden clasps and hats pulled down low over their fierce eyes! As they chased me, their cloaks swirled behind them, catching the wind and rippling in the night air. I reached the lake and there was no escape, so I turned to face them. They were so close that I could see their terrible eyes shining like wolves as they circled me and surrounded me. One of them had a golden earring which glinted in the moonlight. Another had a knife: a long silver blade that he held between his teeth as he advanced.'

Angel sat motionless, simultaneously horrified and enthralled, and Lydia could see her knuckles whiten as she squeezed her hands together in her lap. Encouraged, she licked her lips, her mind racing as she dropped to her knees in front of the other girl.

'The one with the earring caught my wrist and jerked me towards him. I struggled, twisting my arm and trying to shake him off, but his grip was so strong, like a thick rope. He dragged me up the shingle and threw me into the arms of the third man, who waited at the edge of the beach. They laughed and spoke in a strange tongue, or two of them did, for the one with the blade in his mouth was silent throughout. The third man had a strange mark around his neck, a painting of many colours, and when he came close to me I could see that it was the likeness of a serpent that coiled around him, its tail disappearing into his shirt. Its huge striped head was painted across his throat, so that when he swallowed the fangs seemed to move and bite.'

Lydia warmed to her theme, holding Angel's hands in her own and squeezing her fingers, feeling the other girl wriggle a little on the stool and seeing her breath begin to come a little faster, her eyes dewy with partly concealed excitement.

'The serpent-man held me from behind, pulling me by the wrists so that I was stretched up and had to curve my arms around the back of his head, knocking his hat off. That made him angry: he thrust his knee into the back of my legs and grunted something in my ear. His partner, the one with the earring, slapped my face and told me in broken English to be careful, that they didn't want me to be able to recognise them again. Then he leant forward and bit my neck, while sliding his hand down the whole length of my body, pausing just long enough at my breast to squeeze and pinch my nipples. After that he moved lower, lifting up my skirts and showing the Blade my naked thighs.

'The Blade bent over too, and they both inspected me closely; I could feel myself growing hot, blushing beneath their scrutiny, and I twisted, trying to hide from their piercing eyes. The Serpent hissed in my ear, something cruel that frightened me, and I held on to the back of his neck, desperate not to let go and fall to the ground lest the other two pounce on me. The Serpent felt strong and I clung to him. His hands wound round me from behind and grasped my waist, pushing my hips out with a flick of his wrists and tilting me towards the Blade.

'The Blade stood up and stared into my eyes: his were cold and blue, the palest blue that you ever saw, like chips of bone. He stared for a long time, then took the knife out of his mouth and placed it on my breastbone. The point was sharp and I knew that if he applied the slightest pressure it would pierce my skin, slide into me, enter my breast, breach my heart. I was terrified, but then he did something even more horrible.'

She paused, her gaze fixed on Angel's face, aroused by the trembling of the girl's plump bottom lip and the feverish sheen which pearled her pale skin. She gave tiny panting breaths and her eyes were glazed and wide. Lydia knew that she was almost insensible to her surroundings, that she could touch the girl anywhere and the other would think that it was one of the three brigands, for she was totally immersed in the tale.

'He opened his mouth and tried to lick his lips. But he couldn't. Because at some time his blade had worked its cold magic on him. He had only the shortest stump of tongue, thick and hard, and he curled his lips up and leered at me. I knew that although he could not speak, he could use that tongue to terrible effect, so I tried to look unafraid, but inside my body was trembling and petrified. I felt everything turn to water and my limbs became useless as the Blade and the Earring snarled at the Serpent and he laid me down. I could feel the shingle under my back, sand broken with tiny hard stones. I tried to protest, to move, but they filled my mouth with some vile and oily rags; then they turned me on to my stomach and stretched my arms and legs out, driving thick stumps into the ground to tie me to. I struggled and kicked, but they were so strong: the Earring's hand felt like a huge weight that had been dropped on to my left ankle. Strangely, he was also the most gentle, for his other hand crept up my inner thigh like velvet, softly, smoothly, until he reached the crease of my buttock and fingered the bare flesh there. He was like fleece against my tortured skin and I closed my eyes to savour such tenderness.

'Suddenly I felt the point of a knife at my neck and I gasped, almost choking on the oily rags. The Blade sliced my clothes from neck to hem and tore them open, so that I felt the chill of the night air on my back and legs. There was no pause to savour the sight, as before. Almost instantly, I felt cruel fingers prise my buttocks apart and the sharp sound of someone spitting. I felt his saliva hit my bottom, warm and wet, and tried to close myself against him, but I was powerless. The Blade knelt between my thighs and pressed his mouth down, his short tongue pushing against me, the hard stump opening and probing as his teeth grazed the rosebud flesh there. At the same time I felt something hard against my sex, something unyielding and terrible. I thought at first that it was his cock. But no, it was the hilt of his dagger. He pressed it up into me, fucking me with it, plundering me with the dirty plaited leather handle, and while my mind said "No, please, no!", my body betrayed me utterly and I felt myself melt against the rough thing that stretched my tender parts and rubbed me until I bucked my hips. When they saw that, the men became excited, the Serpent and the Earring speaking at once, and one of them pulling the Blade away. He fought them at first, his huge fists flailing while his deformed tongue and the hilt of his weapon did their deed; but they were two against one and he succumbed to their superior strength.

'I thought I was saved and that they would let me go. I felt a blessed relief, but also a strange burning disappointment that flared in me and died the minute the Earring knelt between my outstretched legs. His fingers were gentle, easier to bear than the other's tongue and hilt. He stroked me, opening me softly, and I could feel my bottom flare under his tutelage as he coaxed me. He spent a long time there, easing me open, until I longed for him to do something more.

'I felt his breath on the back of my shoulder as he curved his body to mine, felt the bristle of his spiky chin and smelled the fresh sweat which clung to his body, tempered by the dark odour of his leather coat. He was heavy and I felt crushed beneath him, small and frail but very alive, as his cock pushed neatly between my gaping buttocks and he breached the tight muscle there. Slowly. So slowly.

'He filled me.

'We were both still, and I could hear the slick sound of hand on flesh and turned my head to see that the Serpent had knelt before my face, his wet cock in his hand. He slid his fist up and down the engorged length, and I felt my arousal grow to fever pitch as he pulled the oily gag away and plunged the fingers of one hand into my mouth. He coated himself with my saliva. His fingers tasted bitter, strange, and I knew that I could cause him great pain if I bit down. He knew this too, for he watched me. His eyes became the colour of melting chocolate as his gaze held mine, and I noticed the thick lashes which fringed his eyes: they were so silky and long, and his eyes so soft and pleading, that I did not bite, but simply ran my tongue along the groove between those fingers and wet them as much as I could. He used this to lubricate the passage of his hand along his shaft, and I watched as he stroked himself to full hardness next to my face.

'By the time that he pressed his glans to my lips, I was ready to beg.

'I lay there, pegged to the little stakes, my body a starfish that had been washed up on the shingle of the beach, my mouth full of hard cock and the taste of the sea, while my flesh was stretched and filled from behind by a nameless man who kissed my bare shoulder with lips of fire. I reached with my bound hand and the Blade knelt, fitting himself to my palm, and I pleasured

172

them while they pleasured me, in the dark, by the lake in the silver gleam of the full moon.'

'What happened? Did they – well – you know – did they –?'

'Yes, Angel. They did. But not until I had achieved mine. I felt myself lifted: not bodily, but in my mind. The tingling that began at the top of my spine released my head to float and soar above the scene, and as I felt the first trembling waves deep inside me I could see myself, and the three men, through a blurring haze of sensation as I rippled and tightened on the sand while my mind was set loose and free. They felt it too. The Serpent was the first to come: my tongue was too sweet for him to bear, and I swallowed his lust as he pumped his hips and gripped my head tight with his hard hands. The Earring gasped a string of foreign words and I felt him tense, then release himself. He was hot: hot as the poker when you leave it in the fire, and I felt him scald me inside and clenched myself to keep him in.

'The Blade saved himself for the last victory. His face contorted, and I could see the stump of his tongue as he tried to speak his pleasure, but no words came. His cock jumped in my fist and he reached down to grasp his own balls, pulling and twisting them to milk out the last drop, as it fell on my arm and creamed the nakedness of my shoulder.'

Angel slowly let out the breath she had been holding. She closed her eyes briefly, and when she opened them she fixed them on Lydia's face. Her hands were warm as they slid up to cup her chin and she bent quickly, before Lydia could move, and devoured the other girl's mouth with her own.

They went to the floor in a tumbling embrace. Angel pulled at the laces of Lydia's bodice until her breasts were bare and golden in the dying firelight. Lydia let her stroke and unclothe her, then she closed her eyes as Angel reached between her trembling thighs and pressed a finger into her in mimicry of the Earring. She filled her with fingers, plundering and stretching her tight little sphincter before testing the juiciness of her sex with her thumb.

Lydia arched and cried out, her arousal strengthened by the story she had told. She gasped as Angel used both hands to pleasure her, and then felt her teasing and licking with the very tip of her pink tongue.

When her climax had subsided, she pushed Angel roughly over the stool so that her knees were firm to the floor and her buttocks pushed out behind her. She swept up the petticoats and bunched them on the girl's back with one hand, while the other moved to the slickness between her peachy thighs.

'My name is the Serpent,' she growled, her voice foreign and hard. 'You will feel pleasure and pain in equal measures.'

Her fingers moved to the pucker between the twin crescents of Angel's pale buttocks. She placed the tip of her forefinger there and rubbed gently, teasingly, until the little mouth opened as if to kiss her: then she rammed the finger in as hard and as fast as she could, pushing and probing and revelling in the smoothness that soothed her fingertip and the muscle that gripped repeatedly at her knuckle as if it could swallow.

Leaving the petticoats to tumble to one side, Lydia stroked her other hand across Angel's hip, slipped her fingers under, and then slid them into the creaminess of her sex. She could feel the pleasure, sense the movement that was needed, and she moved accordingly: sometimes gentle, sometimes hard. Slow. Fast. Then still. Angel's soft inner flesh gripped and undulated on her fingers, and she dropped a kiss on the warm curve at the base of her spine, the little hollow that dimpled her beautiful back. She curved her body over Angel's, and they stayed still for a long time, kneeling and watching the light in the grate as the last embers died.

Chapter Eleven

'Where's Lydia?' demanded Madame, peevishly. 'We were supposed to leave at one and the clock has just struck half past.'

She tapped one foot on the slate hearth, her fingers plucking at the ribbon on the front of her sable cloak. She had been pacing the floor for some time, and now she could feel that her impatience was beginning to get the better of her.

'Clancy! Come here this minute,' she snapped. The little page came at a trot, his chubby face split from ear to ear with his usual happy grin.

'Yes, missus.'

'Run upstairs and find out what's happening with Miss Lydia. Tell her that if she tarries any longer I shall go to the Jefferson-Handley's without her.' She sat down heavily on a nearby chair, poked around in her reticule until she found her jewelled snuffbox, and helped herself to a generous pinch.

'I am here now, Madame.' Lydia came lightly down the stairs, pausing to give Clancy an affection tap on the shoulder with her fan. 'Is the carriage at the front?'

'Yes, it is. And it has been for quite some time.' Madame's mouth twisted unattractively as she looked Lydia up and down. Every time she saw the girl, she

175

had to push away an irrational surge of jealousy. Valerian had enjoyed her far more than Claudine had expected. The pearly smoothness of her young skin, coupled with the growing air of confidence and sensuality which seemed to cling about her like an invisible perfume, served to make Claudine feel her own years acutely. She shivered, suddenly cold, as the air cut through to her thin bones. She pulled the thick sable collar closer about her shoulders.

'Come along, we'll be late. They are expecting us for dinner at two.' Turning to Clancy, she sniffed and narrowed her lips to a thin line. 'Make sure you have those red slippers cleaned by the time I get back. I wish to wear them tonight.'

Angel stood at the window near the top of the stairs, a soft cloth in one hand and a three-branch candelabra in the other. She watched the carriage bear Madame and Miss Lydia away from the house, then craned her neck against the latticed glass to watch it disappear from sight.

'They've gone, Angel.' The hair prickled on the back of her neck. 'We're alone now.'

Turning, her pulse skipping feverishly, Angel held the candelabra before her like a talisman to ward off an evil spirit.

'I'm working, milord. See, I've nearly finished this one.'

'Well, finish it then. I have a fancy to see your fingers polish and stroke the brass shafts.'

Angel hesitated.

'Proceed.' Valerian folded his arms across the blue brocade of his long waistcoat and leant back against the wall, his dark eyes fixed on Angel's slender hands. 'Proceed, my dear. Don't make me angry.'

Angel carefully placed the candelabra on the wide window-seat and applied the cloth. She had already given it a reasonable shine, and it was the work of moments to make it gleam. Her slender fingers pushed

176

the cloth up from the base to the curling lip of one of the branches. The thick creamy candle at the top shuddered. Holding her breath, she slid the cloth down again, her hand curving over the cylindrical shaft; her actions made her feel languor instead of her usual quiet rebelliousness.

She moved to the middle section and rubbed the dull brass to a high sheen. Her own face was reflected there, slightly bowed out of shape, moon-like, and she saw that her cheeks had flushed and her bottom lip looked swollen and full as if she had been kissed. Her heart began to beat a little faster, and heat prickled beneath her arms and behind her neck. She knew Lord Hawkesworth was watching, studying her every move, and the knowledge made her rub harder and more diligently as the silence lengthened between them.

She sensed rather than heard him move behind her, his stealth that of a nocturnal animal stalking prey. Angel stood motionless, her nose full of his smell: that slightly acid citrus tang with which he dressed his hair, accompanied by the musky perfume of his clothing as it warmed with his body heat. By contrast, his hand under her chin was cool, his fingertips almost icy, and as she turned she saw that his eyes were glacial as he swept his gaze from the top of her head to the toes of the wooden shoes which peeped out from beneath the hem of her apron.

'On your knees.' His voice was so low that at first she thought she had not heard him correctly. She hesitated, and he gripped her chin, twisting the soft flesh there, forcing her face round to one side. His head thrust suddenly forward and she thought that he was going to kiss her, but his mouth barely grazed her cheek and she felt the heat of his breath on her ear lobe.

'On your knees, Angel.' The sibilance of his hiss tickled at the downy hair that curled at the nape of her neck. She shivered as she heard him laugh, a horrible low sound that reminded her of a metal spoon being scraped around the inside of a saucepan; she gritted her teeth.

'Are you afraid of me?' he asked, bringing both hands up to imprison her face and pull her upward, closer to him. She had to stand on tiptoe to ease the pain in her stretched neck.

She shook her head.

'No.'

'Wrong answer!' The shout was deafening, and Angel stared into his face, her mind rapidly working out all the possible replies.

'Yes, master. I am very afraid of you.'

The grip on her face was released and she dropped back on to the soles of her feet. She bowed her head and waited for him to speak again.

'Very good.' He gently stroked one finger from the hollow under her chin up to her mouth, following the curve of her face until his fingertip dipped between her lips and Angel could taste the bitterness that clung to his nails. She had sampled something similar before, but her head was so full of fear, and a subtle arousal, that she could not recall where. She stood still, her mouth slack around his fingers. He raised an eyebrow.

'You are supposed to be on your knees.'

The words had barely left his lips when his hands descended like weights on to her shoulders. Felled by the pressure, she dropped abruptly to the magenta carpet with a dull thud, her head bowing with shame as she realised what he intended. His left hand cupped her neck and he urged her forward with a light but definite pressure. The tip of her nose touched the immaculate cream fabric of his breeches, and she could detect the masculine smell of him behind the smooth frontage. She closed her eyes.

'Now, my dear Angel. There is something you can do for me. Something you can do for your lord and master. If you do it well then I shall reward you. If not . . . well, I would hardly like to say.'

She kept her eyes tightly closed and swallowed, dropping her chin almost to her chest. He seemed pleased by this gesture of humility, for his hand stroked the back of her neck and he bent to place a kiss on the parting of her pale hair. His mouth, unlike his fingers, was hot and seemed to burn her skin through the smooth layer of her sleekly combed hair.

'Mmm.' He moved his lips against her. 'Like silk. Everything is silk: your hair, your lashes, your eyebrows.' His lips traced the features as he named them, and she could feel the skin beneath his touch tingle and then throb. She swayed slightly on her knees, stimulated by the hot glide of his mouth over her face.

Abruptly, he seized one of her wrists.

'But not your hands, eh, Angel? No, your hands show how far beneath me you really are. Despite the care you take with your toilette, despite your aping of your mistress, you'll never be anything but my servant. A maid. What would you do if I turned you out? Nothing. You'd be on the streets.' His mouth was by her ear now, and she gave a quick little inhalation as he sank his sharp teeth into the fleshy part of her tender lobe. 'So better make it good, Angel.'

She nodded dumbly, unable to speak, determined that he would gain no satisfaction from hearing how near she was to crying.

She sensed him pull away from her and straighten up, his shirt-sleeves whispering over the satin brocade of his waistcoat. Her spine crinkled at the sound of his hands sliding on the sheer material, over his hips to the fastenings of his breeches. The top button gave under the firm pressure of his thumb, and she shuddered, unable to move away although she knew that she ought to. Her every instinct told her to jump to her feet and flee down the stairs, away from him, but her treacherous body would not obey. It made her stay. Still. With the smell of him in her nose and the sound of buttons popping through fabric as he undid himself. Her treacherous body lied to her – or was it her mind lying to her body? – as a gush of cream slicked the curves at the top of her thigh.

She felt the feverish heat of his cock as it bounced against her cheek and then stood by her ear. Without opening her eyes, she could sense the nearness and the readiness of him. She moved her head slightly, just a tilt, and her nose touched him. He was as hard as rock and as hot as a furnace, and her eyes flew open as he gripped the back of her head and levered her round.

'Suck me. Slowly,' he said, positioning her so that her lips were poised at the very end of him, and she had an uninterrupted view down his long, slender length. He smelt divine, so aroused, so ready. There was a tiny glistening drop just within reach, and she flicked her tongue out and over him, taking up the seashell tear-drop and pressing it up to the roof of her mouth, where it mixed with her own saliva and dissolved. She opened her lips and encircled him. He breathed out heavily, his eyes fixed on hers.

'Careful,' he said. He watched her intently as she kneaded the muscles of his thighs, which tightened and then relaxed under her hands. Her thumbs worked up and underneath him, cradling him and then sliding under, moving towards the tip until she could feel the pout of her own lower lip. She lightly stroked the smooth upper surface and then gripped him firmly, between thumb and forefinger, as she had seen the pipers do their flutes in the market-place. She slid her lips a little way down his engorged shaft and gave a tiny suck.

He quivered and rotated his hips. Glancing up, she saw that his head had tipped back a little and his eyes were closed. She could feel the palms of his hands, hot now, against the back of her head as he pulled her on to him with little bobbing motions and his cock slid towards the back of her throat.

Her hands slid under the warm fabric of his breeches, and she hitched them down so that they rested tight just above his knees. Her fingers walked up the back of his legs and nestled under his buttocks, her nails stroking the curve there until she felt his skin pucker and he shivered. Her hands traced the curve of his hips and dragged slightly over his flat belly before meeting over the swollen skin of his cock, which jerked against her palm as she gripped it.

Slipping her fingers gently back and forth, she revelled in the smoothness of velvet over honed steel. Then she softly lapped at the underside, her tongue flat and hard against the musky taste, as she gradually worked her way down his length until her nose ruffled the crisp hairs which collared him. Her fingers slid under and she cupped his balls, cradling them in the palm of her hand and wrapping them in her fingers. He gave a low groan of appreciation, and she felt the hairs on the back of her neck rise in anticipation.

She glided back up to the swollen glans and circled it with the pointed tip of her tongue, searching beneath the soft collar and stroking, licking, sucking lightly, feeling it straining against her. Above her she heard a hoarse moan and a laboured exhalation as he closed his lips and flared his nostrils. She took him in deeply, warming him with the soft insides of her mouth, then slid down and began to move more definitely against him: more pressure, tongue curved, lips tighter as she felt him swell and grow to greater hardness. Her fingers gripped his hard buttocks, preventing any escape, and she felt his hands flutter over her hair, loosening it.

There was a tiny sound as one of her pins fell to the carpet and bounced, coming to rest on the polished timber at the edge of the stair, under the banister. Then silence, as the thick skeins of hair were gathered and bunched around her ears, muffling and shutting out the sound of the world until she felt as if they were the only people in it, the only two people alive. And pleasure the ultimate reward. Her own arousal was hot and thick, and she felt her sex swell, the lips there as pouting and wet as the ones that fellated him.

He came, with sudden white-hot spurts and a heady

pulsating of his cock against her tongue. He gave a sharp cry and thrust his pelvis forward, knocking his glans to the back of her throat, and Angel swallowed around him, her mind on fire and her own juice trickling down her leg as if what she absorbed had gushed through a hollow vessel and pooled on the magenta carpet below. She felt him gradually relax and bend over her slightly, both of his hands stroking her jaw and cheeks. When she looked up, she saw that his dark eyes gleamed as he buttoned his breeches.

'Thank you,' he said. The words sounded unfamiliar on his lips, as if he rarely said them and was not quite sure of their meaning.

'Oh, no, milord. Thank you.'

He raised an eyebrow and then frowned, his hands sliding into the pockets of his breeches and pulling the fabric taut over his subsided cock. Angel dragged her gaze away and looked up to meet his eyes.

A secretive smile curved her lips. She took a step forward until she stood very close to him, the top of her head just level with his chin. Placing her hands on the smooth brocade that stretched across his wide shoulders, she rose on to tiptoes and paused momentarily before kissing him full on the lips. She felt his mouth open a fraction under hers with his surprise, and she felt the tingling contact as she flicked her tongue out, just once, to lightly touch his. Then she turned away from him to pick up the candelabra and cloth.

She hummed a little tune as she began polishing, and was aware that he did not move for a long time: his curious eyes seemed to burn into the skin of her back. Then he was gone, as silently as he had approached, and she was alone again.

She slid the thick creamy candle out of the holder and caressed the rounded end lightly before slipping it into her apron pocket. Kneeling, she rubbed the cloth over the silvery, crystalline patch which caught the light on the dark carpet; it took a few moments, but soon it was gone. Angel sat back on her heels, wondering how long she would have in the privacy of her attic bedroom to slake her own arousal.

'Thank you so much for dinner,' Lydia murmured, her eyes downcast as she tried to avoid the lecherous gaze of Oswald Jefferson-Handley. His grip on her hand, warm and slightly slimy with excessive perspiration, did not lessen, and she thought for one horrible moment that she would have to publicly shake him off. He was a huge barrel of a man, almost as wide as he was tall, but his flesh did not have the jocund ruddiness of many country squires: Oswald was pale and mealy with skin the colour and consistency of cold porridge. A vague odour of urine clung to his clothes, and Lydia privately wondered whether it was his own, or that of the skinny dogs who shadowed his every move.

She gave her hand a little tug; he squeezed her fingers with his own, the pressure turning the nails an ugly yellowish-white. He smiled at her, his pale eyes glassy and his mouth working as if he sought to rid his gums of some remnant of stale food.

'Come now, Ossie!' His wife Rosamunde, the former Honourable Lady Rosamunde Bentley and an old London friend of Madame's, tapped his arm with an ornate fan. 'Leave the girl alone.' She turned to Madame and her mouth curled in a conspiratorial smile. 'Claudine, darling, I shall see you in town very soon. I'm so grateful for your visit: you've quite cheered me up by bringing this delightful young lady to see me. She really is very easy on the eye.'

The two women stood side by side and pushed the odious Oswald behind them, almost out of sight. Lydia felt herself blush to the roots of her hair as their appraising eyes swept the curves of her body.

'Maybe you'll bring her to town?' murmured Rosamunde, her full red lips pursed assessingly. Claudine frowned a little, as if thinking.

'Yes,' she said. 'I think she will do very well there, don't you? With a little training.'

'Yes. A little training would go a long way.' Rosamunde reached a hand up to smooth the light layer of powder on her rich auburn hair. '*Au revoir*, then, my darling. And good day to you, Miss Hawkesworth. Ossie will hand you into the carriage.'

Lydia endeavoured to climb the three steps without assistance, but Oswald was there with a speed which belied his bulk. His hand trailed across her ankle; she aimed a quick little kick sideways and felt it connect with his knuckles. Satisfied, she settled into the corner of the carriage and sulked out of the window, disgusted with Oswald for being so familiar, and furious with Madame for showing her off like a possession.

As the cultivated lawns of the parkland gave way to the tangled hedgerows of the local countryside, Madame sighed and picked at an imaginary piece of fluff on the flawless satin of her full-skirted gown.

'I don't know why you have to be so objectionable, Lydia.'

'I was not objectionable. I was perfectly polite to your horrible friend and her disgusting husband. You have no cause to complain.'

'If you deem it polite to mope over the soup and cast a sour eye over the syllabub, then you English have even worse manners than I have previously credited you with. And as for kicking dear Ossie. It was most unnecessary.' She glanced out of the window and then sneaked a look at Lydia. 'But I have to confess to wishing that I had done it first. You realise that she only married him for his money, don't you? We're all waiting for black-edged funeral invitations and then we can all relax again. Rosamunde will be back on the scene, thrilling all and sundry once more.'

'Was she one of Valerian's lovers, too?' Lydia wished that she had not asked; a sick feeling almost overwhelmed her and she found that she did not want to hear the answer. The snort of laughter that greeted her question served only to deepen her misery.

'*Mon dieu*, no! Rosamunde's wonderful breasts are far

184

too – too – womanly for a man like him. No, Valerian prefers his girls to be like boys.' She straightened in her seat as if to accentuate her own narrow chest and hips. 'That's why you'll never be anything more than a passing fancy, a diversion, as I've said before – why are we stopping?' She tapped her fan on the communicating panel and raised her voice. 'Why are we stopping, coachman?'

There was no reply. Only an ominous silence. Dappling shadows from a roadside tree rippled across the polished interior of the motionless carriage, and Lydia held her breath. She suddenly knew why they had stopped, and she waited to hear the familiar cry of 'Stand and deliver'.

None came.

'This is ridiculous!' Madame gathered her skirts in one hand and leant forward to look out of the window. 'Grief, the man's running away. Come back here: come back here at once!'

A shadow fell across the doorway, and Lydia stifled a giggle. The look of shock on Madame's face was mirrored in Drummond's astonished eyes as he quickly pushed his mask back in place. That he had expected Lydia to be alone was obvious, and for a moment she enjoyed his discomfort at the tangle his audacity had thrown him into. Leaning forward, she grasped Madame's sleeve and shook it.

'Oh, Madame,' she gasped, her voice high and full of feigned alarm. ''Tis an evil highwayman. He'll rob us blind and steal our virtue. What can we do?'

Madame glanced at Lydia with impatiently pursed lips, and then stared back at the highwayman. Her blue eyes travelled the length of his body, and Lydia could see her lecherous thoughts as plainly as if she had spoken them. Her gaze lingered on the muscular thighs which were just visible beneath his short, stout coat, and then drifted up to inspect the width of his shoulders and the bronzed jaw which twitched slightly under her scrutiny.

'Well, well, well,' she murmured, lifting her hand to the neckline of her gown as if to protect her modesty. 'A highwayman! And a handsome one at that, I judge. We mustn't disappoint him: come Lydia, your money.'

'I have none,' protested Lydia. 'Give him yours.'

Madame laughed, her hand patting her reticule which rested on the seat beside her.

'Monsieur Highwayman, it seems we are at your mercy. My friend has no money, and I confess that I too have travelled without any.' Her eyes searched his face, a look of blatant challenge making her blue eyes gleam brightly.

Lydia watched as Drummond coughed into his glove, and she wondered how he would extricate himself without causing suspicion. He stepped nearer to the window and took Madame's hand in his. It lay on the rough surface of his dark glove like a slender flower, pale and delicate and trembling slightly. He regarded the hand for some moments, deep in thought, and then smiled up at its owner.

'My dear lady, it would be rude of me to steal from so gracious and beautiful a traveller. I shall be on my way with nothing more than a kiss to your tender hand.' He bent his head, and Madame remained motionless as he pressed his lips to her bare skin, lingering over her hand. Lydia saw a look of secret hunger stiffen Madame's face: it was as if a mask had fallen over her features, turning her to porcelain. Only her eyes seemed alive, burning as they moved assessingly over the breadth of the man's shoulders. Lydia glanced from one to the other, waiting to see how each would react.

'A gentleman thief,' said Madame, her voice slightly breathless as if the tight lacing of her bodice suddenly constricted her movements. 'Forgive me, sir, but you'll make a poor footpad if all you are going to steal are kisses. I imagine that you will hold fast to the maxim of "your money or your life"? I shall be sorely disappointed if you will not trade.'

Drummond straightened, Madame's small hand still

186

captive in his own. He looked at her, his eyes roving over her face, neck, and breasts, then travelling down over her gown to her tiny feet, clad in damask slippers, which rested on the dusty floor of the carriage. Lydia then met his gaze as it travelled across the floor and up over her body to her eyes. His stare seemed to sear into her, questioning, enquiring, seeking permission of a kind. She curved one corner of her lips upward in a minute gesture of complicity, unseen by Madame.

'Ladies,' he murmured. 'I shall not take your lives, for that would see me branded a murderer, but we could trade. I change my maxim, for today only, and make it "your money or your virtue". Would that be a fair exchange?'

'Yes!' Madame and Lydia both spoke at once, then glanced at each other. Drummond leant into the carriage and grasped Lydia's hand, pulling both women towards him.

'But do I have your word that neither of you will try to run? I am outnumbered two to one, as you see.'

'Oh, come, now.' Madame's voice had an edge of impatience to it. 'A man such as you should be able to keep us both so busy that neither would have energy or chance even to consider escaping. But speed is of the essence, or that damned coachman will have a search party organised and we will be discovered *in flagrante*.' She gave the door a little kick, and Drummond handed her down from the carriage.

Lydia watched him take Madame's wrist and lead her to the shadow of a large oak tree girded by leafy bushes, where he unribboned her sable cloak and spread it, fur side up, before sitting her down. He returned to the carriage and lifted Lydia bodily from the step, pulling her easily into his strong arms and bearing her to the makeshift bed.

He laid her next to Madame and stood above them, his legs astride their feet and his heavy boots firmly planted on the leafy ground. He placed his leather-clad fists on his hips and stared down, as if considering the treasure he had captured. Lydia felt her heart swell with desire for him, and a sensual hunger to see his body twinned with Madame's. Her thoughts weakened her limbs and stirred a trembling lust, which began behind her knees and licked up the soft flesh of her inner thigh to heat the inside of her. She looked sideways at Madame, whose fingers picked at the lacing of her gown and whose legs were revealed up to the knee where she had begun to lift her own skirts, and her arousal deepened as the pale curves of Madame's little breasts were bared. She tentatively reached out and slid the tip of her forefinger over the ruby nipple, which hardened at her touch. She heard Drummond draw breath, and was aware of his sudden movement as he shrugged his short coat off and knelt beside them, his hands joining hers to cup and stroke the soft flesh. Two hands caressed the perfectly shaped breast: one large and leather-clad, one small and milky-pale.

Lydia pulled at the lacing and freed Madame to the waist, her eyes devouring the small bare breasts and flat stomach. Keeping her gaze fixed on Drummond's hands as they massaged and smoothed the other woman's breasts, Lydia unhooked and unlaced herself, sensing other hands – feminine hands – at her back and at the fastening of her skirts. Both women were gradually bared almost to the stockings, Madame retaining her smooth-boned stomacher and Lydia the black velvet-and-pearl cuff which braced her slender neck.

Lydia lay back on the shimmering sable cloak and shivered at the curious, sensual hunger that the fur gave as it slipped and slid under her bare limbs.

Drummond, faced with the two delectable bodies which writhed and tangled before him, wondered how best to satisfy both without neglecting either of them. He feasted his eyes on Lydia's creamy curves, partly covered by Madame's draping thigh, and on the languid softness of her violet-tinged eyelids. He gazed at the deep shadow cast by her lowered lashes, and at the puffy redness of her recently kissed lips. Madame's fingers splayed across the curve of her belly, and Lydia's hips pushed upward as if seeking the pleasure of that hand.

Feeling his cock jerk against the taut fabric of his breeches and the heat which gathered in his loins, Drummond saw in Lydia's wanton thrusting the way to satisfy them all at once: he could give Madame the fuck that she so desired, and have her give Lydia sublime pleasure and hold her there until he could have her himself. He stripped off his gloves, throwing them impatiently aside, then pulled his soft cotton shirt over his head without bothering to unbutton it. The warmth of the sun which danced between the oak branches stippled his skin and lit the curves of his muscular body with gold. He reached for Madame, his hands sliding over Lydia's legs and dwelling on the tender skin of her knees. He parted her thighs with one hand, his other sliding around Madame's hips to lift and position her.

'Kneel for me,' he said, turning her so that she was able to gaze down at Lydia's outstretched body, and he could press his chest against the length of her slender back. Her bare flesh was broken only by the satin corset which clung to her, boning her waist and keeping it tiny. He spread his hand on her thin spine between the sharp fins of her shoulder blades, and then pulled on the laces until the corset was unnaturally tight. Madame gave a tiny moan as her breath was squeezed out.

Drummond leant away slightly to consider her shape and smiled to himself with satisfaction. Her figure was beautifully shaped now, her shoulders and hips flaring above and below a tightly constricted waist. She looked feminine, curving, and wholly desirable. He bent her forward to take her but his cock betrayed him and he came before he was ready.

'Lick her. Lick the girl,' he muttered, his hand spread on her hair as he guided her head. She took no second urging; her body curved forward and she sank into Lydia, her hands spread wide on the tender pads of flesh on Lydia's inner thigh, while her tongue sought and found the hardened bud to which she fastened her lips and tongue. Beneath her, Lydia's eyes suddenly widened and she stared up at Drummond, her gaze a deep emerald which reflected the forest canopy above them, her pupils wide and black as she fixed them on his, and he felt himself drowning, sucked in and under, swirling in the vortex of her desire as she relaxed under Madame's expert tongue.

Unable to contain his own lust, Drummond stroked his hands from the deliciously corsetted waist down over the pale crescents of Madame's buttocks. Her sex was framed by the curve of her white thighs, dark and mysterious and creamed with her arousal. He played a thumb lightly over her, and she shuddered, swelling and opening to him as a fresh gush of liquid heat pouted the already puffy lips.

His nail caught on something smooth and hard and he glanced down, surprised and aroused to see that her labia had been pierced and threaded with a thick gold loop, similar to an earring. It had been positioned towards the rear of her sex and slightly restricted access to her, as well as promising a subtle friction to the entrant.

His need was suddenly urgent. He did not stop to part her or make it easy for her to receive him: he held his straining cock in one hand, rested the burning head against her, and entered, almost savagely, giving a sharp cry as she opened and then gripped him, pushing his tender skin tightly back as he plunged into her. He jerked his pelvis, impaling her in one thrust which hilted him, and he could feel her tight against his balls, the ring hard against his shaft.

He reached up and encircled her tiny waist with his hands, his fingers almost meeting around the satin corset. Using this as an anchor, he pulled out and then drove himself into her again, relishing the softness inside her which unfurled and parted over the steel of his cock. He heard her gasp and felt her legs shift, widening a little to give him better access, and he pushed his own knees forward, deep inside her now, the front of his thighs welded to hers and the sticky heat of her sex splayed against the hairs which covered his belly and groin.

Beneath them both he could see Lydia, her head tipped back and her ebony hair loosened to spill and mix with the dark sable of the pelisse on which she lay. Her eyes were closed, her cheeks flushed, and her slender arms thrown up to frame her head. One of Madame's hands cupped and squeezed her left breast, rhythmically moulding and releasing, while the other was buried deep between Lydia's thighs, and Drummond could only imagine what sensual pleasure her fingers gave as they worked in time with her tongue.

Madame seemed to sense that his attention had wandered from her, for she reached behind her and grasped his hand, roughly pulling it down to grind it over the milky folds that clamped around his cock, forcing his fingers to press and circle the hard, protruding little nub. She worked him with her hand, guiding his fingers until they were coated with her juice and slid helplessly against her. Her sudden seizing of control, her silent demand for fulfilment, made him feel lust and anger in equal measures, and he determined to tame her.

He lifted his other hand to his mouth, moistened his forefinger, and circled it into her anus, waiting for the telltale buck as his knuckle stretched her wide. He pressed down, feeling the slippery glide of his own cock through the smooth membrane separating her two sheaths, and began to move his hand in time with his hips. He felt her tighten on to him, both apertures grasping him, almost sucking at him as she shuddered with the build-up of her orgasm.

He slowed a little, cruising against her, his thrusts shorter and more paced, then he felt her senses spill over and he thrust quickly, rapidly, until she raised her head from Lydia's dark wet sex and cried out – shouted hoarsely – as her vagina gripped and spasmed, and

Drummond felt his own heated climax throb and rush through him, searing his loins and scorching his balls with red-hot sensation.

He jerked out of her and held his surging cock in one fist, crimson needles burning the inside of his eyes, as he watched the hot spurt of his come spray on to the pale skin of Madame's back and darken the crimson satin of her corset.

He fell against her, covering her body with his and pressing into the slick come which branded her. He could smell the dark perfume she had dabbed on her pulses earlier that day, could almost taste it as his lips opened around her ear and he kissed her, sucking the pearlescent lobe and drawing it between his teeth. She rubbed her head against his, and as she shifted, he saw that her hands were buried between Lydia's legs and two fingers were knuckle-deep inside.

'Don't stop now. Oh, help me.' Lydia urged her hips up towards them both, her eyes open now, wide and dark and filled with sensual need. Her hands grasped Madame's and she pulled the woman's fingers deeper into her.

With a hoarse cry, Drummond thrust Madame to one side and scooped Lydia bodily into his arms, beating hard little kisses on to her flushed face and kneading her belly, squeezing her breasts, pressing his chest to hers and seeking her tongue with his own. He could feel Madame's small hands fluttering over his buttocks, pressing his hips and legs; as he sensed what she intended, his body did her bidding, rolling over so that he lay prone and ready.

He lifted Lydia and sat her astride him, feeling the luscious wetness of her sex spreading on the hard muscle of his lower body and his ardour returned in a rush, his body primed and his cock swinging up to hook against the curve of her hip. He saw that her face was almost obscured by her long hair, thick masses of jet-black silk which tumbled to his chest and stroked his nipples. Glossy tendrils of it had caught across her cheeks, and she reached up with an impatient hand to sweep them aside as she flexed her thighs over him.

There was an extra weight on him, and Madame's legs squeezed his as she slid up behind Lydia, her hands gripping the girl's hips and easing her up until the tip of Drummond's straining shaft was poised at her plump lips and he could feel the prickle of her partly regrown pubic hair. He felt the welcoming relief of her juicy flesh engulf him as she sank down on to his body, her thighs framing his waist.

Madame stood, and moved around him on the slipping fur cloak to cup his head between her knees. Her face was upside down above him, with her curious pale blue eyes slanting at him and her rouged lips curving in a smile.

'A gentleman thief. Mmm. How well you ply your trade.' She leant forward, and he felt the butterfly caress of her lips on his for a brief moment before she reached for Lydia, catching her under the chin and pulling her forward for a full-mouth embrace. Her lips were wide on the puffy rose of Lydia's lower lip, her tongue darting and sliding over her small white teeth. Drummond could see their hands entwined in each other's hair; he could feel the tightness of Lydia's sex as she slid down over his cock; if he reached up he could touch the rosehip tautness of two pairs of nipples above him. He sighed with pleasure, and drove himself up into the gripping sheath of one woman, while cupping the hips of the other and urging her over his waiting face.

Madame shifted a little and he caught a drift of her scent, the muskiness of the sexual pleasure he had given her, and as she lowered her sex to his mouth his cock jerked to its full length, almost painfully, and he felt Lydia arch against him. He drove into her, repeatedly battering as if he would gain entry to the very depths of her soul, while his tongue plunged and thrust at the fragrant folds of Madame, drinking her, devouring her, his mouth wide and greedy as he worked her into a frenzy of grinding and writhing above him.

Lydia came first: her frustration from being so aroused and yet unfulfilled as Drummond had pleasured Madame from behind, was suddenly, gloriously, tipped over into a pulsing vortex. Her tongue thrust into the mouth that sucked at her lips, while her pelvis crushed down, grinding sensitive female flesh on to the hard resistance of the man below her. She gasped, climaxing, her head jerking suddenly back and her throat pale and arched in the shaded sunlight. Drummond felt her soften over him, her body suddenly lax and her dark head drooping towards Madame's shoulder, and his hand left the thin woman's hips to probe between her thighs and seek the golden ring that slid alternately over his nose and teeth. Looping his forefinger through it, he gave a slight, almost imperceptible, pull and hardened his tongue against the rigid clitoris which quivered in response.

When Madame came, it was silent, her body suddenly still and stiff, the only sound that of a sudden breeze rustling the leaves above them. He felt her fingers seek his nipples, and he gasped at the sudden intense pain as she pinched them hard, cruelly twisting. As her sex undulated over his mouth, a fresh gush of cream flooding his tongue, he felt his own white-hot response and emptied himself with muscular jerks of his lean hips. He heard Lydia sigh, and felt the oscillation of her muscles as she gripped him with her sex and sucked him upward, lengthening his pleasure almost unbearably.

'You'll have to help me.' Lydia went to step up on to the coachman's seat, her hands gathering the leather reins. Madame was standing beside her on the rutted path, her reticule open, tucked under her arm, and her fingers smoothly applying her customary cochineal potion to redden her lips. She glanced at Lydia, dropping the little pot back into the satin-lined bag.

'I'm not going to help you. I would have thought that you, countrified as you are, could manage to drive a carriage without help from me. Besides, it'll ruin my hands to hold those smelly, dirty reins. I think we should wait here for help.'

She turned away, but Lydia grabbed at her, catching her shoulder.

'Help might not come. That man probably hasn't been paid for weeks: I should think he's cut his losses and gone home. Get up there and help me with these horses.'

'Take your hands off me this minute.' As Madame jerked herself away, her bag dropped to the ground. The button fastening popped open and the contents spilled out at their feet: the jewelled snuffbox, a tiny violet handkerchief, the pot of lip colour, and a velvet pouch which clinked as it hit the hard-packed mud of the road. The neck of it gaped loosely and a handful of glittering gold coins spilled out. Lydia stared at them, then nudged the nearest with the toe of her shoe.

'Why, you had money all the time. There must be thirty sovereigns there! Why didn't you give it to him?'

Madame knocked Lydia's hand off her shoulder, one thinly pencilled brow raised enquiringly as her eyes traced the girl's nose and mouth.

'Would you really have preferred it if I had? And if you say yes, then I shall call you a liar. Now drive the coach.'

Chapter Twelve

'*T*ell me again,' urged Valerian, his voice thick with lust.

Madame was in front of him, her skin naked and softly lit by the dozen or more candles that lined the walls of Valerian's study. She sat on a dark wooden chair, the seat of which had been carved out to leave just a wide rim; the occupant could make themselves comfortable, but also allow access from below. Heavy drapes were drawn across the window to shut out the night, and a low fire glowed in the grate. Valerian knelt on a soft rug, fully clothed, but with a look of naked lechery etched across his handsome features.

'Again?' she asked.

'Yes, tell me again. I want to hear it again.' His hand worked at the crotch of his breeches briefly, but Madame kicked it aside.

'I said that you were not to touch yourself!'

'Oh, please!' he begged, bending at the waist as if in pain. 'Please, if I mustn't, then you do it. I need it.'

'Well, you'll have to need it a little more than that, if you are to satisfy me.' Her long nails played over the flat plain of her stomach and then upward to count each rib that jutted through the translucent ivory skin of her chest. Her gleaming eyes never left his, and her mouth was set in a stern line, rouged this time with a dark shade that matched the amethyst rug on which Valerian kneeled. Her nails reached her breasts and she toyed with them, leading his eyes inexorably to the taut nipples that pushed out to her own touch, the ruby centres proud and stiff as they reared from the flattened discs of her dark areolae. She pulled them, leaning forward slightly as if she would offer them to his mouth, but when he leant forward she lifted one foot and placed it flat against his chest. She raised her eyebrows at his groan of agonised disappointment.

'Exactly which part do you wish to hear again? Would it be the secret dalliance I had with Rosamunde today while the others innocently ate their dinner around us?' Her fingers dropped to her thighs and she stroked them gently, her thumbs easing slowly inward in ever-decreasing circles. 'It was so easy to slip off my damask slippers and do this with my toes. You know how brilliant my toes can be. Altogether more brilliant than my fingers at times. Look: this is what I did to Rosamunde, and not a soul saw, except perhaps the footman, and Rosamunde has him under strict control.'

Her forefingers, in a mime of what her toes had done, slid over the plumpness of her sex and eased back the hood of her clitoris. One thumb, covered with a thimble-like ring, rubbed lightly over the surface. The ring was covered with a series of bumps and grooves, giving it the appearance of a minute bunch of grapes. As she toyed with this, Madame closed her eyes and concentrated on the sensation, her breathing rapid and her legs trembling. To give herself better access, she hooked one leg up over the arm of the chair, knowing that the sight of her – open and vulnerable – would push Valerian to the limits of his endurance.

'Or perhaps you would prefer to hear about this afternoon in the woods, when the masked man bent me forward and pushed my face into your delicious cousin. He opened me from behind and took me savagely, his cock wide and splendid as it stretched me, before thrusting his finger into my arsehole and twisting it until I cried out. I swear, Valerian, he was almost as good as you.'

She pouted her thin, purple-stained lips and leant forward, interested to gauge his reaction. As she could have predicted, his face flushed a dark angry red and the veins in his neck stood proud, bulging lividly above the soft white collar of his shirt.

'No one is as good as me,' he snarled.

'I said almost, my love. Almost.' Her voice was soothing now, soft and maternal; she beckoned him to her. He fell forward on to her lap, and she cradled his head against her breast, her fingers stroking his hair.

'No one could ever be as good as you, Valerian,' she whispered. 'Unless, of course, you had a brother.'

'My brother is dead!' He jerked out of her arms, his eyes black and malicious as he stared at her. 'Don't you ever forget that. He'll never be better than me again and I'll prove it!'

'Show me,' hissed Madame, her eyes glittering, her breasts jutting out and her sex suddenly full and heavy. She loved Valerian when he was roused with fury. His rages were always the most potent aphrodisiac, and she rarely missed an opportunity to provoke him. The ancient rivalry between Valerian and his late brother was a newly discovered vice, and she decided to use it to push his prowess to the limits. 'Show me how much better you can be. Would he do this? Or this?' Her hands moved swiftly from her breasts to her sex, and she used her fingers as if they were a man's penis, hard and stiff against her swelling skin.

Valerian gave a low, throaty groan, the sound of an animal that had been teased beyond all tolerance. He lunged forward, gripping her knees and pushing her back so that her spine hit the chair with a crack. She laughed mirthlessly, her eyes goading him, and her hands fending him off as he struggled to grasp her wrists and pin them forcefully down on the armrests.

'Oh, he'd be stronger than that,' she taunted him.

'He'd overpower me quickly and pin me down to take me: rough and totally in control. He wouldn't care for my pleasure, only his own.'

Valerian stood up, resting his booted foot between her legs at the front of the chair. His mouth curled with distaste, and his hand shot out and grasped a handful of her hair at the top of her head, pulling her upright and curving her body forward so that her sex was jammed painfully against the hard toe of his shiny leather boot. He shook her by the hair, his eyes black and burning, and she felt herself sucked into their bottomless depths as she stared back at him. His mouth came down hard on hers and he ground her lips with his own, his teeth bruising and tearing as if he would devour her mouth. She thrilled at his savagery, her heart pumping and the blood swishing in her ears as she eagerly kissed him back.

Gasping, he jerked his mouth from hers and wiped it with the back of his hand before tearing at the fine lawn of his shirt. The front gave with a loud rending sound which seemed to split the air around them, and he used the pieces to bind her wrists and pull her arms taut above her head, standing on the chair between her legs to tie the ends tightly to a hook set in the beam above them. He dropped back down and stood still for a moment, his upper lip curved in a leering smile.

'Is this the best you can do?' asked Madame, her sex swelling into the hole carved in the seat of the chair, her arms stretched painfully up above her head. 'If your brother were alive, he would have had me by now. I'd be screaming for more and he'd know how to give it to me. You're just a pale shadow of him, that's all you've ever been: that's why –'

'Shut up! Shut up, or I'll make you.' Valerian's hand cracked across her face. His signet ring caught her jaw and she winced, pain sending fresh waves of arousal shooting through her taut body. The look of tortured suffering which clouded his face made a secret frisson of pleasure spiral up her legs, and she curled her toes in anticipation, widening her knees and thrusting her sex forward to show him how ready she was. She could feel the slickness between her thighs, smell the spiciness of her own vibrant scent, and she felt suddenly desperate for his touch – any touch – any satisfaction – as long as it was hard and fast.

Valerian turned and strode away from her, and she mewed with frustration, thinking for a moment that he intended to abandon her. He reached the door and turned the key in the lock, then jerked it out and carried it back to where she sat. His fingers caressed the forged iron key momentarily, then he reached down and prised her sex open before pressing the cold key to her clitoris. She bucked under the pressure and he laughed, a low and malevolent sound, then took one of the torn remnants of his shirt from the floor and bound her, winding the fabric strip around her sex and strapping the icy metal to her. She writhed a little as the narrow, cold key pressed unbearably against her, then she whimpered as he kissed her again, hard and demanding, his tongue probing her mouth and throat until she gagged.

He tore his lips from hers, and dropped to the floor out of her line of vision; she half-closed her eyes, tilted her head back, and waited for the next barrage of cruel sensation to hit her. She could see his long black boots stretched out on the amethyst rug, his toes pointing upward as was the huge bulge in his breeches. She longed to lean forward and grasp him there, to squeeze and knead. But her hands, bound to the beam above, kept her still and in position.

She waited, then jumped as if she had been burnt. Something warm, wet, and soft probed her from below, through the hole in the seat. She squirmed with pleasure, part of her wanting to evade, and part of her needing to press herself down on the circling wetness.

It was his tongue. Long and rigid, he pressed it around her from below, easing it between the engorged folds of her sex, then giving long deliberate strokes to the fleshy grooves. She felt his forefinger penetrate her, and she sighed, tightening herself on to the length of his probing finger; he introduced a second finger, then a third, while his tongue played with the golden ring that pierced her. The combination of soft and hard, stroking and penetrating, cold key and warm breath, made her quiver, and she thought that she would die if he did not fill her. A slick of her musky juice eased his passage, and she sensed a fourth finger stretch her; she moaned, and exhorted him in a low voice to take care. He ignored her, pushing further in, the ring taut now against her full flesh, and she heard him speak through a haze of painful pleasure.

'I'm using my whole hand. He wouldn't do that to you; he wouldn't fill you. I know what you like. Only I know what you desire. Say it. Say you love only me. Say that no other can satisfy you as I can. Tell me the truth: that I'm the best.'

'No,' she gasped, unbearable ecstasy filling her body and tightening her swollen sex on to his hand. 'No. He would do better. You have no imagination. I am nowhere near my climax.'

'God's blood, I'll make you say it!' His other hand reached up, and she felt the sting of his palm as he slapped the cheeks of her arse. His fingers continued to work inside her, filling her to the brim with pleasure, but then a new, teasing sensation opened her, and she felt his tongue prepare the way for his other hand.

She was as full as she could be, her sex wide open and her clitoris throbbing beneath the key, when she felt his thumb ease and twist into her anus. She tried to close against it, sure that she could not accommodate more, but he pushed beyond the tightness of her sphincter, aiming upward and inward until she could feel his fingers rubbing his thumb through the membrane that separated her there. He moved his hands separately, one going inward as the other eased outward, and she felt herself relinquish control and let go, her body turned to water, to cream, to burning oil as she came, hard, on to his hands. He was instantly still, just pressing up, while she rocked and quaked on the chair, a guttural cry wrenched from the depths of her body.

Almost before she had finished, he slid his hands out of her and came up between her legs, his face flushed and his breathing rapid. He knelt before her, then stood to release the bindings that stretched her up. Her arms felt useless, cramped, but he did not appear to know or care; he picked her up like a rag-doll and held her to him, his cock painfully hard against her pubis.

'You'd never come like that with anyone else but me, and you know it.' His lips tore at hers again, biting, licking, covering her mouth with his. He half-carried, half-dragged her to his desk and pushed her over it, face down. She laid a cheek on the cool surface, gently inhaling the waxy aroma of the polish, and thought of the flaxen-haired maid who polished the wood. She imagined her leaning over the desk, duster in hand, wearing her ever so slightly too-small dress, the fabric of which clung so closely to her breasts that the darkness of her nipples could almost been seen through the worn cotton. Madame closed her eyes and shuddered, her thoughts making her insides quiver with longing and loosening a fresh wash of sexual juice to slick her already creamy thighs.

'Oh yes, he would,' she ventured, when she had regained her equilibrium a little. 'No brother of yours would have stopped there. He would have fucked me senseless. Your brother would have fucked me until I hurt, until I begged him to stop, and even then he would have carried on. His stamina was probably greater than yours.'

She yelped as his hand slapped against the cheek of her vulnerable buttock, and she could feel the reddening imprint as he reached for an abandoned riding-crop which lay against a pile of leather-bound books. The plaited leather made a taut 'thwack' as it made contact with her skin, and she gripped the opposite edge of the desk, pain and arousal coursing through her veins like hot treacle. She ground her hips against the timber underneath her, sighing and rubbing her mouth on the desk, kissing the waxy polished sheen and dampening it with her hot breath.

'Come on, little brother. Give it your best shot,' she goaded him.

She heard him grind his teeth near her ear, and felt the weight of his body as he moulded himself to her. The scent of fresh sweat caught in her nostrils, and she could feel the slickness of his chest, the perspiration that beaded him as he pushed against her with unsuppressed rage. She expected him to take her conventionally, for his hot cock to slide in front of the ring that pierced her labia; so, when the burning head of his shaft probed between her buttocks, she felt the thrilling shock of his unpredictability.

One of his hands spread her cheeks wide, the other she could feel below, and she winced as the tip of his finger caught at the gold loop and pulled it downward, dragging and pulling her anus into a vertical oval. He rotated his hips, easing himself into her with the familiar screwing motion she had seen him employ on the countless young men of his acquaintance.

Excited and hurting all at once, she jutted herself back out at him, her hands leaving the slippery table-top to come behind and grip his thighs. She held her breath momentarily, then jerked herself backward as she pulled him into her.

'Little brother, little brother,' she taunted him, through gritted teeth. 'Show me who is the best of all. Oh, *nom de dieu*. Valerian. Fuck me hard. Do it harder than your brother could ever dream of!'

Their bodies heaved and writhed; she could feel the slap of his tight balls on the back of her thighs as he drove into her, his movements frenzied and irregular. He felt huge, stretching her almost unbearably, and she wished that he had filled her sex instead. Reaching down, she used her own fingers to fill herself, pushing into her wet, aching body and squeezing her eyes shut, her forehead bumping on the desk and her breasts pressed flat on the cool wood.

She felt him stiffen and strain against her, then the familiar lambent heat as his cock resonated and jerked with muscular little tugs deep inside her. She gave one last, desperate thrust with her fingers and felt herself teeter on the brink, her senses flailing in the infinite second before she fell, gasping, into orgasm, her body gripping his with invincible, rhythmic strength. She clutched at the desk with her free hand, her head twisting round and her lips seeking his.

He gripped her neck and pulled her to him, his mouth hard against the corner of her mouth, and his breath hot as it cut across hers.

'Is it me?' he whispered.

'It's always you,' she replied, her lips stroking his and her throat constricting at the sight of his flushed and beautiful profile.

'Sam? Sam, are you in there?' Lydia tapped on the wooden panel of the stable door. Shafts of afternoon sunlight cut diagonally through the open door and caught the motes of straw dust that danced in the warm air of the stable. Dandy Beau, the old mount who had belonged to William Hawkesworth, and whom Valerian was determined to send to the slaughterhouse, whickered, and Lydia gently stroked his velvety nose.

'Still here, old boy?' she murmured, nuzzling him with the tip of her nose. He smelt of hay and saddle polish, and she felt a sudden wave of nostalgia for the days when her Uncle William had ridden him every morning, and she and the boys had followed on their ponies.

Glancing around, she wondered where the groom was. She had a letter that she wanted him to deliver, and Sam was one of the few people that she trusted not to gossip. Fingering the wax seal, she studied the curving black ink that spelled the name of the solicitor, Mr Lavendale. He had promised help if she ever needed it, and she had decided to call in the favour and appeal to him on Drummond's behalf.

Shuffling and a barely audible moan sounded through the boards just above her head.

'Sam, are you up there?'

She moved away from the stalls and stood at the bottom of the ladder that led up to the hayloft. There was silence. Dandy Beau, behind her, shifted his huge hooves on the straw, and for a moment she thought that her ears had deceived her and that his movement was what she had heard.

There was another moan, this time accompanied by a long inhalation, and she was convinced that there was someone up in the loft. She tucked the letter into her pocket, kicked off her scarlet-heeled shoes, and began to climb the sturdy wooden ladder. At the top she paused for a moment to accustom her eyes to the gloom and pick a piece of straw from her hair.

At the far end of the wide loft, a half-open door let the sunlight in from a window beyond. The corner of a low pallet was just visible, and sitting on it was the groom, his shoulders hunched and his head bowed nearly to his knees. A loose shirt hung from his body in tatters, the yellow linen stained with the slowly spreading crimson of fresh blood; as she tiptoed nearer, Lydia could see that the wide muscular back was criss-crossed with inch-wide weals.

'Sam.' She spoke softly, partly because she did not want to startle him and partly because of the thick lump that had risen to her throat. He glanced up as she reached the door, and she rested her hand on the frame to steady herself. His deep brown eyes fixed on hers, and she read in them a combination of fear and helplessness mixed with an angry dash of vengeance. He did not move or speak, and Lydia pushed the door wider before sinking to her knees in front of him. As she took his huge calloused hands in hers, she was aware of the stable odour that clung to him: the leather and hay mingled with honest male sweat and the piquant tang of tobacco from the open pouch that lay on the blanket next to him.

'Did Valerian – Lord Hawkesworth, I mean – did he do this to you?'

'Aye,' murmured the groom, his auburn head dipped as if in shame. His shoulders heaved, and Lydia frowned, reaching up so that her hands lightly touched his powerful shoulders.

'Sam, look at me,' she said gently. 'Please. I am so sorry. My cousin is an animal with no respect for people or things. I apologise for his behaviour, and I will do my best to ensure that this never happens again.'

Her fingers slid under his chin and she tilted his face up. His eyes glowed like bronze coals, and his thick brown lashes shone with unshed tears. The pallor of his skin made the sprinkle of freckles prominent on the bent curve of his nose, and a muscle worked in his jaw as he met her gaze.

'Miss Lydia, you don't have to apologise. It weren't your fault. Everyone knows what the master's like, but it don't mean that we think any less of you. We only stay because of you, and the hope that Master Drummond might one day come home. Everything will be all right then.'

'Oh, Sam. If only that could be soon.' Remembering the letter, she thrust it into his hands. 'Take this into the town for me, would you? You would be helping me more than you know.' As he rose and turned away, she stood and touched his flailed skin lightly with one finger. 'Wait. Let me wash the blood from your back: those marks look sore, and they'll heal better if they're clean.'

When she returned with freshly drawn water, she saw that he had gone to stand near the open window; a twisting spiral of golden smoke rose from the pipe in his hand and was drawn by the current of air from the casement. On a low table beside him was a mug and a leather-bound bottle which Lydia uncorked. Sniffing it, she wrinkled her nose, and then slopped a generous amount of amber liquid into the mug.

'Here. Have some of this. It might help.'

He did not take the mug from her, merely stood very still and stared down at her. She was aware of how close to him she was standing, of the proximity of his bare torso and the scent of him that clung in her nostrils. She wondered whether she should step back, move away, but found that her legs would not do her bidding. He frowned, his brow creasing with a deep vertical cleft which mirrored that which divided his stubborn chin.

'I'm no coward,' he said.

'I know you're not. But it will hurt. Drink some.'

As he took the mug, the hard tips of his fingers grazed the back of her wrist and she jerked away, clasping one hand with the other as if it had been burnt. The sensation that flashed through her body at his touch was amazing, almost as if a closed fist had punched into her belly, and she stepped back as he moved, shocked by the strength of her own desire.

Sam, his strong face set and the frown still clouding his brow, sat heavily on the edge of the nearest mattress and slugged back the brandy. Lydia stirred herself from her contemplation of the way his thighs strained at the fabric of his rust-coloured breeches. She began to tear up one of the sheets, then refilled his cup. She took a mouthful herself before dipping the corner of one of the calico cloths into the bucket of cold water.

Drawing a lantern nearer, she inspected the groom's back and winced, almost able to feel the smarting of his skin. Valerian had given him a thorough beating: the pale, freckled skin was bright red and criss-crossed with countless lash marks beaded with blood.

His body recoiled as she touched the cold cloth to his back, his muscles flickering under the skin. He hunched forward, shoulders rounded and russet head dipped so that all she could see were the rugged cords of his neck and the clean stubble of his hairline. As her fingers moved tenderly over him, she became aware of a curious stillness in the warm, scented air of the hayloft, and she slowed down, wanting the moment to last as she cossetted the fragile skin of the youth on the bed beside her.

'Does that hurt?' she asked, deliberately pressing a hard seam into one of the raw wounds. Sam shuddered and jerked forward a little, then straightened himself and leant back, shaking his head. The straw mattress rustled underneath him, and Lydia leant forward, her fingers playing over the skin of his back from his shoulders down the tapering line of his ribs to his waist.

She could feel him shuddering, trembling under her touch, and she knew then that he had felt it too: that flash of tense desire when their hands had met accidentally. She knew that he wanted her, that he was hungry for her, that his trembling was as much that of lust as of pain from his wounds. It also came to her that he would not do anything about it, that he would not move first, for he was a servant, and she the lady of the house.

Her forefinger reached the firm waistband of his breeches and she let it rest there, dwelling on the rough texture of the fabric, as she tried to imagine the hard flesh beneath. Her heart was pumping quickly, her breathing a little more rapid than normal, and she tried to slow it down, to control herself. But it was no good: she was beyond control, and she knew it.

Placing both hands squarely on his shoulders, she raised herself to her knees on the mattress behind him, her silk-skirted gown whispering against the rough blankets. She placed her mouth very close to his ear and felt him tense his muscular frame beneath her, his body bent forward slightly under the firm pressure of her breasts, like a supple bow being drawn ready for the arrow. When her nose was almost touching his hair, she breathed softly into his ear and spoke.

'Sam,' she murmured. 'Sam, are you obedient to your master?'

'Yes, miss.'

'Are you obedient to your mistress?'

He did not reply, but she could feel the labouring of his breath as he steadied himself and absorbed the import of her words. He moved his head in a tiny dipping movement that she took to be affirmative.

'Look at me,' she whispered, her nose so close to his cheek that she could feel the scratch of the short bristles that stubbled his jaw and she closed her eyes, filling her senses with his animal smell and the warmth that emanated from his half-naked body.

She felt him shift on the mattress, his body twisting, and she kept her eyes closed as his hands gripped her waist and raised her up and over; over until she lay across his now supine body and their combined weight settled into the bed. His hands were tight on her hips now, and she could feel the rigidity of his thighs beneath hers and the smooth, hard flesh of his chest under the silky fabric of her bodice.

'I would never disobey you. I am your humble servant, and I would give my life for you, Miss Lydia.' His voice was hoarse, and she opened her eyes to look at him, to study the ruddy planes of his young face and trace the mobile curve of his bottom lip.

'I'm not asking for death, Sam. Only pleasure.' She dropped her mouth to his and felt a sense of glorious relief as his lips opened and she felt the warm touch of his tongue on hers. He tasted of liquor and tobacco, and she drank in his flavour as she kissed him, her lips questing his and her tongue seeking more as she felt his arms encircle her and his hands close over her.

They kissed for a long time, the mattress rustling under every tiny movement. The gentle breeze from the window gradually fanned Lydia's hair into tangled skeins which coiled and twisted like ebony serpents across the calico sheet. There were no words, only touch, and she felt her arousal like a hard shell in the pit of her stomach that abruptly cracked, falling open to reveal a molten gold yolk that trickled through her veins until it reached the farthest corners of her being.

She felt feverishly hot, then shiveringly cold; the tiny

hairs on the back of her neck lifted under the light touch of his fingers as he pulled her hair aside. She waited for him to unhook the fastenings at the back of her gown, to open it, to peel it back, to stroke her pale bare skin with the coarse tips of his workman's fingers. But he did nothing. Merely kissed her again and shifted beneath her.

She waited for him, silently begging him to undress her, but he did not move. His eyes were closed, and she raised herself on one elbow to study the shadow that his lashes cast across his cheeks. She was struck by his youth: he was younger than she was – eighteen, nineteen at the most. A sudden thought came to her in a rushing revelation.

'Sam, you have been with a woman before, haven't you?'

His eyes flickered open, deepest brown with wide black pupils that almost drowned her as she gazed into them. He blushed and frowned, his eyes dipping and a look of intense shyness colouring his face.

'No, I haven't, miss. I never have.'

Lydia was touched by his bashfulness; she stroked his hair and rested her forehead on his, forcing him to look up into her eyes.

'I'm surprised, I really am. I thought that stable-lads had the run of every wench in town. Why not you?'

'Well, there aren't many willing ones out here at Hawkesworth. The maids in the house don't care for us on the outside, so that only leaves ancient Tessie in the dairy, and I don't quite . . .'

'No, I can imagine,' agreed Lydia, smiling. Her hands slid between their conjoined bodies until she felt the hard curve of his cock beneath the buckskin front of his breeches.

'So, no girl has ever done this to you?' She arched one eyebrow enquiringly. He shook his head, a dark flush creeping up his neck accompanied by a sharp intake of breath. His eyes anchored hers, and she felt herself tremble a little as the thought of untouched flesh finally sank home.

Pushing herself away from him, she sat astride, arranging her petticoats high around her legs so that he could see the pearliness of both thighs above the opaque blue of her stockings. Her knees were tight on his ribs, and beneath the curve of her buttocks she could feel his ramrod stiffness as his cock shifted inside his trousers.

'Oh, Sam. You're in for a treat,' she breathed, her fingers smoothing over the satin of his chest to dwell on the hardening discs of his brown nipples. His hands twisted out from beneath the drifting silk of her skirts and he gripped her wrists, stilling her and pulling her forward slightly.

'This isn't right,' he said. 'You shouldn't do this. Not with me.'

'Oh yes, I should. I want to. Just relax and it will be all right.'

'But, miss –'

'No buts, Sam. I know you want this as much as I do. Don't you? Or are you trying to tell me that you don't like me? Aren't I beautiful enough? Perhaps you wanted someone better for your first time?'

'Someone better?' He snorted derisively. 'You're the most beautiful lady I've ever set eyes on, but a lady is what you are, miss, and –'

'And a man is what you are, Sam. So let's stop talking and find out just what kind of a man you can be.'

Her lips were hard on his this time, partly to silence him and partly because she could wait no longer. The feel of his muscular body underneath her was almost unbearably sweet. She pulled his tongue into her mouth as she ground herself on to him. His cock jerked in reply, the hardness of his erection straining at the fabric that separated them; Lydia twisted her hands downward and wrestled with his buttons until she felt the warmth of his exposed skin. Easing her body back, she pulled her mouth from his and sat up to look at him.

He was big: long and hard with gorgeous twisting

veins and two tight balls that seemed to want to fight with each other for proximity to the base of his cock. He curved up and out of his fly with the strength and vigour of a young tree, and it was all Lydia could do to stop herself from falling on to him and taking him in her mouth then and there, but the agonised expression on his face told her how near the edge he was. Having a girl so close, and having her put her hand on him and pull his cock out of his breeches was the nearest to sexual ecstasy that the lad had ever been; Lydia decided to tread carefully for fear of having him come too soon. She wanted pleasure, too.

'Help me,' she said, sitting back and arcing her leg over and away.

She unlaced her stays, guiding his fingers to the places that needed his touch and smiling at the waves of awed wonder that broke across his face at the baring of each new piece of female flesh. The pads of his thumbs were coarse on her skin, and the callouses teased her breasts as she closed her hands around his and made him cup her, coaxing his thumbs up and over her nipples.

His touch was tentative at first, his eyes timid and his handling of her wary, but as he saw her pleasure and felt the puckering of her skin under his touch, he became more sure. Lydia found his movements inexperienced but sweet, his fingers careful but delicious as they moved down to loosen her skirts.

'Here, let me.' She stood up to let the cascade of silk and linen drop to the floor, and she saw him draw a deep breath, his hand going involuntarily to his cock. He stroked himself, and as she watched his movements, Lydia felt a welcoming rush of syrupy juice slick her insides and impatience to possess him seized her.

She moved to the edge of the bed, the late afternoon sun gilding the glossy new hairs that curled around her sex. She could feel the warmth on her naked back and relished the last moment before she conquered the youth on the bed. Then she raised one leg and swung it over his hips.

'Wait, miss. I don't think this is right. We shouldn't.' She heard his voice as if it came from a far-off place, and she frowned down at him. She could feel the heat rising from his body, the febrile warmth of his straining cock. She placed the flat of her hand against his chest and pushed him into the straw mattress.

'Shut up, Sam.'

She crested him, her warm sex unfurling as she hovered, butterfly-like, over his straining helmet. She watched him through half-closed eyes, a hint of emerald glinting between her thick lashes as she drank in the sight of the vanquished stable-boy. He lay flat against the calico sheeting, his big hands thrown wide and his head tilting, so that his strong chin jutted up as if he would kiss the lath ceiling. His Adam's apple bobbed with each swallow of the air that he gulped, and Lydia could feel by the tense stillness of his hips that he would come if she moved so much as a muscle.

'How does that feel?' she crooned, her fingers drifting lightly over his taut stomach.

He groaned and shook his head, unable to speak, but she could feel him under her, could feel the contraction of his lean buttocks as he eased himself up into her with tiny jerks, quick, slow, gasping and gritting his teeth. Leaning forward until the tips of her pointed nipples brushed lusciously against the satin of his hairless young chest, she placed her mouth close to his ear.

'Let it go. Let it go, Sam. We can do it again later.'

With a groan of long suppressed ardour, he swung his hands round to grasp her hips and hold her still while he thrust himself upward. She felt her sex anoint his shaft as she sank on to him, felt her lips wrap tightly around his length until the hard grind of his balls pressed against the gentle curve of her buttocks. With him deep inside her, she held her breath, her sex fluttering on to him and then losing him as he withdrew slightly.

He was clumsy, his fingers knotted first into her hair and then white-knuckling as he slipped down to grip her thighs with iron hardness. His movements seemed unpredictable: one thrust, then two, then a long pause as he grunted and mouthed her earlobe. Then fast, fast, fast, in a quick succession of feverish, frantic jerks that culminated in a long, hot leap of his cock as he pushed hard into her, almost hurting her as he buried himself deeply, practically punching himself into her womb. Surprised, Lydia felt a shimmering release strum along her spine and open over her hips in thick, rippling waves which resonated on to his suddenly still cock.

He tilted her chin and gazed into her face, wonder and uncertainty lightening the brown of his eyes to an amber clarity.

'Was that the same for you? Did you feel that too?' He wound his burly arms around her body and crushed her to him, his mouth bruising hers with a desperate, hungry kiss. When he was still, she let her tongue coast over his face with a myriad of tiny licks before tucking her head under his chin and resting her cheek on his chest.

She felt a contented warmth steal through her limbs and smiled, her fingers sliding around and beneath him to wedge tightly in the fold of his neat buttocks. She felt sensual and languid, satisfied and free, yet hungry for more, and she ground her sex on to the crisp slickness of his pubis in a promise of further pleasure.

As she dozed, the reason that had sent her to seek Sam in the first place shot unbidden to the forefront of her mind. She sat up and prodded the sleeping figure below her.

'The letter,' she said. 'Sam, will you take the letter now? It must reach Mr Lavendale before he closes his business for the day. Will you go? I'll come back here later, but please go now.'

Chapter Thirteen

When she tiptoed through the yard in the dark of night, Lydia thought that she would find Sam alone, and that he would have found a pretext to send his fellow groom away. She was surprised to find, when she pushed open the door to the stable, that two young men awaited her. One lounged on a pile of soft, fragrant hay, his familiar body and auburn hair lit by the soft glow of a lamp. The other, tall and dark with the slender coltishness of youth, sat on a bale, tentatively chewing his thumb. He started when she entered and glanced sidelong at his friend, who had the grace to look slightly abashed.

'Evening, Sam. Evening, Jemmy.' She leant against the closed door and tucked her hands behind her in the curve of her back. She watched them covertly from the shade of her lashes for a few moments. Sam was the first to rise: he dropped nimbly from the bale of straw and approached her slowly, caution making his steps hesitant.

'Miss Lydia,' he began, stopping just in front of Jemmy, so that the light was interrupted and the other boy was cast into darkness. 'I thought that we could show Jem what we did. He's never done it either, and if you could just show him, he'd be very happy and grateful.'

'Are you mad?' Lydia's imperious voice cut across the young man's speech, sounding like her cousin even to her own ears. She drew herself up to her full height, very aware that even on tiptoes she was a full head shorter than Sam; if he chose to, he could force her to submit, although she imagined that he wouldn't have the courage or brains to do that. 'If you imagine for one moment that I have come here to give myself to you in full view of another stable-hand, then you are very much mistaken. Jemmy, leave us, please.'

She stepped forward into the circle of light thrown by the lantern and placed both hands on her hips. One foot tapped impatiently on the lightly strawed wooden floor, and she tipped her chin upward to give herself an authoritative air. Sam frowned and thrust his big hands deep into the pockets of his breeches; his face was red and his russet head drooped a little as he studied the floor.

Behind him Jemmy stood up, uncurling his long slim body from the pile of loose hay on which he had been lounging. Lydia could not see his face clearly because of the shock of silky brown hair that flopped over one eye, but she could see that he was deeply embarrassed and, if it was possible, even redder in the cheeks than Sam. He glanced towards her, one long brown hand sweeping his hair back over his head, and Lydia was struck by the innocent disappointment that lurked in the depths of his deep blue eyes. He gave her a mischievous half-grin and shrugged before turning to go.

Lydia watched him walk away, fascinated by the movement of his long legs as he stepped over the obstacles that littered the floor of the stable. She took a step forward and brushed against Sam, suddenly acutely aware of the warmth of his body and the evocative smell of saddle polish and tobacco that reminded her so forcibly of events that afternoon.

She felt a constriction in her throat and a sudden pull at her sex which belied her previous words of indignation and hauteur. Making a sudden decision, she

216

reached out to take Sam's hand, enjoying the rough feel of his palm against her own skin, and then she called to Jemmy as he disappeared into the darkness at the back of the stable.

'Jemmy! Wait! I was too hasty. If you can find some way of barring this door so that we are not disturbed, then I would like you to stay.'

The sudden tightening of Sam's hand on hers was small but telling, and as Jemmy bounded back into the circle of light, looking for all the world like a delighted and energetic puppy, Lydia found herself laughing with excitement and anticipation. Jemmy laughed too, his eyes crinkling at the corners, as he grasped her other hand, and between them the two stable-lads drew her towards the fragrant mound of piled hay.

'I think I shall bind you, my sweet.' Madame pressed her nose to Valerian's, her mouth a wide smile, her eyes hard and calculating. 'And blindfold you, I believe. Then you will have only your ears and your imagination to give you clues.'

Her mouth crushed his in a hungry kiss and Valerian moaned against her lips, his fingers fumbling feverishly at the fastening of her long robe. She slapped his hand away and encircled his wrist with her own, leading him to the bed. Pushing and pulling at his limbs, she arranged him in the widely spread position she desired. He lay on the slippery sheets, his skin luminous and pale against the harsh black and scarlet satin.

She had stretched his arms far above his head and manacled his wrists to the bedposts, while his legs had been pulled wide apart, his ankles and feet encased in yards of soft black leather ribbon which she had wound around the legs of the bed at the foot.

'I want to see you,' he protested, as she advanced with a trailing length of silk in one hand.

'Well, I don't want you to see me,' she replied. 'Look now, then. One last glimpse to fuel your appetite, and then I shall blind you.'

217

She opened her robe and raised one eyebrow. He gazed at her, his eyes devouring her from neck to toe, and she was gratified to see the sudden twitch of his erection as it strained towards his belly. When she had blindfolded him, she ran her hands down the length of his body, feeling the shiver of his muscles and the tension through his legs. Then she stood above his feet, dipped her head, and fastened her lips around his toe, sucking and rubbing the underside with her tongue. He groaned, his head dropping to one side and his fingers cramping into tight fists.

'That was pleasure,' murmured Madame. 'Now feel pain.'

She reached into her pocket and placed two heavy golden clamps on his thighs. She slid them slowly across his skin until she saw his balls tighten at the approach of the cold metal. He cried aloud as she fastened the clamps to his sac, the weight of the gold dragging and pulling at the tender skin, but his cock seemed to grow and swell while his hips thrust upward as if seeking more.

'Patience, *cheri*,' she whispered. 'This is only the beginning.'

The bracket of the piping grated ominously against stone, and Drummond paused in his climb. Below him shadows fell away, the depth of four or five men, to the level of the rose beds, and he knew that if he fell that far he would be injured or even killed.

Cussing softly under his breath, he eased himself up a little farther until Lydia's window-ledge was within reach. He was fairly certain that the room was empty, although it was past midnight, because he had stood on the path below for what seemed like an age, tossing pebbles up against the glass, but she had not come to the window.

'Either she's not there, or she's a very heavy sleeper,' he murmured to himself, grunting slightly as he used the sill to heave himself up to a sitting position. His legs dangled over the side and the ledge was precariously narrow, but he could see in by a combination of twisting and leaning sideways. The leather of his gloves creaked in the cool night air as he reached up and rubbed at the panes with the flat of his hand.

The room was dark: only a slight glow from the grate lit the hearth-rug and a chair nearby. On the far wall he could just make out the big bed, partly curtained against the chill of the night, and the long pale bolster that had fallen to the floor beside the night-stand. He adjusted the black velvet mask he wore, pressed his nose to the glass and tried to see whether the humped shape just visible was Lydia, or merely blankets and linen heaped up. He knocked gingerly on the panes and waited, but there was no movement, no shift in the shape on the bed.

He debated whether to slide back down the piping and trudge through the forest to his warm mattress. As he wiped his face with the back of his gloved hand, he could feel the bristles of his unshaven chin even through the tough leather; he needed a shave, and a bath. The initial excitement of living in the woods was beginning to pall. He made his decision: Lydia, and hot water.

Twisting lithely, he then held his scarf against the window and, with his fist bunched, brought the heel of his big hand hard against the leaded glass. There was a tinkle as the broken bits scattered on the timbered floor below, then silence.

The room was warm and fragrant as he strode to the fireplace to light a taper. He set it on the nearby table and covered the room with two strides, one hand reaching out and tearing back the damask curtain to reveal a rumpled but very empty bed. A chemise lay across the pillow, and he scooped it up, holding the soft fabric to his face to inhale the lingering scent of Lydia's body: jasmine and rose-petals simmered in his nostrils and he felt his chest tighten as a sensuous heat spread across his lower belly.

Where was she?

* * *

219

The candles were burning low, some guttering in the iron sconces, but neither Madame or Valerian noticed. Valerian, still blindfolded and bound, was in the throes of orgasm, his cock twitching against his belly while Madame milked him with one hand. She had encased his hard length in a spiral of pearls, her own beads, and was using this to rub and manipulate him to his climax.

When he was spent, she leant over his face, her rouged lips almost close enough to kiss his cheek.

'I think you deserve a reward, my love,' she whispered. 'I shall go and awaken your delectable cousin. Would you like that?'

The lantern flickered, and Lydia stared down into the luminous brown eyes of the youth who knelt before her. His auburn head was tilted back, but the tip of his tongue, and his nose, were buried in the scented folds of her sex. She inhaled deeply, heat flickering through her veins and the beginnings of true pleasure building and growing towards the devouring abandon that she knew was within her grasp. Sam's large hands gripped her naked hips, and she could see in the lamplight the difference between his sun-toughened flesh and the pale, lustrous sheen of her own skin.

She tipped her head back until she felt the sweep of her long hair brush lightly across the curve of her buttocks. When she felt it grasped by another hand, she knew that Jem had taken a silken hank and was winding it around his slender wrist, tighter and tighter until she could no longer raise her head, and she was captive. Caught between two young men whose only desire seemed to be to give her blissful, delicious pleasure.

She felt Jemmy's other hand slide up her back, his fingertips soft and sensual as they stroked and kneaded along her spine to the nape of her neck and back down to the crescent of her bottom. His fingers drifted, feather-light and barely touching, to the neat little parting between her buttocks, and followed the line down and under. She pressed herself back out towards the seeking hand, arching her back and sighing deeply. Sam, momentarily denied the honey that bathed his lips, pulled her forward again and pushed his tongue more firmly across her swollen flesh, until she felt a sob well up from the depths of her being.

'Jemmy ... push your finger into me. Put your hand under me and find where Sam is ... please!'

Two long and slender fingers trembled between her legs, Jem's inexperience making him hesitate against the warm, wet folds, unsure of his ground, uncertain of Lydia's intent. She murmured, begging him, and felt utter, blissful relief as Sam's hands parted her thighs a little and cupped Jem's hands, guiding them, teaching them, much as she had shown him earlier that day.

Jemmy's fingers were long, filling her completely, and she could feel the fascinating combination of his slippery, petal-soft hands working into her, aided by the coarse hardness of the callouses on Sam's thumbs. She could feel the one urging the other, giving motion to Jem's nervous stillness, and she sighed again as she felt the two pairs of fingers work together, sliding inward, out, and then in again, moving together in a gliding rhythm to the accompanying sound of her own juicy arousal.

She reached sideways until she felt the hard beam of one of the stalls beneath her hands, and she gripped it, steadying herself as she felt the rising sweep of languor course through her body. A fire seemed to light up her fingertips, burn her scalp, and she moaned out loud, perspiration sheening her body like dawn dew, as the motion of the two stable-hands brought her to the brink of release. The smell of her own body, mingled with the soft, fragrant hay and the scent of the two healthy young men whose muscular bodies glistened below her, tipped her, spiralling, into a glorious, gasping, full-bodied shudder.

The door creaked a little as it swung open, and Drummond leapt back and behind it, flattening himself against the wall. A small dark shape, satin robe glistening in the dim light from the single taper, stepped into the room.

'Lydia! Thank God!' Drummond caught her and pulled her into his arms, his masked face dipping to bury his nose in the unbound hair that covered her shoulders.

'What a pleasant surprise.' The voice was foreign, as was the scent that clung to the hair which clouded around his face. Drummond jumped back, dropping the woman and spinning her round. The shoulders beneath his strong hands were thin, narrow blades of bone that seemed to cut through the rich fabric of the negligee. Raising his eyes to her face, he saw beautiful porcelain skin and glass-pale eyes that seemed to burn with excitement and intensity.

It was Madame de Chaillot.

'Why! It's the gentleman thief,' she purred, stepping forward so that the toes of her slippers touched the tips of his postilion boots. 'Are you here to rob us, or have you come seeking intimate knowledge of Miss Lydia's bedchamber?'

'Where is she?' demanded Drummond, easing back to escape her heady scent. He felt the wall, cold and firm, against the back of his coat as he stared down at her, frowning at the determination which hardened the planes of her oval face. She smiled, a cat-like curving of her lips which hardly reached her cool eyes.

'Where is who?' she sighed, one hand reaching up to lie flat against the coarse linen of his shirt-front. Drummond was disturbed by her nearness: the smell of her reminded him of their previous, memorably sensual, encounter in the woods, and he felt himself harden, blood rushing through his veins to concentrate in his groin and thighs.

'You know who,' he said, trapping her hand beneath his glove, for it had begun to wander towards the bare skin of his chest which showed through the unbuttoned portion of his shirt.

'I have no idea where she is. I heard the sound of glass breaking and came to see if she needed my assistance. Instead I found you, the masked marauder.'

Madame leant close to him, her face upturned and her eyes narrowed. He could feel the sleek front of her robe as she pressed her body against him, her free hand sliding up around his neck and pulling his face down to hers. He tried to resist, but his nostrils were full of her smell and he could feel her pulse beating rapidly against his gloved thumb. When her lips touched his, he groaned and crushed her body against his chest, sinking his mouth to hers and devouring her with big, hungry movements.

He felt her hands flutter against him, pushing back his thick coat and letting it drop to the floor before tearing at the leather front of his waistcoat. He pulled his arms free and tossed the garment aside, pausing only to grasp her wrists and pull her to him once more. She seemed to thrill under the hurried roughness of his caresses, her body quivering against him and her mouth trembling with half-suppressed excitement as he bent her backward and fastened his lips to her neck.

His eye was caught by a flash of white on the floorboards near the bed: the drifting linen of Lydia's discarded nightgown. It was as if a cold douche had been thrown over his head, icy trickles running down his neck under his loose shirt. He thrust Madame from him, cursing as he untangled himself from her fingers. She did not open her eyes, merely clung to him, her head extended and her throat pulsing as she waited for more kisses. He shook her lightly until her eyes snapped open.

'Where's Lydia?' he said, his jaw hardening and his fingers biting into her upper arms. She did not reply at first, the surprise in her face slowly replaced by a spiteful narrowing of lips and eyes.

'I don't know, and what's more, I don't care!' she spat, reaching out to grasp his shirt-front and jerk him towards her. Her other hand went to his breeches and she outlined his cock with her palm. 'I want this, gentleman thief. You liked it last time, in the woods, and so did I. Give me that pleasure again. Now. Come here.' Her tone became almost wheedling and she snuggled against his chest, her face softening again. He paused, torn, as she dipped her head and rubbed her soft hair against the bristle of his chin. 'You want to, *cheri*. You know you do. And Lydia, the poor fool, will never know.'

Hearing her speak Lydia's name so carelessly made Drummond feel an intense anger. He thrust her away from him again, his face flushing. He heard her swear in her native tongue and watched her bristle, hands on hips, as she faced him and he saw how cold her eyes seemed, how thin and mean her lips were. All his desire for her fled, drained away, replaced by a slow-burning fury.

'I want to see Lydia,' he said, trying to stay calm and reasonable.

'I want! I want? What about what I want?' demanded Madame. 'I want you to fuck me, you idiot. Look! How can you refuse? No one ever refuses me!'

She ripped the ribbons which closed the front of her dark negligee and dropped it to the floor. In spite of himself, Drummond felt a pull at his guts. She was beautiful: a small, pale frond that glowed in the soft light, her body cinched by a leather corset with impossibly tight lacing, which pinched her waist to a handspan size and swelled above and below to encase her narrow hips and cup the buds of her breasts. Her nipples were huge and stuck out from her body like succulent fruit. As if she knew that these were one of her best assets, Madame raised her hand and toyed with one, pulling and squeezing, teasing it until it was red and hard and as long as her thumb. Drummond swallowed.

'Where is she?' he repeated hoarsely.

Madame's hand left her breast and slid down, over the lacing and leather that honed her figure to hourglass perfection, towards the creamy flesh at the tops of her thighs. Her legs were encased in dark stockings which glimmered slightly, and she ran her fingers lightly over the woven tops, sliding one finger inside to rest momentarily between the silken fabric and her skin, before pressing upward so that both hands met at her sex.

She cupped herself, framing her glossy curls with her flower-like hands and squeezing inward so that her sex puckered up, juicy and inviting.

Drummond caught a tang of her musky scent and shook his head as if to clear it.

'I want to see Lydia,' he said, repeating it like a mantra to protect him against the temptation that was being offered so lasciviously in front of him. Madame raised one eyebrow, her lips curling contemptuously.

'Your sweet Lydia is probably out fucking. Perhaps being tupped by one of her cousin's lusty henchmen. I forget which is her favourite now. Is it the Norseman? Or is it the Negro? Perhaps she told you?'

Drummond gave a roar and pushed her aside, blundering forward to sweep up the nightgown from the floor. He brandished it at Madame.

'You lying whore!' he shouted. 'Where is she? What have you done with her?'

'Oh, she's the whore.' Madame smiled sweetly. 'But I think they're so much more exciting that way, aren't they? Now are you going to have me or not?'

Drummond gazed at her: he felt revolted now by the sight that had previously seemed so deliciously inviting. He saw her fingers delve quickly inside herself and watched as she withdrew them, her eyelids flickering closed with pleasure, before she sank them knuckle-deep again.

'Get out,' he said, with quiet loathing.

Her eyes opened and she met his look with one of pure venom.

'You'll regret this, gentleman thief.'

She picked up her robe and slammed the door behind her.

* * *

225

Lydia slid her lips along the length of the hard cock, her mouth rounded and her tongue flat. He tasted wonderful, like a delicious meal that she could eat over and over again until she was sated, blown with her own gluttony. His hands slipped around the crown of her head and pulled her into him a little more, his slender fingers looping into the loose strands of ebony silk and winding them between his knuckles, playing with her. Above her, she could see the curve of his jaw, the shadow of his young beard, and as he smiled she caught a sparkle of his white teeth between full, pink lips.

'Oh, that's good,' he sighed. 'Your mouth feels so . . . you're so warm, so nice.'

She had slipped all the way to the tip, and then moved to lap her tongue along the underside. He tasted different there, salty, and she savoured him, giving him long licks until she reached the tightness of his balls. She drew them into her mouth until they both lay, warm and slightly fuzzy, against her palate, then she closed her lips and gave a small suck. He gasped, jerking his hips with the intensity of the sensation.

'Christ, woman. Be careful, I might – well, you know.'

'He means that sometimes, when he thinks I'm asleep and the blankets move fast over his hand, he spurts some spunk and that it might not be polite to do it near you.' Sam chuckled, his breath warm on Lydia's back as he nestled up behind her.

'All right, all right,' protested Jem, blushing to the roots of his hair. 'You do it too: I've heard you in the dark, batting against the sheets.'

Lydia sat back, smiling and curving her fingers around Jem's swollen, straining length.

'Do you ever do it together?' she asked. 'At the same time, I mean. I think if I heard someone doing that in the bed next to me, I'd be tempted to go along with it and enjoy myself too.'

The silence that followed, and the sheepish way that Jem glanced at Sam, suggested to her that they had. The thought excited her, and she leant forward to take the swollen head of Jemmy's cock between her lips again. As she sucked, she heard a rustle in the hay and stopped to watch as Sam lifted up her corset and petticoats and gestured to Jem.

She sat back, stroking the soft underside of her thighs as Sam laced Jem into the corset, fumbling a little and concentrating hard on the eyelets as he threaded the lacing and pulled it tight. Next he set the silken drift of white petticoat around Jem's lean hips and fastened it, propping the split open around the rearing cock which brushed against his hand.

Lydia watched, fascinated, hardly daring to breathe, as Sam hesitated, then caught the swinging rod in his fist and stroked it with clumsy reverence. He was shorter than Jem, his auburn head grazing Jem's ear, but it was only a moment before he turned his face up and caught Jem's soft pink lips with his own. Lydia moaned softly, her heart swelling as if it would burst, and a beating, rushing sound echoed in her ears. She stood up and fumbled in the pocket of her discarded skirt for a moment, before pressing herself against the two hard bodies.

Their arms entwined around her, drawing her into their charmed circle, and she felt Sam's lips press against her temple and Jem's hand slide up the curve of her back. She opened the tiny pot of cochineal that she had retrieved from her pocket, and, with a trembling finger, applied a slick of crimson to Jemmy's mouth. He smiled at her, looking for all the world like a beautiful painted doll, and she rose up on to the tips of her toes to kiss him, thrilling at the taste of the crimson salve and the unaccustomed sensation of a hard male mouth made slippery with a woman's make-up.

Sam had watched her with interest and unconcealed excitement. When she drew back from kissing Jem, he replaced her mouth with his own, his lips firm and open. Lydia, only inches away, could see Jemmy's scarlet pout soften and his tongue catch at Sam's. She was almost overcome with lust, and leant forward again to join her own mouth to theirs, feeling them welcome her with tiny licks and sucks, and she knew she was drowning in sensual pleasure, sinking into delirium as their strong arms clasped her in a muscular embrace.

She felt herself being moved by Sam's big hands. He pushed her to her knees and coaxed her head forward until she took Jem into her hot mouth again, her hands clasping the softness of the petticoats that covered his strong thighs. She felt her hips being eased back, her body arched until she was open and ready; then she heard Jem groan as he watched Sam sink down behind her. His knees eased hers apart and she felt his fingers on her buttocks, firmly prising her open. She stuck her bottom out farther to welcome him in. At first he eased her with long languorous strokes of his fingers until she was wet and creamy, a trail of juice slicking her thighs and his palm. She was so aroused that she felt like screaming, crying out, but her mouth was so full of the seashell taste of Jem that she could not – would not – because she did not want to leave this feast of cock. Instead, she stayed still, shivering under Sam's suddenly expert handling of her body.

He had come a long way from the tentative virgin boy of that afternoon, she decided, as his hand slid around her belly and his fingers delved into the softness of her sex to seek and stroke the tight little bud that protruded there. She arched her back further, pleasure flooding through her and filling her from toes to scalp with tingling, bubbling bliss.

When she had coated his fingers, and her pleasure had been elevated to an almost unbearable level, she felt Sam change his position behind her. He rested the burning head of his shaft against her and she felt herself tighten under the sudden hot contact.

'Please, sweet love. Please let me in.' His voice was soft and humble, his tone filled with suppressed lust. She felt her sex soften and pushed herself out against him.

'Thank you. Oh, that feels so good. You're beautiful, you feel so tight and creamy on me.'

He gave a moan as he pushed in, easing his width into her, and she was motionless for a moment. Waiting. Afraid to close her mouth on to Jemmy for the moment. When she felt him all the way in, his cock stretching her impossibly wide, she took Jem in her hand and eased him back between her lips, feeling totally at home, utterly fulfilled, as Sam began to move behind her and Jemmy's hips contracted and pushed his hardness to the back of her throat.

She could not keep still, could not wait passively for Sam to get his rhythm and take her. She moved herself, easing back and forth on to him in short, compact strokes; she squeezed him, milking him with her muscular sex while he gasped and grunted and held her hips, one hand still framing her sex from the front. The sensations were hot and hard, gripping at her insides and making her breath hard and fast, her nostrils flaring as she strove to maintain the clamp of her lips on Jemmy. She ground herself against him, harder and faster until it almost hurt and she felt him shudder, his cock stiffening deep inside the smoothness of her body. Aware that he was about to come and that she had neglected Jem, she let Sam take over and relaxed beneath his tempo as he found the pace she had set.

Both her hands cupped Jem, one catching his balls and pulling down, squeezing and coaxing, while the other curled around the upper reaches of his shaft, hard against the crisp hairs at his root, while her mouth worked – hard and soft, wet as a butter churn – around his helmet. She felt a flash that tore through her body as Sam came, his guttural cry like music to her ears, and she redoubled her efforts with her lips. The pumping of the huge cock inside her made her cream against his fingers, and she felt him press and rub until she came too, arching herself and trembling at the spasm of pure, hot, molten treacle that flooded her veins.

Jem opened his eyes as he ground his hips into her

face, and she watched him, their eyes locked, as he muttered and swore, his lips still smeared with rouge. When he came it was hot, sticky and searing, as she felt him pulse at the back of her mouth and she swallowed in a reflex action, gulping him and gripping his lean hips to pull him farther in. Sam's body curved over her, warm and protective, and she could feel his breath on her shoulder as he bent to kiss her cheek. Leaning back, one hand still on Jem's spent shaft, she turned to kiss him and felt him lick the tiny salt droplets from the corner of her mouth.

Chapter Fourteen

Drummond stepped out into the hallway. Madame had disappeared into the inky shadows, leaving behind her a trail of heady perfume and angry spite. The big house was dark, a warm velvety blackness, and he could smell the once-comforting aromas that he thought he had forgotten: polish and flowers, musty wall-hangings and ancient carpets scented with the dust of generations. The smell of home, although in some strange way it no longer seemed like home. It had changed. It seemed like a stranger's house now; his absence had been too long.

He turned left outside Lydia's room, his feet taking him almost without conscious thought to his own bedroom door. Inside, he could see the shadows of unfamiliar furniture and smell Madame's perfume. On the floor by his foot lay a drift of diaphanous fabric and a casually discarded piece of jewellery. Everything that he had once called his own had disappeared. Hastily, he pulled the door closed. It was no longer his room: it had been changed and given to another, used as a guest room, all trace of his presence erased. His heart felt heavy and his steps faltered as he went towards the room that had once been, and maybe still was, his brother's.

Outside, he paused momentarily, undecided. His heart skipped with a sudden nervousness and he wondered what he would do if Valerian was inside. On the stone wall near to his head an ornamental sword hung in a metal bracket, and he lifted it down, testing its weight in his hand, rubbing the blade lightly with the calloused pad of his thumb. His brother was unpredictable, he knew. It would be as well to have some means of defence.

The door opened smoothly on well-oiled hinges and Drummond was surprised to see that the room was partially lit. Candles of varying sizes and colours stood around the room, lighting the shadowed corners with ghostly flickering. On the huge bed at the far end of the room, a man's pale body lay spread like a heathen sacrifice on a crimson and ebony altar, the eyes blindfolded, the hands and feet bound to the four corners.

As he drew closer, Drummond saw that Valerian was relaxed, possibly sleeping, and that he had partaken in some bizarre sexual game. The evidence of his previous arousal was silvery on the skin of his belly, slowly hardening and crisping the curling hairs around his navel.

Drummond was almost unable to absorb the scene. His overwhelming desire was to laugh, to shake with mirth at the sight of his notorious brother bound up by a woman and inadvertently delivered to his, Drummond's, avenging hands. He walked quietly across the room, his boots stealthy on the soft tiger-skin rug. At the side of the bed he paused, noticing the sudden alertness of the body in front of him, the raised hairs on the forearms, the tension in the muscles.

'Claudine?' whispered Valerian.

In reply, Drummond raised the sword in his hand and gently rested the tip at his brother's waist. The point created a small dip in the even surface of the smooth skin, but did not pierce it.

'Claudine, what are you planning now? Your head is full of evil, wonderful games. Prick me again.'

Drummond obliged, his mouth widening into a grin. This was marvellous, so much better a confrontation than he had anticipated. He slid the sword along Valerian's flank until it rested on the side of his thigh. A tiny red scratch appeared in its wake. Valerian inhaled audibly, his chest rising and then falling. The sword slipped around, skirting his loins.

Drummond paused. Emasculating his brother had appeal, but he swiftly discounted such barbarity and moved around the bed until the point of the weapon pressed into Valerian's ribs. He saw with amusement that his brother's erection was beginning to stir, and decided to end the game before he was forced to see it fully aroused.

Dragging the tip of the sword up to Valerian's throat, he bent over him and placed his lips so close to his ear that he could almost taste him.

'No, dear brother. It is I.'

There was a momentary pause.

Then the figure on the bed convulsed, hips rising off the bed, claw-like hands clutching at the air, while his wide mouth twisted into a frenzied snarl.

'Untie me! Untie me, you bastard!' Valerian raged, the tendons in his arms buckling and twisting into knotted cords.

'Careful,' warned Drummond. 'Be still, or I shall accidentally run you through.'

Valerian, the tip of the sword still pressed to his throat, slumped back, his body flaccid and the only movement the rapid rise and fall of his chest.

'You coward. Won't you even untie me and fight me like a man?' he goaded him.

The point was pressed closer to his throat, the skin around it blanching.

'A man? Is that what you call yourself? You didn't exactly fight like a man when you gave me this scar I bear,' hissed Drummond, his amusement gone and replaced by a hard determination which left his face pale and his eyes narrowed to golden slits. 'Never fear,

I am not going to kill you. Merely enjoy the sight of you trussed up like a chicken ready for the broiler. Look at you! If Father could see you now, he'd turn in his grave.'

'Father can roast in hell. And you, too. Now untie me or I'll have you horsewhipped before I have you killed.'

Drummond threw back his head and laughed. The sound echoed coldly from the walls.

'Have me killed?' he mocked. 'You just don't see, do you? Oh, I forgot. You can't see, can you? Your lovely mistress has blindfolded you. Dearest brother, let me uncover your eyes and perhaps you will see the seriousness of your predicament.' Drummond moved the sword and, with a quick flick of his wrist, sliced the side of the blindfold and the strip of black fell, catching at the side of Valerian's head and resting on the scarlet pillow. 'You don't have the power to have anyone horsewhipped or killed. Least of all me.'

He slid the tip of the sword downward until it rested centrally on Valerian's chest, the point digging in a little, the blade rising and falling under the harshly beating thud of Valerian's heart.

'Where is the will?' demanded Drummond, his face hard and uncompromising.

'I don't have it,' sneered Valerian. 'And even if I did, you wouldn't want it. It'll do you no good.'

'I'll ask you again. Where is Father's will?'

There was the sound of a sharply inhaled breath behind him, and Drummond half-turned to see Madame rushing across the room, her arms outstretched and her red robe flying behind her like a cascade of blood. Her face was a white mask of hatred, and her teeth were bared as she launched herself at Drummond, flinging the full weight of her small body against him. He threw up an arm to fend her off, but she leapt on to his back, her nails clawing at his face and her teeth snapping at his neck like a vulture preparing to tear its food apart.

'Leave him alone!' she screamed.

There was a cry from beneath him as Drummond felt

her weight bend his body forward and his chest pressed on to the hilt of the sword. He experienced a momentary stillness and then he felt the ornamental sword yield beneath him. Thinking that it had broken, snapped beneath their combined weights, he twisted his head and saw in horror that the blade had pierced his brother's chest, and a dark wash of crimson was slowly spreading over Valerian's milky skin. Finding his strength, he pushed at the harpy who tore at his hair, sending her crashing to the floor.

'Valerian!' he cried, his hands trembling as he cupped his brother's face. Valerian's dark, tortured eyes fixed on his, and Drummond saw unremitting hatred deep in the dilated pupils.

'You'll hang for this.' A bubble of scarlet, air laced with blood, slowly formed at the edge of his lips and he gasped, his eyelids closing slowly as if he were deeply tired.

Drummond gripped his brother's shoulder.

'Oh, Christ. Oh, God. Quickly, send for a surgeon. A surgeon, woman!'

He span around, almost falling in his haste. Madame stood behind him, her pale eyes wide and ringed with dark shadows. As he moved towards her, she threw her hands up before her as if to ward him off. Then she began to scream.

The room was bright with light as Lydia pushed open the door. The scene was frozen for an instant as she took in the significance of the sword and the reed-like body of Madame who stood, as motionless as Lot's wife, at the foot of the bed. The air was rent with the sound of her screams.

Hardly pausing, Lydia turned and ran down the stairs, back to the stables, her heart frozen and her body numb.

'Quickly! Sam, take one of the horses: go to the surgeon and bid him come. Hurry! My cousin may be dying. Get Mr Lavendale, Jem. Waste no time!' As she spoke, she began to drag open the low stalls and pull at Dandy Beau's saddle. The stable-lads, kicked into action by the urgency in her voice, swung up and were away almost before she had buckled the last strap. Hardly pausing to watch them disappear into the blackness of the yard, she raced back to the house and took the stairs two at a time.

Madame turned and caught at her as she ran past, long nails raking across Lydia's forearm. She shook herself free and rushed towards the bed, but stopped as she heard Valerian emit a choking, guttural sound. Frozen, unable to move, she saw that Drummond had cut the bindings and removed the sword; he was staunching the flow of blood with the sheets. Valerian's face was creased and pale, his breathing shallow and rapid.

The screaming stopped as suddenly as it had begun and the room was blissfully silent. There was a whisper of movement as Madame went to the other side of the bed, her hair tumbling across Valerian's face and chest as she bent over him to take his hand in hers.

'Oh, my love. *Mon pauvre petit*. Speak to me, *mon amour*. Valerian, speak.'

'Is he dead?' Lydia dropped to her knees in front of Drummond, her hands fluttering over Valerian's face. His eyes opened, met hers briefly, and then left to search for Madame's face.

'Take me away, Claudine. Take me away from these . . . people,' he muttered, his voice shadowed with pain. 'Tend me, Claudine.'

'The surgeon, thank God!' Lydia rushed to the door and drew the portly little man into the hall. 'Quickly, there is a man upstairs who is wounded. Come now! Bring your bag.'

When she had shown the doctor to Valerian's room, Lydia hurried down the stairs. Drummond was sitting on the bottom step, his knees curled up and his head drooping forward. Lydia gently laid one hand across the back of his neck, filled with tenderness and concern.

236

'Drummond, what happened?' she murmured. 'How did that sword come to be in him?'

'It was an accident. An accident. Not that anyone will believe me. If he dies, I'll be swinging from a gibbet before sundown tomorrow.' He lifted his head and she saw that his bronzed skin was pale and his face haggard. She drew him to her and rocked him, like a baby, in her arms.

'Sssh,' she whispered. 'You won't hang. They won't hang you: you're Lord Hawkesworth, now.'

'Never,' he said, dragging himself upward and away from her. 'There's nothing for me here, now. This house has forgotten me. It's not my home any more.'

'What do you mean? It has always been your home. It always will be.'

'No.' He shook his head, biting at his lower lip thoughtfully. 'I can never live here, not now. I'm going back to sea. That's where I'm truly happy.'

'Drummond, please. Don't be so hasty. We need you here. You can't let this . . . this . . . *accident* ruin all that.'

'*Accident*. You see, even you aren't sure. Even if the surgeon saves him, I can't live here with everyone glancing sidelong at me and whispering "Fratricide" whenever I pass. I'm leaving. My brother is welcome to the house and the title.'

'Don't go.' Lydia stared uncomprehendingly as he stood and moved away from her. 'Drummond, this is a mistake. Everyone knows the threats he made against you: they will understand that you killed him in self-defence.'

He turned towards her, his eyes tired but gentle, and a tiny smile lifting the corner of his mouth.

'My love, I wish that were true,' he said. 'I must leave now, before the lawyer comes. I could have been happy with you, but I cannot stay and let them hang me. Be careful.' His arms enfolded her and she felt his lips bruise hers as he kissed her, fiercely, on the mouth. Then he was gone, the huge studded door banging behind him.

The surgeon materialised at Lydia's elbow. He sighed impatiently.

'Madam, I can be of no service here. I am a doctor, not an undertaker. The gentleman upstairs is dead.'

'The will has always been in my possession, Miss Lydia. It is my regret to inform you that I acted under the instructions of Valerian Hawkesworth – er, the late Valerian Hawkesworth, I should say.' Mr Lavendale stood in front of the fireplace in the library, his coat raised slightly to allow the fire to warm his legs. Lydia, her hand paused over the brandy decanter, looked up at him with some surprise.

'Do I take it that Valerian gave you financial remuneration for this deviousness? I should not have to remind you that he was not the true Lord Hawkesworth.'

'Indeed, madam. You are more correct than you know. There is no Lord Hawkesworth. There has been no male incumbent since your uncle's death.'

'What can you mean?'

'Oh, dear, Miss Lydia. This is so very difficult.' Lavendale sighed and rubbed his chin, a deep frown creasing his wide brow. 'Your cousin Drummond, he . . . well . . . he incurred the wrath of Lord William when he left. It was seen by his father as a defection, a betrayal, you understand. And as time progressed, it was clear to Lord William that Valerian had neither the inclination nor the sanity to manage an estate of this size and wealth. He changed his will some four months before his death and cut both of his sons right out. They were to receive nothing under the terms of the new will.' He sighed again. 'That is why Master Valerian chose to act as he did. He felt that Hawkesworth was rightfully his. He did not want the new beneficiary to inherit. At all.'

'And you colluded in this?' Lydia stared at him and he fidgeted uncomfortably.

'I did. I agreed with him that he was more able than the selected beneficiary. I was wrong.'

238

'And who is this beneficiary that you all deemed so incapable?' Lydia lifted a glass from the tray.

'Yourself.'

The glass fell to the floor and smashed at her feet. She stared at it dazedly, thinking irrelevantly how pretty the shards of crystal were as they caught the light and formed clusters of tiny rainbows on the polished floor.

'Me?'

'You, Miss Lydia. Indeed it is a tangled web. However, I hope that you will see beyond my temporary lapse of professionalism and maintain me as your advisor? Your dear uncle would have wanted it so.'

'We shall see, Mr Lavendale. We shall see.' Lydia selected another glass and slowly poured a generous measure of brandy. Without offering him any, she drained the glass.

Lady Lydia of Hawkesworth Manor, she thought. It really sounded very satisfactory.

Sitting back in the winged chair, she slowly crossed one stockinged leg over the other and folded her hands in her lap. She took a deep, calming breath and met Lavendale's heavy-lidded gaze.

'Exactly how much did you say the estate is worth?'

One Year Later

As the bow of the enormous ship hit a wave, a spray of ocean spume washed up and over the rail to darken the planking of the deck. Lydia waited a moment until the swell had eased, one hand on an adjacent pile of ropes to steady herself. She tipped her face towards the morning sun and inhaled the fresh saltiness of the open sea, letting her hood fall back on to her shoulders and the brisk wind tease her hair into long ebony skeins. A sense of enormous happiness and well-being swelled in her chest, and she moved forward and up the steps to stand by the rangy figure whose weathered brown hand loosely guided the wheel of the ship.

They had been at sea for almost a month, and were halfway to the Americas. Lydia had sold her inheritance, and a vast fortune in gold now swelled the securely padlocked coffers that were stowed in the ship's hold. She had left England with a vague feeling of regret, tempered with anticipation to see the New World that Drummond had once described to her. She was extremely wealthy, she had her health, and above all she had her youth and beauty to guide her through whatever awaited her on the other side of the vast ocean.

She took her hands out of the mink muff that had warmed her fingers, toying for a moment with the sparkling ring that adorned her left hand: a wide band of gold set with rubies and emeralds that fitted snugly to her finger and emphasised the narrow paleness of her hands. The man at her side glanced down, his blue eyes warm and interested, his vigorous white-blond hair escaping from under his scarlet bandanna with each successive tug of the wind. He was taller than she was, and broad; his shoulders stretched the seams of his leather jerkin while the bare V of his chest showing at the neckline of his open shirt gleamed like beaten copper in the sun.

'Thinking of your late husband, Mistress Hammond?' he enquired. Lydia glanced up at him, then her brow cleared as she remembered her assumed role of a grieving widow bound for the Americas to seek out her late husband's family.

'It gets a little easier each day, Captain Jefferies,' she replied, smiling and tucking her hands back into the muff. She paused to admire his lean hands, watching with fascination the easy way they commanded the ship through the polished timber wheel. Capable hands, strong hands. She found herself imagining how they would look set against the whiteness of her thighs, then roused herself to enquire nonchalantly: 'How much longer before we have sight of land?'

Towards dinner-time, Lydia returned to her cabin. It was on the seaward side and had been newly decorated with velvet to befit lady passengers. Having closed the door behind her, she leant one hand against the timbered wall.

'When will I get my sea legs?' she sighed.

'Probably when we disembark,' came the wry reply. Angel, beautifully attired in black mourning taffeta, smiled and patted the place on the settle beside her. 'Come here. I do believe he's smiling. The wet-nurse says that it's the wind, but look! Look at that!'

241

The baby on her lap gurgled and cooed, then his chubby face split into a toothless grin. His shock of unruly brown hair stuck straight up from his round head, and his golden eyes crinkled with jollity.

'Oh, Angel. He's so beautiful. And that is definitely a smile, I don't care what Gertrude says.' Lydia stroked the baby's round cheek with her forefinger, her heart swelling with love for her little boy. At that moment, from the carved wooden crib beside them, a strident wail cut the air.

'Oh, Lord,' cried Angel. 'Here, miss. Take him. His majesty has woken, and about time too. I thought he was going to sleep all day.'

She carefully settled the smiling child on to Lydia's lap, and reached into the crib to lift out an identical baby boy. The only differences between the twins were in their eyes and hair: the newly awoken cherub had jet-black hair and dark sloe eyes that stared imperiously at the world.

Lydia gestured for Angel to hand him to her, and settled back into the soft cushions with her sons. She nuzzled their delicately scented hair and closed her eyes, conjuring up images which tried to remain hidden in the back of her mind: Drummond striding through the woods of Hawkesworth with his cloak billowing and his unruly hair ruffled by the wind; Valerian in his tall leather boots and immaculate white stock, sitting astride his magnificent stallion.

Would she ever know which of these strong but flawed men had fathered her children, she wondered. As the babies snuggled happily against the silk of her bodice, she let the images fade and sighed contentedly, deciding that she did not really care: perhaps it had been both.

BLACK LACE NEW BOOKS

Published in March

RAW SILK
Lisabet Sarai
£5.99

When software engineer Kate O'Neill leaves her lover David to take a job in Bangkok, she becomes sexually involved with two very different men: a handsome member of the Thai aristocracy, and the charismatic proprietor of a sex bar. When David arrives in Thailand, Kate realises she must choose between them. She invites all three to join her in a sexual adventure that finally makes clear to her what she really wants and needs.

ISBN 0 352 33336 7

THE TOP OF HER GAME
Emma Holly
£5.99

Successful businesswoman and dominatrix Julia Mueller has been searching all her life for a man who won't be mastered too easily. When she locks horns with a no-nonsense Montana rancher, will he be the man that's too tough to tame? Will she find the balance between domination and surrender, or will her dark side win out?

ISBN 0 352 33337 5

Published in April

HAUNTED
Laura Thornton
£5.99

A modern-day Gothic story set in both England and New York. Sasha Hayward is an American woman whose erotic obsession with a long-dead pair of lovers leads her on a steamy and evocative search. Seeking out descendants of the enigmatic pair, Sasha consummates her obsession in a series of sexy encounters related to this haunting mystery.

ISBN 0 352 33341 3

STAND AND DELIVER
Helena Ravenscroft
£5.99

1745, and England is plagued by the lawless. Lydia Hawkesworth feels torn between her love for Drummond, a sea-faring adventurer turned highwayman, and her all-consuming passion for his decadent younger brother Valerian. With the arrival of the icy Madame de Chaillot, Valerian's plans to usurp his brother's position and steal his inheritance turn down a sinister and darkly erotic path – one which Lydia is drawn to follow.

ISBN 0 352 33340 5

To be published in May

INSOMNIA
Zoe le Verdier
£5.99

A wide range of sexual experience is explored in this collection of short stories by one of the best-liked authors in the series. Zoe le Verdier's work is an ideal reflection of the fresh, upbeat stories now being published under the Black Lace imprint. Many popular female fantasies are covered, from sex with a stranger and talking dirty, to secret fetishes, lost virginity and love. There's something for everyone.

ISBN: 0 352 33345 6

VILLAGE OF SECRETS
Mercedes Kelly
£5.99

Every small town has something to hide, and this rural Cornish village is no exception. Its twee exterior hides some shocking scandals and nothing is quite what it seems. Laura, a London journalist, becomes embroiled with the locals – one of whom might be her long-lost brother – when she inherits property in the village. Against a backdrop of curious goings-on, she learns to indulge her taste for kinky sex and rubber fetishism.

IBSN: 0 352 33344 8

BLACK LACE BOOKLIST

All books are priced £4.99 unless another price is given.

Black Lace books with a contemporary setting

ODALISQUE	Fleur Reynolds ISBN 0 352 32887 8	☐
WICKED WORK	Pamela Kyle ISBN 0 352 32958 0	☐
UNFINISHED BUSINESS	Sarah Hope-Walker ISBN 0 352 32983 1	☐
HEALING PASSION	Sylvie Ouellette ISBN 0 352 32998 X	☐
PALAZZO	Jan Smith ISBN 0 352 33156 9	☐
THE GALLERY	Fredrica Alleyn ISBN 0 352 33148 8	☐
AVENGING ANGELS	Roxanne Carr ISBN 0 352 33147 X	☐
COUNTRY MATTERS	Tesni Morgan ISBN 0 352 33174 7	☐
GINGER ROOT	Robyn Russell ISBN 0 352 33152 6	☐
DANGEROUS CONSEQUENCES	Pamela Rochford ISBN 0 352 33185 2	☐
THE NAME OF AN ANGEL £6.99	Laura Thornton ISBN 0 352 33205 0	☐
SILENT SEDUCTION	Tanya Bishop ISBN 0 352 33193 3	☐
BONDED	Fleur Reynolds ISBN 0 352 33192 5	☐
THE STRANGER	Portia Da Costa ISBN 0 352 33211 5	☐
CONTEST OF WILLS £5.99	Louisa Francis ISBN 0 352 33223 9	☐
BY ANY MEANS £5.99	Cheryl Mildenhall ISBN 0 352 33221 2	☐
MÉNAGE £5.99	Emma Holly ISBN 0 352 33231 X	☐

Black Lace anthologies

PAST PASSIONS £6.99	ISBN 0 352 33159 3	☐
PANDORA'S BOX 2 £4.99	ISBN 0 352 33151 8	☐
PANDORA'S BOX 3 £5.99	ISBN 0 352 33274 3	☐
SUGAR AND SPICE £7.99	ISBN 0 352 33227 1	☐
SUGAR AND SPICE 2 £6.99	ISBN 0 352 33309 X	☐

Black Lace non-fiction

WOMEN, SEX AND ASTROLOGY £5.99	Sarah Bartlett ISBN 0 352 33262 X	☐

-------✂------------------

Please send me the books I have ticked above.

Name ....

Address ....

....

....

.... Post Code ....

Send to: **Cash Sales, Black Lace Books, Thames Wharf Studios, Rainville Road, London W6 9HT.**

US customers: for prices and details of how to order books for delivery by mail, call 1-800-805-1083.

Please enclose a cheque or postal order, made payable to **Virgin Publishing Ltd**, to the value of the books you have ordered plus postage and packing costs as follows:
   UK and BFPO – £1.00 for the first book, 50p for each subsequent book.
   Overseas (including Republic of Ireland) – £2.00 for the first book, £1.00 for each subsequent book.

If you would prefer to pay by VISA or ACCESS/ MASTERCARD, please write your card number and expiry date here:

....

Please allow up to 28 days for delivery.

Signature ....

-------✂------------------